A CHRISTMAS KISS

Without warning, his finger slid beneath her chin, forcing her face up to meet his mocking gaze. "Could it be I have unintentionally offended you? Or is it that you hold me to blame for young Jimmy's injury?"

Her heart forgot to beat at his touch.

"Neither, Mr. Charlebois. I am simply busy."

"So I see." The blue eyes darkened as he lowered his head to brush his lips over her temple. "Butter." His lips moved to tease at her cheek. "Flour." He covered her trembling mouth with a tender kiss. "And ginger." Slowly he pulled back, his slumberous gaze sweeping over her flushed features. "You taste of Christmas."

Pleasure as thick and delicious as warm honey slid through her body at his touch. His slender, clever fingers trailed down her jaw, his touch sending jolts of dazzling sensations straight to the pit of her stomach.

Oh . . . he was wicked.

Wondrously, magnificently wicked.

"Mr. Charlebois," she breathed.

"Raoul."

All Sarah wanted was to press against that hard body, to part her lips and give in to the potent temptation of his kiss. To drown in his heady beauty, and the artistic skill of his seduction . . .

Books by Deborah Raleigh

SOME LIKE IT WICKED

SOME LIKE IT SINFUL

SOME LIKE IT BRAZEN

BEDDING THE BARON

SEDUCING THE VISCOUNT

SEDUCE ME BY CHRISTMAS

Published by Kensington Publishing Corporation

SEDUCE ME
By CHRISTMAS

DEBORAH RALEIGH

ZEBRA BOOKS
Kensington Publishing Corp.
http://www.kensingtonbooks.com

ZEBRA BOOKS are published by

Kensington Publishing Corp.
119 West 40th Street
New York, NY 10018

All Kensington titles, imprints, and distributed lines are available at special quantity discounts for bulk purchases for sales
promotion, premiums, fund-raising, educational, or institu-
tional use.

Special book excerpts or customized printings can also be created to fit specific needs. For details, write or phone the office
of the Kensington Special Sales Manager: Attn.: Special Sales
Department. Kensington Publishing Corp., 119 West 40th
Street, New York, NY 10018. Phone: 1-800-221-2647.

Zebra and the Z logo Reg. U.S. Pat. & TM Off.

ISBN-13: 978-0-8217-8046-6
ISBN-10: 0-8217-8046-8

First Printing: October 2009

10 9 8 7 6 5 4 3 2 1

Printed in the United States of America

Chapter 1

It was a typical London day for late November.

In other another word . . .

Miserable.

The streets were shrouded in a damp, frigid fog, and had long since been abandoned by the glittering *ton* who preferred the comfort of their countryseats. Those unfortunate souls who were forced to remain behind huddled near their fireplaces or when pressed to venture outdoors, dashed from one place to another with their heads bent low and their faces covered with heavy mufflers.

Well, at least most did so.

Raoul Charlebois, on the other hand, did not huddle or dash. He did not even waddle, despite the icy slush.

Nature had bestowed upon him a languid, elegant grace that had made him famous upon the stages of London (almost as famous as his stunning cobalt-blue eyes and silver-blond curls that framed his finely crafted countenance perfectly), and with a measured gait he stepped down from his carriage to stroll up the short walk and enter the modest house on Lombard Street.

It was an elegance thoroughly appreciated by the handful of elderly widows that contributed the lion's share of tenants in the quiet, growingly shabby neighborhood. Oh, they might later agree that they disdained the arrogant set of his wide shoulders beneath the multi-caped greatcoat, and the sardonic smile that curved his sensuous lips, but peering through the lacy curtains at his magnificent form, there was not a one who could halt their hearts from skipping a beat or a whimsical sigh from slipping between their lips.

He was . . . spectacular.

The sort of gentleman who seemed created for the sole purpose of fulfilling a woman's fantasy.

No matter what her age.

Gloriously indifferent to the avid gazes that followed his every step, Raoul used the key the land agent had sent round earlier in the day to unlock the door. Then stepping into the small foyer, he paused to absorb the familiar scent of pipe tobacco and leather-bound books.

He smiled, slipping off his coat and hat. With only a little effort he could envision Dunnington waiting for him at the top of the steps, or Ian and Fredrick racing down the long hallway to the kitchen, whooping at the top of their lungs.

Raoul had been ten years old when his father had sent him to this small town house. At the time he only knew that Mr. Dunnington was starting a select school for boys of excellent, if not legitimate birth. Bastards. And that he was the first student to arrive.

Not surprisingly, he had been terrified when his father, the Earl of Merriot, had quite literally dumped him on the front stoop.

It wasn't that he'd been happy at his father's grand

estate in Cheshire. Lord and Lady Merriot made little effort to disguise the fact he was the one blight on their otherwise perfect life. After all, what leaders of the fashionable world desired to have a bastard underfoot when they were entertaining their influential guests with one lavish party after another?

Still, he had not known what to expect from the thin, bespectacled tutor who had opened the door to this non-descript house and led him up the narrow steps to the schoolroom.

Thankfully, it had taken only a handful of days in Dunnington's presence, not to mention the arrival of Ian and Fredrick (two of his fellow students), to realize that coming to London was nothing less than a miracle.

Suddenly his days were more than an attempt to melt into the shadows and disappear.

He had a kind, intelligent man in his life who offered him an unwavering affection and respect he had never before experienced. He had two friends who he bullied and loved and raised as if they were his own brothers. And he had the opportunity to create a career that had not only made him famous, but wealthy beyond his wildest dreams.

Actually, the only kind thing his father had ever done for him was dumping him on the doorstep of this house, he acknowledged wryly, moving down the shadowed hall to enter the library.

An hour later, he had the Holland covers tugged off the solid English furnishings and a cheerful fire blazing. Seated in Dunnington's favorite leather chair, he propped his feet on the walnut desk and sipped deeply from the bottle of brandy he had the foresight to bring along.

He closed his eyes, the chill slowly easing from his body.

Yes. This was what he had needed.

Nothing could bring back Dunnington. Or heal the sense of loss that had plagued Raoul for the past year. But there was a measure of comfort in breathing life back into this house that had been shrouded in darkness for too long.

And perhaps, someday, he would . . .

His vague future plans for the house were forgotten as Raoul stiffened in surprise. Was that the front door?

He frowned as the click of the door was followed by the slow, steady tread of boots on the floorboards. Damn, it was.

Who the devil would bother him?

The weather was nasty enough to keep the old tabbies from barging in to sate their rampant curiosity. And he hadn't shared his intended destination with anyone beyond his groom.

Besides, whoever was approaching was making an obvious effort at stealth. As if hoping to catch Raoul unaware.

On the point of rising to his feet, Raoul's annoyance suddenly eased as the intruder stumbled, knocking a figurine off a hall table, and muttered a low curse.

He recognized this particularly clumsy gentleman.

"*Mon Dieu,* Fredrick, halt your tiptoeing around and come in before you break your fool neck," he called, the French nurse who had cared for him as a tiny lad leaving her mark on his faint accent even after all these years.

Turning his head, he watched the slender man step into the library. Fredrick Colstone, heir apparent to Lord

Graystone, tossed his greatcoat and hat onto a nearby chair before moving toward the desk.

"How did you know it was me?"

"You always did have the grace of a drunken sailor."

Fredrick's singularly sweet smile curved his lips, adding to the impression of angelic beauty. As a youngster, Fredrick had detested his fragile features and honey curls that had made him the target of ruthless bullying. Thankfully, maturity had added an edge of masculinity, although he would never acquire that annoying arrogance that came as easily as breathing to most aristocrats.

Raoul hid a smile as he noted the dust marring the rumpled cravat and ink staining the cuffs of the charcoal-gray coat. It wasn't even teatime and already his friend was a mess.

"No doubt my lack of grace explains why I became an inventor rather than a burglar," Fredrick readily agreed.

"That and the fact you cannot distinguish a Gainsborough from a nursery school scribble," Raoul pointed out.

"True enough."

Waiting for his companion to settle in a chair on the other side of the desk, Raoul held up the bottle still clutched in his hand.

"Brandy?"

Fredrick reached beneath his jacket to pull out a silver flask. "I have come prepared."

"So you have." Raoul arched a pale, golden brow. "Which begs the question of why you have come at all."

"I was passing by and noticed Nico standing guard by the carriage out front." Fredrick waved a hand toward the bay window that overlooked the street. "If you wish to travel incognito, then you should hire a groom that does not quite so closely resemble a cutthroat."

"You were passing by?" Raoul demanded, ignoring the insult to his groom. Nico did look like a cutthroat. Possibly because that was precisely what he had been before Raoul took him on as a servant. "Since when does your route take you through Lombard Street?"

"I pass by quite often when I am in London," Fredrick confessed with a grimace. "Ian would claim I am plagued by maudlin sentimentality, but . . ."

"There is no need to explain, *mon ami,*" Raoul interrupted, his heart twisting with that ruthless sense of emptiness. "Not to me."

"This morning, however, I came with a purpose."

"Ah, then it was not fickle fate that crossed our paths?"

"Did you know that the house was recently purchased?"

Raoul took a deep drink from the bottle. "I had heard such rumors."

"And by any chance, do you know the new owner?"

"Intimately."

"You?" Fredrick's silver-gray eyes narrowed as Raoul dipped his head in acknowledgement. "Bloody hell."

"Does the thought trouble you?"

"Quite the opposite. I am delighted to know the house will belong to someone who will appreciate what Dunnington accomplished here." The unnerving gaze swept over Raoul's carefully guarded expression. "But I am curious. You already possess an obscenely large town house. What the devil do you intend to do with the place?"

Raoul glanced toward the towering shelves that were stuffed to the ceiling with leather-bound books.

"I have yet to decide," he hedged, not yet willing to commit himself.

"Then why purchase it at all?"

"As you said, maudlin sentimentality, no doubt," Raoul mocked his desperate need to cling to Dunnington's house. As if the memories that echoed here could somehow fill the hollow ache in the center of his chest. "Or perhaps I am merely becoming batty in my old age, as Nico has kindly suggested."

Easily sensing Raoul's reluctance to discuss the intimate reasoning behind the purchase, Fredrick took a drink from his flask and allowed his gaze to wander around the room.

"Do you recall the last time we gathered here?"

Raoul nodded, his mind conjuring the memory of Fredrick and Ian seated near the fire, while he paced the floor. They had just returned from Dunnington's funeral, then endured the pain of listening to their beloved tutor's last will and testament being read by the solicitor.

The shock that had gripped all three of them still lingered.

"How could I forget?" His short, humorless laugh echoed through the library. "It was a memorable day."

"Indeed, it was." Fredrick grimaced. "Not only were we mourning the loss of Dunnington, but we'd just learned that he had left us each a legacy of twenty thousand pounds."

"Twenty thousand pounds that the wily old fox had managed to extort from each of our fathers to hide their deepest, darkest secret."

There was a pause as they contemplated that long-ago afternoon, then Fredrick's expression abruptly softened. A certain sign he was thinking of his beautiful wife, Portia.

"So much has changed since then," Fredrick murmured, his voice distracted, as if he were imagining rumpled sheets and a warm woman.

"Certainly for you, *mon ami*," Raoul murmured, pretending it was not envy clenching his stomach in a painful vise. "It is not every bastard who discovers he is heir to a noble title, and a damned fine estate. And, of course, you have been blessed with a wife who is not only *très belle,* but absurdly devoted to you."

"And for Ian as well," Fredrick added. "Whoever could have predicted the gentleman toasted as Casanova would so happily settle into married life and devote his days to his tedious investments?"

Raoul snorted. He had shared dinner with Ian and his wife, Mercy, only a week ago.

"There is nothing tedious in the manner that Ian invests." He shook his head as he took another swig from the bottle. "I had nightmares after he confessed he had risked near fifty thousand pounds on a shipment of spices from the far East."

Fredrick chuckled. "True enough, he is neck or nothing in everything he does. He is fortunate that Mercy possesses nerves that are not easily overset."

"He has most certainly been dealt a winning hand when it comes to his wife." His lips twisted. "Not to mention in his mother and uncle, who I gather are determined to make amends for the past."

"They have certainly done their best."

"Indeed. Although, I am not certain Ian would have wished for their amends to be quite so . . . lavish."

The log snapped in the fireplace, the heat of the dancing flames battling back the gloomy chill of the day.

"Ah, you have heard that Lord Norrington is building Ian a grand new country manor house in Surrey?"

"As well as the sad tidings that it is also to be home to Mercy's parents." Raoul shuddered. He had met the Vicar and Mrs. Simpson only once, but that had been more than enough to assure him that he'd rather have his throat slit than live beneath the same roof as the quarrelsome couple. "*Mon Dieu*. No house, no matter how lavish, would be worth having to reside with those two hideous creatures."

Fredrick shrugged. "Unfortunately, when it comes to families, we must accept the bad with the good."

Raoul knew that his companion was no longer speaking of Ian.

"Such as a vindictive stepmother?" he asked, softly.

Fredrick grimaced. "And a ridiculous buffoon for a stepbrother."

Raoul raised his bottle in a mocking toast. "To families."

Fredrick readily raised his flask. "Families."

They both drank, a comfortable silence filling the room. For a long moment, Raoul allowed his thoughts to drift back to the evenings spent listening to Dunnington read from one of the numerous books that lined the walls, or indulging the boys in a game of chess.

Simple, uncomplicated days.

Damn, but he missed them.

At last aware of Fredrick's unwavering regard, Raoul turned his head to meet the steady gaze.

"Is there a reason that you are studying me as if you expect me to sprout a set of horns?"

Fredrick continued to stare, unapologetic. "I am wondering if the rumors are true."

Raoul's lips twisted. Over the years he had become accustomed to the gossip that swirled around him. Hell, he had encouraged most of it. A part of his success on the stage was a reflection of his carefully crafted image offstage.

He was seen only with the most beautiful women. The parties he attended were the most exclusive in London. And he never, ever allowed anyone to see the man beneath the façade that was Raoul Charlebois.

He was an enigma, a mystery.

And that was what kept the jaded members of the *ton* titillated.

"I find rumors in general to be untrustworthy, but that does not seem to keep them from spreading like a virulent plague."

"So, the magnificent Raoul Charlebois does not intend to retire from the stage?" Fredric demanded.

"That is hardly a rumor, Fredrick," he drawled. "I made the announcement myself."

"Why?"

Raoul smiled with a rueful flare of humor.

It was a question he had no answer for.

At least none that made any sense.

"The most important talent any actor can possess is an immaculate sense of timing," he said smoothly. "That includes knowing when to take my final bow. I have no intention of having all of London watch me become a decrepit wreck of a man, deluding myself that I am still in my prime."

Fredrick frowned. He knew Raoul too well to be easily fooled.

"For God's sake, Raoul, you are far from becoming a

decrepit wreck. I would say you are at the very pinnacle of your career."

Raoul shrugged. "What better moment to walk away?"

Far from satisfied, Fredrick studied Raoul for a long, discomforting moment, then with a shake of his head, he accepted Raoul had said all he intended.

Instead, he smiled wryly.

"It is certainly causing a sensation throughout London."

"It must be if word has managed to penetrate to the dark, musty bowels of your workrooms, *mon ami*."

"My workrooms are not musty," Fredrick protested. "I am not quite the hermit you think."

"No? Then tell me, was it Portia who informed you of my recent retirement?"

"I . . ." Fredrick laughed, realizing he would never be able to lie beneath Raoul's penetrating gaze. "Damn you, yes."

Raoul chuckled. "You will never change, Freddie, and in truth, I am glad of it. The world would be a sadder place without your odd combination of plodding logic and fanciful dreams."

"Maudlin, indeed." Fredrick tilted his head to the side. "Tell me, what devil is plaguing you, old friend?"

"The devil that plagues many gentlemen who have reached my advanced years." Raoul grimaced. "Quite simply, I am bored."

"And you believe retiring from the stage will relieve your boredom?" Fredrick demanded. "What the devil will you do with yourself?"

"I have taken an urge to travel."

"The continent?"

"Cheshire."

"Ah." Fredrick's puzzled expression cleared as if by magic. "So the thorn has at last festered, has it?"

"A charming analogy," he muttered, recalling Fredrick saying those precise words near a year ago, when they had first discovered the truth behind Dunnington's legacy.

The silver gaze never wavered. "You seek to uncover your father's dark secret?"

Raoul kicked his feet off the desk and rose from the chair, suddenly struck by a flare of restless discontent. Not an uncommon sensation. At least not when the mention of his father, Lord Merriot, entered the conversation.

Reaching the bay window, he peered down at the icy street below. "Yes, *mon ami,* I find that I must discover what my father was willing to pay twenty thousand pounds to keep hidden."

"Be careful that is all you discover."

Raoul snorted.

Both Fredrick and Ian had gone on their quest to uncover their fathers' secrets, only to return with brides.

"There is no fear of that." Raoul's gaze shifted to his slender servant who leaned against the gleaming black carriage. Despite the nasty weather, Nico refused to wear one of the dozen fancy uniforms that Raoul had purchased for him. Instead he preferred a plain woolen coat and loose breeches that made him look more a dockworker than valet for London's most famous actor. Not that many people noticed his clothing. Not with those lean, swarthy features that were finely honed and edged with a promise of violence. Women trembled at the dark, Latin beauty and smoldering dark eyes that perfectly matched the long, raven hair he kept pulled into a queue. Gentlemen instinctively gave him a wide berth. At least they did if they desired to see another day. "While I have the greatest appreciation for the fairer sex, I have yet to encounter one that can claim more than a passing interest. I am resigned to my future as a bachelor."

Rising to his feet, Fredrick moved to reclaim his hat and coat from the chair.

"Never dare fate, Raoul. It has a nasty tendency to make a fool of a man."

"Not of me."

"We shall see." Fredrick offered a mocking bow. "Happy hunting, *mon ami*."

December 9
Cheshire

It had been twelve years since his last visit, but Cheshire was precisely as Raoul remembered it.

Rolling timberlands that were dotted with occasional fields and meadows, along with the dangerous kettle holes locally known as meres. The tiny villages were mostly notable for their black-and-white timbered buildings, and the native red stone used in the local cathedrals.

A sleepy, peaceful corner of England that was content to allow the world to pass them by.

Greeted by a light, icy rain that was not at all uncommon for early December, Raoul discovered he was not entirely disappointed by the familiarity of his surroundings.

Odd. His memories of the particular neighborhood were hardly worth cherishing. Hell, most of them still gave him nightmares.

He could only suppose there must be some need within every man to know there is a place in the world that never changed.

Of course, it helped that he had chosen to settle in the small but elegant hunting lodge loaned to him by Sir Harold Baxter, rather than his father's lavish estate simply known as the Great House.

He would never be able to claim Fredrick's raw intelligence or Ian's sheer cunning, but he did understand human nature.

In all its noble glory, and with all its fatal flaws.

And more importantly, he understood his father.

Lord Merriot was a handsome, fiercely proud gentleman who was accustomed to others bending to his will. Predictable, if annoying. The Merriots were by far the most important family in the entire county. Who would dare stand against them?

He would be infuriated that his bastard son would arrive in Cheshire without a formal invitation. And even more infuriated that Raoul had not yet presented himself at the Great House like a proper sycophant, to beg for his father's approval.

Soon enough, his conceit would overcome his dignity, and he would seek out Raoul.

In that moment, Raoul would gain the upper hand.

Until then, unfortunately, he had little to occupy his time.

Unlike most sons of a wealthy nobleman, Raoul had never developed a passion for hunting, and his one attempt to join in the local society by attending a ball at the assembly rooms had caused a near riot among the local ladies, one of whom had actually swooned at being in the presence of the notorious Raoul Charlebois.

Even a brief luncheon at the village pub had created an embarrassing fuss.

Conceding defeat, he awoke his fifth morning in Cheshire and gathered his restive horse from the stables. Then, ignoring the gray clouds that threatened snow, he deliberately took a path leading away from the village. Soon enough, the natives would be accustomed to his presence. Until then it seemed best to avoid stirring the mobs.

For well over an hour he meandered through the countryside, enjoying his ride despite the decidedly brisk breeze.

He had forgotten how soothing the silence could be.

Savoring his rare sense of peace, Raoul was completely unprepared for the small form that appeared from seemingly nowhere to dart across the path.

Before he could react, his horse reared and instinctively struck out. Hercules had once performed at Astley's Royal Amphitheater and was exquisitely well-mannered, but his nerves were no match for the unexpected disturbance.

Much like his owner, Raoul decided as he vaulted from the saddle to study the fair-haired urchin laying with a terrifying stillness on the frozen ground.

"Damn."

Bending beside the boy, he studied the large bump already forming on his forehead. What he knew of children could fit into a thimble, but he put the youngster at eight or nine years of age, and seemingly well-fed beneath his heavy wool clothing. Fortunate, since he would heal far quicker if he were not malnourished.

There was a rustle from the side of the path, but on this occasion, Raoul was prepared for the impetuous lad who burst through the hedgerow and dashed to stand beside the unconscious body.

"Jimmy. Sweet Mother of God." Clutching a well-used cricket bat, the boy stabbed Raoul with a worried gray gaze. "Is he dead?"

This one was older, maybe twelve, but with enough resemblance to the lad on the ground to suggest they were brothers.

"No. Knocked senseless." Raoul kept his tone nonchalant, sensing the boy was hovering on the edge of panic. "Which is more than the impetuous cub deserves darting into the road without regard to unwary travelers."

As hoped, the boy's threatening tears were forgotten, and a flare of anger stiffened his spine.

"It was an accident, sir. Jimmy was chasing after our cricket ball. If you're worried for your horse . . ."

"I suggest you swallow the remainder of that insult, Mr. . . . ?"

A flush touched the thin face framed by a thick mane of brown curls.

"Willie."

"Master Willie," Raoul continued, easily scooping the unconscious boy off the ground and cradling him to his chest as he straightened. "And instead make yourself useful by directing me to young Jimmy's home."

"Aye, sir." With a surprising air of maturity, Willie squared his shoulders and nodded his head toward the massive black horse. "Shall I lead your mount?"

"No need." Raoul gave a low whistle. "Hercules."

The gray eyes widened as the horse readily moved to stand at Raoul's side.

"Hellfire."

"Does your mother allow such language?"

"Ain't got a mother." Willie turned to lead Raoul through the gape in the hedgerow. "She did a flit three years ago. Miss Sarah takes care of me and Jimmy."

It was not an uncommon story. Too many young women were left alone to raise children they either did not want or could not afford. Most were simply incapable of providing a proper home.

"And who is Miss Sarah?"

"The finest lady in all the land."

Raoul hid his smile at Willie's fierce loyalty. The scamp was barely old enough to be out of shortcoats, but it was obvious he considered it his duty to protect his brother, and the mysterious Miss Sarah.

Such loyalty was something Raoul not only understood, but appreciated. It was precisely what he had felt toward Dunnington and his two friends, Ian and Fredrick.

"She is no doubt a fine lady, but not terribly wise to think she can give two rapscallions a cricket ball and bat without dire consequences."

Willie nervously cleared his throat. "Well . . . as to that . . ."

"Ah. Did you steal them?"

"Nay." Hurt pride flared through the gray eyes, sharply reminding Raoul of Fredrick when he was just a lad. "We might be poor, but me and Jimmy are no thieves."

Raoul grimaced with regret. "Forgive me. That was shockingly rude."

Willie led the way through an overgrown field, his back stiff and his chin high. Raoul was wise enough not to press, instead following in silence.

At last, Willie halted to pull open a gate set in a low stone wall.

"Just through here, sir."

Stepping through the gate, Raoul came to a sharp halt.

He recognized the timber-framed cottage that was charmingly set beside the tiny stream. When the hell had he crossed into Merriot land?

"*Mon Dieu.*"

Willie stopped to regard him with a puzzled frown. "Something the matter?"

"This is the old gamekeeper's cottage," he breathed.

"Aye. Miss Sarah's father was the gamekeeper for Lord Merriot afore he died some seven years ago."

Vaguely, Raoul recalled spotting Jefferson's raven-haired daughter occasionally about the estate during his rare visits. She had been at least five years younger than himself, and while a pretty little thing, of no real interest to an unhappy bastard who was already dreaming of a life far from Cheshire.

"Miss Sarah, she is not wed?"

"Nay, nor does she ever intend to wed. She says she is happy to be an old maid."

Old maid? Egads.

Without undue vanity, Raoul comprehended the power of his appearance on women. How could he not? They had been fawning, fluttering, and occasionally fainting since he had left the nursery.

And old maids were always the worst.

"Perhaps you should run ahead and prepare her for my entrance," he commanded, poised for flight. It was bad enough to be on his father's land, without having the added annoyance of fighting off a desperate female. He would hand over Jimmy and bolt. "I would not want to send Miss Sarah into a swoon at the sight of her wounded lamb."

"You don't know Miss Sarah if you think anything

would send her into a swoon. She didn't so much as bat an eye when I fell from the tree and broke my arm." Willie glanced toward his brother's limp body, gnawing his bottom lip. "Still, I wouldn't wish her to be thinking poor Jimmy is dead."

Raoul's impatience melted. Poor lad.

"Go on," he urged, gently. "The little one is safe in my care."

The gray gaze studied him for a long moment, then seeming to find something trustworthy in Raoul's lean features, he abruptly turned and sprinted across the frozen ground, and disappeared into the cottage.

Alone in the cramped front garden, Raoul distracted himself from the impending confrontation by ensuring that Hercules was happily destroying a small bush next to the gate, and then by studying the warm bundle cradled in his arms.

Ugly little bugger, Raoul decided, with his face all thin angles and sharp points. So ugly that Raoul could not possibly feel a tug at his heart at the boy's small frown of pain. And certainly his arms did not tighten as Jimmy shivered in the sharp breeze.

There was a welcome distraction as a woman stepped from the cottage, and lifting his head, Raoul watched as she briskly crossed the short distance.

No, not a distraction.

A . . . bolt of lightning.

Or at least that was what it felt like to Raoul as he haplessly gaped at the exotic vision swaying across the frozen ground. She was dark, he inanely noted. Thick raven hair tugged into a haphazard knot at her nape, and black eyes that were faintly tilted and surrounded by a thick lace of black lashes. Even her skin held a hint of gold, rather than ivory, reminding Raoul that her mother had been a foreigner, reputedly of gypsy blood.

An old maid?

Sacrebleu. With her lush curves perfectly revealed beneath the plain blue gown, and those lips that were full and tinted with rose, she could make a fortune on the London stages.

Or gracing his bed . . .

Abruptly Raoul realized that far from fending off a hysterical female, *he* was the one staring like an idiot. As if he had been kicked in the head, instead of poor Jimmy.

Rueful amusement helped to ease the sense of unreality that gripped him, and with a measure of composure, a very small measure, he managed to meet the dark, steady gaze.

"Miss Jefferson, I believe I have something that belongs to you," he murmured.

"So I see, Mr. Charlebois," she retorted, proving she was well aware of his identity. Just . . . indifferent. Astonishing. "If you would be so kind as to bring Jimmy into the parlor?"

His amusement deepened as she turned, and with the same brisk movements led the way back to the cottage, clearly expecting to be obeyed.

As if it were England's most notorious actor's duty to tend to her precocious scamp.

"Of course."

A few flakes of snow drifted from the gray clouds, twirling in the icy breeze. Nearby a dog barked in warning. From the cottage wafted the scent of wood smoke, and more distant the potent scent of freshly cut evergreens.

The sights and smells of Cheshire in December.

Ducking his head, Raoul entered the cottage and followed Miss Jefferson through the cramped foyer into the parlor. He had a brief impression of wooden floors and an open-beamed ceiling with plastered walls. The furnishings were plain and ruthlessly polished, and despite the woman's obvious housekeeping skills, there was no way to disguise they were growing shabby. Oddly, Raoul had the vague feeling he had seen them before as he settled his small burden on a brocade sofa.

It was a feeling he readily dismissed as his beautiful companion moved to stir the coals in the vast stone fireplace.

His breath became elusive as he watched her graceful movements, feeling as focused as a hound on point as she slowly straightened and brushed past him to settle on the edge of the cushion next to her young ward.

As if sensing her presence, Jimmy managed to lift his lashes just a crack, revealing a hint of pale blue eyes.

"Miss Sarah . . ."

"Sssh, poppet, all is well," she murmured, motioning toward Willie, who had just entered the room carrying a basin filled with lavender-scented water. He set it on the floor and stepped back as the woman reached into the water to withdraw the cold compress, pressing it with tender care to the lump on Jimmy's forehead. Only when the boy sighed and drifted back to sleep did she lift her head to regard Raoul with a calm expression. Clearly, Willie had not exaggerated. Miss Jefferson was quite prepared for any disaster. "What happened?"

Raoul hid a smile as he felt Willie stiffen at his side. "The fault is mine, I fear," he said smoothly.

She arched a perfect raven brow. "Yours?"

He smiled, readily disregarding the truth. "My mount is a high-spirited beast that took exception to the poor lad as he stood beside the path."

The dark gaze shifted toward the window where she had an unimpeded view of Hercules, patiently awaiting his master.

"Oh yes, quite spirited, I see."

"Beyond question."

"And no doubt there was an unexpected noise that spooked the poor creature?"

"A covey of quail in the hedgerow, I believe."

"Ah." Her gaze slid to the suspiciously innocent expression on Willie's countenance before returning her attention to the equally innocent Raoul. "I do hope there was no harm done?"

"Only to poor Jimmy. Do you wish me to fetch the local surgeon?"

"Thank you, no." She turned her head to smile tenderly at the unconscious urchin. Raoul's heart gave a peculiar flop. "I believe all I shall need is a length of rope and apple tarts."

"Rope?" Raoul shamelessly vied to regain the minx's attention. "I do trust that the rope is not destined for my neck?"

As hoped, the dark gaze lifted. "Actually, I intend to tie this impossible scamp to his bed so he cannot sneak out and do even more damage to his battered brain."

"And the tarts?"

"They tend to make any wound a bit more bearable for the boys."

"Actually I believe it is you, Miss Jefferson, that makes wounds, not to mention life in general, more bearable for the boys."

Chapter 2

Sarah Jefferson had known Raoul Charlebois was in the neighborhood.

How could she not?

All of Cheshire was buzzing with the excitement of having such an important personage attending the local assembly, and even taking luncheon at the local pub.

She had not, however, given him much thought.

It never occurred to her that their paths would cross. After all, she didn't move in society, and for the most part, she was kept far too busy tending to the boys and working on her paintings to join in the village amusements.

Now she discovered herself strangely . . . unnerved by his close proximity.

It was not just his magnificent beauty, although that was enough to make any woman weak in the knees. Pale golden curls. Cobalt blue eyes that were framed by indecently long lashes. Finely crafted features that included a wide brow, an aquiline nose, full lips, and chiseled cheekbones. Or even the odd sense that she had seen the precise face before, but on another person . . .

No, it was the shock of his powerful presence that seemed to overwhelm the small cottage.

Gads, it was little wonder critics claimed he could light an entire stage without the benefit of gas lamps.

Thankfully, Sarah was a sensible woman who was content with her life without foolish dreams. Her mother had taught her that every day was a blessing that was meant to be enjoyed to the fullest. They were words she had taken to heart.

Which was why she was capable of ignoring her racing pulse and the pleasurable flutters in the pit of her stomach.

Raoul Charlebois was like Christmas punch.

Far too potent for more than a small sip once a year.

"It was very kind of you to bring Jimmy home, Mr. Charlebois, but I believe we have imposed upon you long enough."

A stillness settled about his large form. "My dear, Miss Jefferson, am I being dismissed?"

Distracted by her tingling awareness of the gorgeous gentleman, not to mention concern for Jimmy, Sarah missed the dangerous edge in his smooth voice.

"I am certain you have a better means of passing your afternoon."

"Not particularly." His lips curved into a practiced smile that could make a woman swoon at a hundred paces. "Master Willie, will you see that Hercules is given water and perhaps a few oats?"

Pleasure flared through the gray eyes as Willie bolted toward the door.

"Aye, sir. You can depend on me."

Belatedly, Sarah realized her error.

Lud, she'd taken care of her father after her mother's

death when she was just fourteen, and for the past three years she'd tended to two spirited boys who were as skittish as untrained colts.

She, better than anyone, knew better than to directly challenge a male.

Especially a male accustomed to women fawning at their feet.

It was the one certain way to ensure they dug in their heels and did the precise thing you did not want them to do.

Clumsy, Sarah, very, very clumsy.

Hiding her annoyance behind a serene smile, Sarah waved a hand toward a nearby chair.

"Please make yourself welcome. There is sherry on the sideboard. I fear I never keep stronger spirits in the house."

"A wise choice with two inquisitive boys underfoot." He tossed aside his hat and greatcoat to reveal an exquisitely tailored blue jacket and buff breeches before sprawling with elegant ease in the wing chair. Then, slipping his hand beneath his ivory waistcoat, he removed a silver flask. "As you see, I am always prepared for emergencies."

Sarah busied herself by wetting the compress in the basin of water. Why was her throat dry? Surely it could not be because Raoul's expensive attire molded to his hard muscles with wicked perfection?

Or because those impossibly blue eyes were skimming over her as if he was considering the pleasure of devouring her?

"I assume you are staying at the Great House?" she asked, pleased to discover her voice revealed none of her inner disturbance.

"You assume wrong, *ma belle*," he drawled. "I have accepted Mr. Baxter's generous offer to occupy his hunting lodge while he is forced to take the waters in Bath."

She returned the compress to Jimmy's lump, pleased by the hint of color returning to the boy's cheeks. It wasn't his first, or even worst, injury, but a head wound was always worrisome.

"Do you come with a party?"

"No, I am quite alone, unless you count my valet and groom."

"Ah, so this is what they call a repairing lease?"

"*Mon Dieu,*" he breathed. "Now where would a young, innocent maiden hear such a vulgar term?"

She shrugged. "It is a common enough occurrence here in Cheshire."

"No, *ma petite,* I have no need to retrench." There was a pause. "More a journey of discovery."

"Really?" She refused to glance in his direction. Pretend indifference, and eventually he would go away. "And what is it you hope to discover?"

"I am not entirely certain," he said meditatively.

"Then how will you know you have discovered it?"

He gave a startled chuckle. Gads, even that was heartbreaking.

"An astute question."

"And the answer?"

"Not nearly so astute." She heard him shift, as if discomforted by his inner thoughts, then he deliberately turned the conversation. "I was very sorry to hear of your father's passing. He devoted many an afternoon to teaching me to fish, or how to shoot without causing too much carnage among the neighborhood."

The familiar pain tugged at her heart. "I miss him every day."

"You live here alone?"

The question and his tone were unexpectedly abrupt.

"I have the boys and Maggie Stone, who comes daily to help with the laundry and heavy cleaning."

"I am surprised Lord Merriot would rent his cottage to a young maiden and her two strays. He was always such a judgmental ass."

Why would her living arrangement matter to this man? Unless . . .

"The cottage and the surrounding gardens were given to my father by the Earl as a portion of his salary some years ago. It was passed to me upon his death."

"An unusual arrangement."

Common sense was forgotten as she turned to stab him with a proud gaze.

"From my understanding, the lands east of the paddock are not part of the entail."

A golden brow lifted, his sinful lips curving into a smile. "You need not jut that lovely chin at me, *ma petite*. I am a bastard, not the legal heir keeping count of every pence and pound of my birthright. If it were in my power, I would offer you the entire godforsaken estate. My dislike is a natural concern for the thought of a lone woman and two young boys living in such an isolated spot."

Oh. She battled the urge to blush.

"Not so alone," she corrected. "If you would peek into the back garden, you would discover two very large and very protective dogs that I bring into the cottage during the night. Besides, there are few in the vicinity I haven't known since I left the cradle."

"There are others beyond the local residents who

can pose a danger to a beautiful young woman," he strangely persisted.

"Others?"

Something that might have been bitterness darkened the blue eyes.

"As I recall, Lord and Lady Merriot enjoy hosting lavish parties with guests that linger for weeks. There are few creatures more dangerous than a bored nobleman. They possess an unshakable belief that the world and all who inhabit it are simply here to serve their pleasure."

She frowned, silently wondering if the bitterness was directed toward Lord Merriot, or those bored noblemen.

"You have been gone a long time, Mr. Charlebois."

His gaze deliberately skimmed down to the modest cut of her bodice before returning to her face.

"True, but I am uncertain what bearing that has on our conversation."

She refused to be flustered. "There are never guests invited to the Great House. Lord and Lady Merriot have remained in deep mourning since their son's death."

"Still?" There was genuine surprise in his voice. "Peter drowned what . . . three, or is it four, years ago?"

"There are some tragedies that no amount of time can heal."

"I suppose that explains their absence from London."

Having been raised in a loving family, Sarah was startled by his seeming disinterest.

Of course, he had been barely ten when he was sent to London, and his occasional visits had halted altogether after the birth of Lord and Lady Merriot's only child. Perhaps it was not unexpected he would feel a measure of resentment.

"You did not know?"

"Does that astonish you?" His smile remained, but Sarah sensed the darkness beneath the smooth charm. "I have not been invited to Cheshire since Peter's birth, and certainly my father has never made an effort to correspond with his bastard son. I daresay you are far better acquainted with Lord and Lady Merriot than myself."

"Perhaps your arrival in the neighborhood will ease their suffering."

He snorted. "More likely it will terrify them into boarding over the windows and barricading the door."

Realizing that she was allowing the dangerous man to stir her fascination, Sarah determinedly returned her attention to Jimmy. She was a confirmed spinster. There was no place in her world for magical creatures that were surely made of mist and enchantment.

"Very dramatic," she said, dryly. "You should consider a career on the stage."

Again that delicious chuckle. "Brat."

"Do you truly believe they will not desire your company?"

"I believe they will demand me to make an appearance at the Great House, but not because of any desire for my company."

"People do change, you know. It could be your father will be anxious to heal the rifts with his only remaining son."

"Only if you believe in miracles, *ma petite*."

"It is the season for them, Mr. Charlebois."

"Season?"

"It soon will be Christmas."

Beneath the tender stroke of her hand, Jimmy sighed and struggled to open his heavy lids.

"Will we have plum cakes, Miss Sarah?"

She hid her smile of relief. His words were clear and coherent.

"I promised, did I not, poppet? Although . . ." She heaved a faint sigh.

"What?" The guileless blue eyes that should have belonged to a saint, not a mischievous imp, gazed at her with growing concern. "What is it?"

"Well, I fear that boys who are sickening from a pain in their head must content themselves with gruel."

"I ain't . . ." He swiftly bit off the word. Sarah demanded proper speech, as well as the ability to read and do sums. It was the only means by which two boys without family or money would ever make something of themselves. "I mean, I am not sickening, I swear. Why, I can show you I'm as right as rain."

She gently pressed on his shoulder, keeping him flat on the cushions.

"Oh yes, I can see you are a determined young man, which is precisely how I know you will balk at being sensible enough to remain abed until you are fully healed, thus ensuring that by Christmas day you will be laid up with a fever and scattered wits. I should not be at all surprised if you shall be too weak to even hang the holly wreath." She offered a sympathetic smile. "Still, I am certain you will feel that sneaking from your bed the moment my back is turned will be a grand jest and well worth missing our simple celebrations."

"Nay," he breathed, horrified by the mere notion. "I swear I won't stir without permission."

"You swear?"

"Aye." He brushed a hand over his chest. "Cross my heart."

"Well then, I suppose I shall be baking plum cakes after all."

Jimmy flashed his lethal dimples. "You might even need a double batch seeing as I shall be dreadfully hungry from all that nasty gruel."

"Scamp." Bending down, Sarah brushed a light kiss on the tip of his nose. "Close your eyes and rest, and I shall put the kettle on."

"Are there any biscuits?"

With a soft laugh, she rose to her feet. "We shall see."

She had barely taken a step toward the kitchen when a large, decidedly male body was blocking her path. With effort, she resisted the urge to back away from the imposing form, and instead tilted up her head to meet the amused blue gaze.

"Deftly done, Miss Jefferson," her intruder drawled. "You have a frightening talent for forcing your will without need of ropes. I shall keep that in mind."

"Pardon me?"

He offered a dip of his head, then turning, he collected his coat and hat before crossing toward the door.

"*Adieu, ma belle.*"

December 12
Cheshire

Baxter's hunting lodge was not the finest house in the neighborhood. Certainly it could not compete with Lord Merriot's grand mansion, or even the local squire's tidy Queen Anne home.

Still, it was comfortably shabby in a masculine fashion, with a back parlor, a dining room, a large billiards room, and a surprisingly well-stocked library that overlooked the small, currently frozen lake.

Settled in a large wing chair that was situated close to the marble fireplace, Raoul absently leafed through a book that described some traveler or another who seemed to have spent an inordinate, not to mention uncomfortable, amount of time among the African natives.

It wasn't that he was incapable of enjoying a good book.

The library in his London town house was the envy of many devoted bibliophiles, with a collection that was as wide and varied as Raoul's interests.

On this cold afternoon, however, he was far too distracted to properly concentrate.

And not distracted in the manner that he should be distracted.

Slamming the book shut, he tossed it onto a walnut pier table. Why the devil couldn't he get the image of a raven-haired, dark-eyed minx out of his mind?

It wasn't as if she were the sort of woman who usually occupied his thoughts.

She was beautiful, certainly. Astonishingly, breath-takingly beautiful. And there was a compelling vibrancy shimmering about her that would capture the fantasy of even the most jaded gentleman. So blessedly different from the boring, languid grace of society women.

And that lush body . . .

His blood heated for what seemed to be the hundredth time since he'd left the cottage three days ago.

Sacrebleu. He was an idiot. Miss Sarah Jefferson might look like a woman who could offer a man paradise, but she was in truth, the most dangerous creature known to man.

A proper, virginal maiden.

His dreams should not be filled with visions of ripe, cherry lips nibbling over his chest. Or full breasts spilling over a modest corset.

And most certainly, he should not be obsessed to know why such a beautiful, intelligent woman was content to become a spinster. And why she would take in two high-spirited lads who seemingly had no connection to her family.

He should not.

But . . .

His broodings were disturbed as the door to the library was thrust open. Nico crossed the polished wooden floor to toss a folded message, along with a shilling, on top of the book Raoul had so recently discarded.

Raoul pocketed the shilling and absently fingered the thick ivory parchment paper that had been folded and impressively honored with the Merriot seal.

"Ah, so it has arrived." He studied the message, unable to sort through the mix of emotions warring through him. "Excellent."

"Lucky bastard," Nico muttered, his dark, handsome features hard with annoyance.

When they had arrived in Cheshire, the servant had stewed and fretted at Raoul's refusal to directly call upon Lord Merriot. The one-time thief was a master of disguise and capable of ferreting out any information Raoul might desire, but he had little experience with nobility. Nico was quite convinced that the Earl would never lower his pride to contact his bastard son.

Convinced enough to bet a shilling on the outcome.

"Bastard, most certainly, but it is a painful understanding of my father, not luck, that allowed me to win this particular wager," Raoul drawled. "He is nothing if not predictable."

Nico grimaced, smoothing a hand over the dark hair he had tied into a tail at his neck.

"Are you not going to open it?"

"In time." Raoul stretched out his legs and crossed them at the ankle, the fine gloss of his Hessians reflecting the flames from the fireplace. "First I desire to know if you managed to acquire the information I requested."

Nico snorted. "You mean, did I snoop around and spy like you wanted?"

"I asked for a *discreet inquiry*."

"And the difference?"

"One sounds less offensive than the other."

"Ah."

"What did you discover?"

Nico moved to lean against the black marble chimneypiece, holding his hands toward the fire. Although he'd left Rome when he was just a child, the cutthroat still cursed the damp, frigid winters of England.

"Surprisingly little, despite my extraordinary skills."

"So modest."

A dangerous smile curved his lips. "The meek might be destined to inherit the earth, but the gutters will always belong to the bold."

Raoul tapped the folded message against the arm of the chair.

"You must have learned something."

"Miss Jefferson lives very quietly in her cottage and, from all I could discover, is beloved by the locals for her talent with herbs."

"Ah yes, I seem to recall her mother possessed a similar talent." His eyes narrowed. "There are no scandals?"

"None that the natives are willing to share."

"And no disapproval at a young, beautiful woman living alone with two abandoned waifs?"

"I believe there was an elderly nurse who lived with her until a year or so ago, but after the nurse's death Miss Jefferson was apparently determined to remain independent, and claimed her advanced years as reason enough to spurn the need for a chaperon."

The vivid image of tilted black eyes and sun-kissed skin seared through his mind.

"*Mon Dieu,* the chit is closer to the nursery than her dotage."

"Does it matter?"

Raoul's brows snapped together. "Of course it does."

Nico turned, leaning his back against the mantel, his expression thoughtful.

"I must admit I am baffled."

"Why?"

"If she is as young and beautiful as you claim, then surely you would prefer she not be guarded by some bitter old gorgon, or worse, a hot-tempered relative who would slice off your manhood for a stray glance?" The dark eyes studied Raoul's suddenly wary expression. "Unless I have mistaken your interest in her."

With a smooth motion, Raoul was on his feet and headed for the door.

"The mistake is no doubt mine, Nico."

Hercules was no more pleased than Raoul to be urged out of his warm stall to confront the brutal wind and icy roads. In truth, Raoul had debated ignoring the short, imperious summons from his father.

It wasn't that he was hurt by the cold, impersonal demand that he present himself at the Great House. How could he be?

This was exactly what he had been expecting.

No, it was merely a healthy aversion to freezing his balls on the two-mile ride, only to have them further twisted into knots by his father when he reached the Great House.

Dismissing his foolish reluctance, Raoul attired himself in a jade coat and gold-stitched waistcoat that were matched with buff breeches and a modestly tied cravat. Although he had never been a particular friend of Brummell, he did appreciate the tailored simplicity that he had made fashionable.

Then, wrapping himself in his coat, hat, and gloves, he gathered Hercules and set out.

Despite the chill in the air, there were several hearty folks out and about. A few farmers tending to their animals, a handful of children collecting Christmas holly for the mantel, a dairy maid that gave a small squeal and darted away when she caught sight of him.

He aimlessly allowed his gaze to roam over the frozen landscape, following the familiar landmarks, until he caught sight of a low stone wall.

Mon Dieu.

He had deliberately chosen the path that would take him directly past Miss Jefferson's cottage.

With the gentle pressure of Raoul's knees, Hercules came to a halt. He should ride on. He had no business here. None whatsoever . . .

So why was he sitting there like a great big lump of stupidity?

As if to mock his strange paralysis, the sound of

barking split the air and two large mutts came charging toward the wall, closely followed by a familiar lad with brown curls and far too perceptive gray eyes.

Hercules stirred at the commotion, and bringing him swiftly under control, Raoul glared at the advancing dogs.

"Enough, you revolting beasts," he snapped, his hand lifting in command. "Sit."

It was too much to hope the unruly curs would actually obey, but they did stop in their tracks and eye him with obvious wariness.

"Sir." A pleased expression lightened Willie's narrow countenance, although Raoul suspected it had to do more with the sight of Hercules than himself. "Wait a moment. Sampson. Delilah. Come."

With surprising ease, Willie corralled the dogs into the long stone building attached to the back of the cottage. No doubt it had once been the stables, although Raoul doubted Miss Jefferson possessed the funds to keep a horse and carriage.

Not nearly as annoyed as he should be at being more or less trapped, Raoul urged Hercules through the open gate and vaulted onto the hard, uneven ground just as Willie came dashing towards him.

"Hard at work with your chores, Master Willie?" he murmured, glancing toward the pile of split firewood.

The boy grimaced. "Aye."

"I believe that I possess something that belongs to you."

"Me?"

Reaching into the saddlebag, Raoul removed the scuffed cricket ball he'd unearthed from the hedge three days ago.

He had been careful not to examine the reason for the

hour he had spent looking for the ridiculous thing. Or why he had hoarded it like some sort of treasure.

"Here." He tossed the ball to the startled Willie. "I would suggest you hide the evidence until suspicion of Jimmy's accident has passed."

"Thank you, sir." The lad hastily tucked the ball into his pocket. "I appreciate you not telling Miss Sarah about our little game. We aren't supposed to take the bat and ball out of the garden."

"I held my council only because I believe the two of you have learned your lesson."

"Aye." Genuine regret darkened the gray eyes. "Jimmy was stuck in his bed until this morning. Poor bugger had nothing to do but study his sums and practice his penmanship."

"I presume he is up and about again?"

"He is up, but Miss Sarah has him scrubbing floors today. Says the air is too crisp for him to venture out."

Raoul smiled ruefully. Miss Sarah had clearly devised the perfect means of ensuring the boys never again played cricket outside the garden.

Clever as well as beautiful.

Dangerous, indeed.

"A true Machiavellian mind," he murmured.

"Beg pardon?"

Raoul shook his head in self-derision, giving into the inevitable.

He had come this way for one reason only.

To try and pretend otherwise was foolish.

"If you do not mind sharing the garden with Hercules, I believe I shall call upon Master Jimmy and assure myself he will suffer no lingering harm."

"I should say I don't mind," Willie breathed, running

a reverent hand down Hercules's neck. "Wherever did you get such a sweet-goer?"

"He spent his younger years performing at Astley's, but much like myself, he has retired to obscurity."

"He's a beaut."

"He's a shameless *prima donna* who will dance a jig for an apple."

Willie lifted shimmering gray eyes, his excitement touching something deep inside Raoul.

"May I?"

Once again reaching into the saddlebag, Raoul pulled out an apple and handed it to the charming lad.

"Just mind the hoofs. I fear I am already in Miss Jefferson's black book for injuring her youngest chick. I won't be accused of doing you both in."

"Aye, sir."

Sensing Willie's innate skill with animals, Raoul readily left his mount in the youngster's care and headed for the back door of the cottage.

His father could damn well wait.

He was done fighting his need to see Miss Sarah Jefferson.

Busy sifting the flour for the gingerbread cake she intended to serve with tea, Sarah had been aware of Raoul Charlebois's presence the moment he arrived.

Pretending that she was indifferent to his company, and that she had not been stupidly let down when she had not seen him over the past three days, Sarah struggled to keep her gaze from straying to the window overlooking the back garden.

There was no need to gawk at him as if she were a

giddy schoolgirl. She knew he was shockingly beautiful, and that he resembled someone she could not quite recall, so why did her gaze continue to linger on that chiseled profile? Almost as if she wanted it engraved on her mind.

Enough.

Concentrating on her pastry, Sarah reminded herself of all the reasons a gorgeous male, one who had reportedly bedded a princess no less, would have no interest in an aging spinster.

There was any number of them, each more logical than the last, so by the time the gentleman boldly entered her kitchen without so much as a knock, she was quite prepared to greet him with a distant smile.

"Mr. Charlebois."

He removed his hat and gloves, performing an elegant bow. "A good afternoon, Miss Jefferson. I have come to inquire after Master Jimmy."

"And to return the missing cricket ball?" she murmured.

He clicked his tongue. "That, *ma petite,* is a subject between gentlemen."

Dear . . . God, he was beautiful.

Sarah's mouth went dry, her heart lodged somewhere in her throat. Sheer survival had her ducking her head to concentrate on her cake.

"Hmmm."

There was the sound of footsteps and the scent of sandalwood as Raoul Charlebois moved to lean against the counter next to her.

"I trust Jimmy is on the mend?"

"He is."

"And you have had no ill effects from the shock of his injuries?"

Sarah wondered if she imagined his sharp intake of breath as she chuckled at his absurd question.

"I have long ago accepted that young, spirited boys and injuries go hand in hand."

"How long have they been in your care?"

"Nearly three years."

"They are fortunate to have such a devoted, yet understanding guardian."

Her heart melted at his words. And not because of his low, seductive tone. The boys, and the care she offered them, touched her where she was most vulnerable.

"I consider myself the fortunate one." She wiped her hands on the apron that covered her primrose muslin gown, suddenly anxious to be rid of her unexpected intruder. "Was that all?"

"Now why are you always so eager to dismiss me, Miss Jefferson?" Without warning, his finger slid beneath her chin, forcing her face up to meet his mocking gaze. "Could it be I have unintentionally offended you? Or is it that you hold me to blame for young Jimmy's injury?"

Her heart forgot to beat at his touch.

"Neither, Mr. Charlebois. I am simply busy."

"So I see." The blue eyes darkened as he lowered his head to brush his lips over her temple. "Butter." His lips moved to tease at her cheek. "Flour." He covered her trembling mouth with a tender kiss. "And ginger." Slowly he pulled back, his slumberous gaze sweeping over her flushed features. "You taste of Christmas."

Pleasure as thick and delicious as warm honey slid through her body at his touch. His slender, clever fingers trailed down her jaw, his touch sending jolts of dazzling sensations straight to the pit of her stomach.

Oh . . . he was wicked.

Wondrously, magnificently wicked.

"Mr. Charlebois," she breathed.

"Raoul."

All Sarah wanted was to press against that hard body, to part her lips and give in to the potent temptation of his kiss. To drown in his heady beauty, and the artistic skill of his seduction.

Instead, she forced herself to swallow her revealing groan, backing away from his lingering touch. She didn't know what role Raoul Charlebois was currently playing, but she was too sensible to join in the cast.

"Mr. Charlebois . . ."

Chapter 3

Raoul was in swift pursuit, following her steps until she was backed against the wall. Then, planting his hands on either side of her shoulders, he effectively trapped her, studying her flushed features with a brooding gaze.

This was not supposed to be happening.

Hell, he had told himself he would not even think about the dark-eyed gypsy, let alone force his way into her cottage and take shocking advantage of her.

But with the taste of her ripe lips still clinging to his mouth, and the feel of her lush curves imprinted on his body, he didn't give a damn.

She was what a woman was meant to be.

Warm and giving with a hint of exotic spice.

Exactly what he wanted Father Christmas to leave in his stocking.

"Yes, it was quite unforgivably forward of me, and I am an utter cad who should have his face slapped," he interrupted her words of censure, flashing his most potent smile.

A smile that had felled countless women.

A smile that Countess Campelli had claimed was blessed by the angels. Or by the devil.

A smile that was wholly and utterly ineffective when it came to beautiful spinsters.

Instead of melting, Sarah lifted her hands and pressed them firmly against his chest.

"I would say you are more a rake who has so often had his way with women that you cannot imagine there might be one who has no interest in your attentions."

His gaze dipped to the demure line of her bodice, deliberately lingering on the frantic beat of her heart.

"Not even a small measure of interest?"

"My hands are filled with caring for two highly demanding, at times infantile lads. I do not need another to fuss over, thank you very much." Her verbal blow delivered with the expertise of Gentleman Jackson, Sarah ducked beneath his arm and moved to pull open the kitchen door with a dismissive smile. "You will have to forgive me, Mr. Charlebois. I have a cake to finish."

"I'll be damned."

The trip to the Great House was a short ride. Less than a mile. Thank God. Raoul didn't need time to dwell on the strange, near volatile sensations rushing through his blood.

He should be furious.

He, Raoul Charlebois, the most sought-after rake in all of London, had just been given a crushing set-down by an old maid.

But he wasn't furious.

He was . . . hell, he was almost giddy.

As if champagne were bubbling through his veins.

And all because a spinster who smelled of gingerbread instead of orchids, who preferred snotty-nosed orphans to elegant gentlemen, who charmed the village with her skills at herbal healing rather than her undoubted beauty had shown him the door.

He was batty.

A complete and total loon.

Or maybe it was the season, he wryly told himself.

Father Christmas was known to play merry jests on the wicked.

Perhaps this was his punishment for any number of sins.

Thankfully, he had no time to ponder the ridiculous notion as the path slowly widened and, cresting a low hill, the Great House came into view.

Raoul shivered as the wind suddenly seemed colder, sharper, and the clouds more threatening as he studied the building that was spread across the rolling parkland.

A combination of Tudor and Elizabethan, the main structure was built of the local red sandstone bricks that had mellowed with age. When Raoul had been just a boy, the Earl had added two long wings with matching courtyards, and a formal rose garden.

The overall effect was clumsy rather than gracious to Raoul's discerning eye, although the locals all seemed readily impressed by the sweeping avenues, flanked by elegant statues and a large reflecting pool at the base of the circle drive.

Ignoring the urge to give Hercules his head and race past the reddish monstrosity, Raoul instead approached the large portico at a dignified pace and awaited the young groom to rush from the stables.

Raoul slid out of the saddle and tossed the reins

toward the servant before he climbed the wide stairs. His foot barely hit the landing when one of the double oak doors was pulled open to reveal the short, pudgy butler with a fringe of gray hair, attired in the Earl's uniform of hunter green and black.

The pale eyes that always appeared leeched of color briefly warmed before he was stepping back, offering a stiff bow of welcome.

"Mr. Charlebois."

"Hawkins." Shrugging off his outer garments, Raoul cast a covert glance about the inner hall, grimacing at the two life-sized silver lions standing guard beside the double marble staircase that curved toward the upper vestibule. He recalled the foyer when it was darkly paneled and filled with shabby furnishings. He preferred the simpler style. "How are you?"

"Quite well, sir. The master requested that I show you directly to the library."

Raoul's lips twisted in a humorless smile. "He was so certain I would come?"

"I cannot say, sir."

"Lead onward, Hawkins."

Moving up the stairs, Raoul allowed himself to be led down the long gallery, resisting the urge to roll his eyes at the green and black plasterwork that covered the walls in honor of the Merriot colors. And the golden crest that was painted in the center of the frescoes decorating the ceiling—narcissism at its finest.

They had nearly reached the end of the gallery when Raoul realized there was something . . . strange about the mansion. No, not the actual mansion.

It was the atmosphere.

As if the brittle gaiety that had always spilled

through the massive house had been swallowed by a lurking darkness.

Darkness that not even the gilt tables and sparkling chandeliers could dispel.

"*Mon Dieu,* it is more a mausoleum than home," he breathed with a shudder. "Has it been this way since Peter's death?"

"The young master is never spoken of, sir," Hawkins warned, his expression unreadable as he pushed open the door to the library. "Mr. Charlebois, my lord."

"Thank you, Hawkins, that will be all." The muffled voice of the Earl had the butler swiftly scurrying away.

Raoul very nearly scurried behind him.

Only pride, and his cork-brained determination to uncover his father's mysterious secret, forced his reluctant feet over the threshold and into the vast library.

For a cowardly moment, he allowed his gaze to roam over the towering shelves that framed the high arched windows that overlooked the back terraces. In the center of the room, the rarest manuscripts were kept encased in glass and walnut cabinets, along with the Earl's fine collection of dueling pistols.

This had always been his favorite room in the entire house.

Not because of the heavy, masculine furniture or polished wood floor. Or even the fine coved ceiling.

But because he could easily hide behind the crimson velvet curtains and disappear into one of the numerous books.

At last weary of Raoul's hesitation, Lord Merriot stepped away from the heavy walnut desk and waved a hand toward a silver tray that was setting on a low marble-topped table.

"Come in Raoul and have a seat. A brandy? Or would you prefer tea?"

"Neither, I thank you."

Raoul strolled across the room, lowering his tall form into one of the numerous leather wing chairs. Then, with a deliberate nonchalance, he stretched out his legs and folded his arms over his chest.

"You summoned me?"

The Earl's florid face darkened with annoyance, and Raoul suddenly realized that the older man had aged.

Once a massive, barrel-chested sportsman with heavy features and a larger-than-life personality, Jonah Spearman, the fifth Earl of Merriot, seemed to have shrunk over the years.

The heavy frame was stooped beneath the brown jacket, and the black curls were thickly threaded with gray. Even his forceful features seemed to have shriveled, becoming almost gaunt.

As if he was merely a ghost of his former self.

Of course, one thing hadn't changed.

The wary contempt that shimmered in the dark eyes.

"Surely you must have been expecting it?" he said, his voice gruff.

Raoul arched a brow, for the first time in his life in a position to control the confrontation with the Earl of Merriot.

"Why would I?" he drawled. "We have not exchanged so much as a word in the past ten years. I assumed you had long ago dismissed any memory of your bastard son."

An ugly crimson began to crawl up the Earl's neck to the heavy jowls.

"Dismiss the renowned Raoul Charlebois, when your name is forever filling the pages of the newspapers and being bandied about in drawing rooms as if you were royalty?"

Raoul studied the gold ring he wore on his little finger. "Ah, how vulgar of me not to realize my need to put food on my table and a roof over my head might be bothersome for you and Lady Merriot." Slowly lifting his head, he offered his father a sardonic smile. "You will be relieved to discover that I have recently retired, and soon enough another will capture the fickle attention of London society."

"Retired?"

"We all grow older." Raoul shrugged. "I prefer a graceful exit to being jeered from the stage."

Merriot paced with jerky steps to a nearby window, his profile hard with displeasure.

"This is unacceptable."

"*Mon Dieu*." Raoul's sharp, disbelieving laugh echoed through the too silent air. "You were just complaining that my fame was bothersome, and now you are displeased by the thought of my retirement. You are a difficult gentleman to please, my lord."

With obvious effort, the older gentleman struggled to maintain his composure.

"If you truly are retired, then why would choose to bury yourself in the wilds of Cheshire? A gentleman at his leisure is able to travel anywhere."

"This was once my home."

Merriot snorted, knowing damned well that Raoul had hated this sprawling mansion almost as much as he hated his father.

"And you have always claimed it dull as dishwater."

"Perhaps maturity will allow me to view it with fresh eyes."

"Highly doubtful." Merriot turned to glare at Raoul, his once handsome face lined and careworn in the gray light slanting through the window. "For heaven's sake, Raoul, there is little here to amuse a young, handsome gentleman. Certainly it cannot compare to the entertainments to be found in London, or even Brighton."

Raoul's lips twitched. It seemed that the entire population of Cheshire was devoted to making him go away.

"If I were a suspicious man, I would think you were trying to be rid of me."

"I am only thinking of you, Raoul."

"I see." Raoul made no attempt to hide his rampant disbelief. "Your continuous devotion quite overwhelms me. Was a son ever so fortunate in his father?"

Almost as if Raoul's low words struck a nerve, which was absurd, Lord Merriot moved to the silver tray and poured himself a large measure of brandy. Tossing it down his throat, he at last returned his attention to the patiently waiting Raoul.

"What is it you want of me?" he rasped.

Raoul narrowed his gaze. Merriot was obviously disturbed by having his bastard staying in Cheshire.

The question was whether it was simply a natural distaste at having Raoul underfoot, or if he had another reason to be uneasy at his son's arrival.

"Who the devil said I desired anything of you?"

The brown eyes that Raoul always thought of as muddy suddenly widened, a hint of relief touching the lined countenance.

"Ah. Of course. Now that you are retired, you will no doubt be in need of funds to . . ."

Raoul was on his feet, his expression hard with disdain. "If I wished to hang on your sleeve, my lord, I would have arrived on your doorstep, hat in hand."

Merriot winced. "You must want something."

"May I remind you that I am comfortably settled in Baxter's hunting lodge, and it was only by your insistence that our paths were ever forced to cross?"

"Bah. You have some purpose in coming to Cheshire, and I do not believe for a moment any sentimental nonsense of this being your home."

"Well, I should never use the words sentimental and home in the same sentence," Raoul mocked. "You and Lady Merriot made certain of that, but not even you can deny that a portion of my childhood was spent in the neighborhood."

Merriot's expression was sullen. "And you were suddenly overwhelmed with the need to visit your old haunts?"

Raoul's lips twisted in an unwittingly wry smile. "I am rarely overwhelmed by anything, although I have discovered I am susceptible to a pair of midnight eyes. Who would have thought?" He shook his head, trying to dismiss the sudden image of Miss Sarah Jefferson. "Still, you are correct. At least in part."

"What part?"

"I have returned to my 'old haunts' as you call them, not out of sentiment, but for information."

"Information?" There was no mistaking the fear that briefly flared over Merriot's face. "What information?"

"Does it matter?"

The older man licked his lips, his body stiff. "Naturally, I am curious."

"Yes, that is obvious."

Merriot squared his shoulders and tilted his chin,

doing his best to intimidate Raoul as he'd done so often in the past.

"Do you mean to tell me, or do you prefer to shroud yourself in mystery?"

Raoul smiled. Genuinely smiled.

This man no longer had the ability to bully and terrorize him.

Hell, the only thing that Raoul felt at the moment was . . . contempt.

"No, that is a role I will leave for you, Father," he drawled, readily calling upon the story he had invented before leaving London. "If you must know, I have rashly agreed to allow a friend of mine who happens to be under the hatches to write my memoirs."

His father poured another brandy, tossing it down with the ease of a hardened drinker.

"The devil you say."

"My reaction precisely, however my friend is convinced that he can earn a few pounds with the story of my life, gullible clod, and since he was clever enough to request my consent while I was three sheets to the wind, I am now obliged to honor my commitment."

Merriot paced back towards the desk, his brow knit with annoyance.

"This friend is in Cheshire?"

"He remained in London to collect embarrassing tales from my fellow actors and lurid details from my past mistresses. I haven't a modicum of hope that any of them will have the least amount of discretion," Raoul expertly lied. It was his profession, after all. "It is my task to provide him with charming antidotes from those who knew me as a grubby lad and, of course, the history of my family. In particular, *your* history."

"What the blazes does he want with my history?" Merriot barked.

Raoul's lips curled. "As distressful as it might be for you, my lord, you are my father. My friend is convinced the public will wish to know of your past, and how you came to producing a by-blow during your travels through France. The more intimate the details of my mother and inevitable conception, the better he will be pleased."

The glass slipped from the older man's fingers to shatter against the polished wood floor.

"Have you taken leave of your senses?"

"A question I have asked myself any number of times over the past year."

"Then return to London, and forget this stupidity."

"Why does it trouble you?" Raoul demanded, growing certain that his father's secret did indeed have something to do with his misbegotten bastard. Why else would he look as if a ghost had just appeared before him? "Most gentlemen enjoy boasting of their youthful escapades. Indeed, it is usually impossible to halt such boastings."

"No," the Earl choked out, his color an alarming shade of crimson. "No, I forbid it."

Raoul glanced down at the shards of crystal scattered across the floor. So fragile. So easily broken.

A chill inched down his spine.

"Forbid what?"

"I will not have the Merriot name bandied about in some repulsive book. It is an old and honorable title."

Raoul snorted. "And were you considering the Merriot name when you were foisting a bastard on some poor French maid?"

"Enough, Raoul." The Earl squared his shoulders. "I

have said no, and that is the end of the matter. You may tell your friend he will have to discover another means of replenishing his empty coffers."

The words were nothing less than a royal command, filled with the conceited arrogance that was the sole domain of the aristocracy.

May their souls rot in hell.

Raoul did a bit of shoulder squaring of his own. "I was not asking your permission, Father, merely explaining my presence in Cheshire."

"You intend to go against my wishes?"

"So it would seem."

"I am not without power, Raoul," the older man warned.

Raoul's smile was blasé. "Did I claim that you were?"

"I have only to send word to London to ensure that no one dare publish your . . . vile manuscript."

"You are certainly welcome to try," Raoul drawled, inwardly amused at the irony of battling over a memoir that was never going to be written. "Although there are always those unscrupulous printers who enjoy tweaking the nose of the rich and powerful."

"Very well." The Earl headed toward the door that connected with the Countess's private parlor. "I might not be able to prevent the memoir from being published, but I most certainly do not intend to assist in the vulgar scheme."

Raoul shrugged, careful not to overplay his hand. For now it was enough to have a suitable excuse for asking questions of his father's past around the neighborhood.

"It never occurred to me that you would provide me with anything, Father." His eyes flicked dismissively over his father's stooped form. "I learned at a very young age that I have no one to depend upon but myself."

The crimson faded from the Earl's face, leaving behind a sickly gray at the accusation.

"I did my duty. I did . . ."

"You did what?"

Merriot swayed, his hand reaching out to land against the door, as if unable to stand on his own.

"I did what had to be done, damn you," he rasped. "Why will you not leave us in peace?"

Stupid concern lanced through Raoul as he took a step toward the older man.

"Father?"

"Go." The Earl held up a dismissive hand. "Just go away."

Once again, Raoul glanced down at the splinters of broken crystal. Then, turning his back on the gentleman who had long ago turned his back on Raoul, he left the library.

He had what he came for.

Lord Merriot was indeed hoarding a secret.

And Raoul suspected that it had something to do with his bastard son.

Entering the pale blue and ivory parlor, Lord Merriot studied the silver-haired woman seated on the rose-wood sofa.

Mirabelle, Lady Merriot, had always been slender, but now she appeared little more than a skeleton attired in the heavy black bombazine gown that made her skin unpleasantly sallow. Even worse, the laudanum she laced in her tea left her once beautiful brown eyes dull and lifeless.

Merriot's heart twisted with a familiar pain. This woman had once been a vivacious hostess who had so charmed King George III, he had pronounced her a Diamond of the First Water.

Now she was a listless shadow of her former self, plagued by guilt, and mourning the son that had been stolen from them.

At his entrance, the Countess lifted a trembling hand to the silver locket pinned to her bodice. Merriot knew that hidden in the locket was a picture of their son, Peter.

"Did you speak with him?" she demanded.

"Yes, for all the good it did," he said, headed directly for the crystal decanter of brandy.

His wife survived the days in an opium haze, while he preferred the fog of well-aged brandy.

They were a fine pair.

A querulous expression settled on her bony countenance. "Why is he here?"

"He has decided to have his memoirs written, arrogant pup, and he has come to meddle in the past."

"No." She fluttered with predictable panic. "You must send him away."

Merriot downed the brandy. Dammit, did the woman think he hadn't tried?

"Calm yourself, Mirabella."

"Calm myself?" She leaned forward. "What if his *meddling* allows him to discover the truth? What if . . ."

"There is no means of him discovering the truth."

"How can you be so certain?"

"Because we have covered our tracks too well." His

voice was edged. They'd had this argument on a dozen occasions since Raoul's arrival in Cheshire. "There is no evidence that could possibly remain after all these years."

"So confident?"

Merriot shuddered, pouring more brandy down his throat. "The papers have all been destroyed, along with those belongings that would reveal our connections to France."

Her lips twisted with a dark, ugly emotion. "It was not my fault that horrid little man recognized the diamonds."

"I warned you . . ." Merriot bit off his words. What was the point? The damage had been done. "It no longer matters. Dunnington is dead."

"What if he said something to Raoul before he died?"

"The interfering worm never suspected more than a small portion of the truth. Besides, I paid a bloody fortune for him to keep his lips shut."

"Deathbed confessions are . . ."

"A figment of overactive imaginations," Merriot growled. "Dunnington died nearly a year ago, and yet Raoul is just now traveling to Cheshire." He shook his head, refusing to dwell on the disaster if Raoul ever learned the truth. It was how he had survived the past twenty-five years. "No, it is nothing more than ill fortune that brings Raoul here."

"Ill fortune." Mirabelle's laugh was edged with madness. "Oh yes, I well believe that. We have had nothing but ill fortune since you convinced me . . ."

"Do not point the finger of blame in my direction, Mirabella. It was as much your notion as mine."

"If I had known the price we would be forced to pay, I would never have agreed," she hissed.

"And do you think I would? If I could go back . . ."

He glanced around the room that had been decorated with the finest furnishings that money could purchase. He had demanded nothing but the best for the Merriot estate when it had been refurbished. Now it felt like a cold, elegant grave. "But I cannot. Nothing we do can change the past."

"Perhaps not, but I cannot bear the constant reminder." Tears formed in the dull brown eyes. "I do not want him here, Jonah. He carries evil with him."

The Earl struggled to fight back his bitter anger, and reassure the woman who he had once loved.

"I have no more desire than you to have the boy underfoot, my dear, but I have no authority to command him back to London." His expression hardened. "Especially since he was disobliging enough to take up residence in Baxter's lodge. That ill-bred ass has never forgiven me for refusing to back his scheme to build a canal through the neighborhood. Certainly he would never agree to toss my bastard from his estate."

"Perhaps not, but you could certainly make it uncomfortable for him to remain in the area."

Merriot grimaced. He had already made the attempt. And failed miserably.

Obviously his position as Earl could not compete with the notoriety of a famous actor.

"I could if he were anyone but Raoul Charlebois. The entire neighborhood is already aflutter with excitement at his arrival."

With effort, his wife rose to her feet, her expression one of bitter accusation.

"You must do something."

"What would you have me do, Mirabella?" With a flare of frustration, Merriot paced toward the elaborately carved mantelpiece. "Knock him over the head and drag him back to London?"

Mirabelle's sob echoed through the room. "What I want is to forget the day Raoul Charlebois ever entered our lives."

Chapter 4

Friday, December 13
Baxter Lodge

The day dawned with a promise.

Although there was a decided nip in the air and the windows of Raoul's temporary hunting lodge were etched with a fine spiderweb of frost, the morning sky glowed with a welcome splash of golden sunshine.

Unfortunately, the ill-fated day swiftly lived up to its reputation. By midmorning, a bank of threatening clouds had blocked the sunshine, and by luncheon, the first snowflakes had started to fall.

Sensing the brewing storm, Raoul hastily sent Mrs. Dent and her daughter back to the village. He had hired the two women to come in daily and tend to the housekeeping, as well as keep his kitchen stocked with plenty of plain, well-cooked meals. A decision that his palate fully approved of, considering Mrs. Dent's deft hand with cooking, though his nerves often regretted being forced to endure the young Miss Dent's incessant urge to giggle whenever he passed by.

Pouring a glass of warm cider that Mrs. Dent had left on the mantel in the library, Raoul aimlessly moved to stand before the tall bank of arched windows, choosing one that overlooked the front gardens rather than the lake.

For once, he was utterly alone in the house. His groom had disappeared to the stables shortly after breakfast, and Nico had left the house not long after with a predatory smile that did not bode well for his intended prey.

Raoul might have appreciated the peace if it hadn't offered such a ceaseless opportunity to dwell on his meeting with Lord Merriot.

And the lingering indigestion that always came after time spent in his father's company.

The snow thickened, swirling as the wind increased. Within an hour it was nearly impossible to see more than a few feet from the window.

Nearly impossible.

Not completely.

Thank the good Lord.

Still leaning against the window, Raoul was startled by the vague shadow of a form struggling to make its way through the blinding snow.

What sort of fool would be out in such weather?

An inconsiderate fool, he decided as he grudgingly headed for the foyer and pulled on his coat. It would serve them right to leave them to freeze.

Unfortunately, the snow was bound to thaw eventually, and then he would be stuck digging a grave for the idiot.

Muttering some of the finer curses he had picked up

over the years in the theater, Raoul yanked open the door and began battling his way through the gathering drifts.

Teeth gritted, he ignored the blast of wind that threatened to topple him backwards, and made his way to the nearby road. He frowned as he neared the traveler, realizing he was far smaller than he'd expected.

Was it just a child . . . ?

His heart came to a perfect halt as the wind viciously whipped down the narrow path, tugging at the heavy cloak wrapped around the stranger, knocking the hood back to reveal a tangle of raven-black curls and a perfect female profile.

"*Mon Dieu.*" Stepping directly in front of Miss Sarah Jefferson, Raoul grasped her shoulders and stared at her in furious disbelief. "Have you no sense at all?"

"I am generally held to be quite sensible, thank you very much, Mr. Charlebois," she said, her stiff attempt at dignity ruined by a sharp shiver.

"I see." Raoul's jaw knotted with anger at the sight of her reddened nose and frost-kissed cheeks. "Walking in the midst of a blizzard is held to be quite sensible? Clearly the reasoning in Cheshire is vastly different from that in London."

Her lips thinned. "It was not a blizzard when I set out."

"Well, it is now. Where are the boys?"

She yanked up the hood of her cloak, not nearly as relieved at being rescued from the storm as she should have been.

"The Vicar's son, Simon, requested that they spend the night so they could try their hands at writing a series of short charades for the Christmas luncheon we host for the local orphanage."

"The Vicar must be an idiot to allow you to leave with a storm threatening."

"No one *allows* me to do anything, sir," she retorted, her voice as cold as the biting wind. "I have been making my own decisions for a number of years."

"Which explains so much," he muttered.

"I beg your pardon?"

Shifting, he gripped her elbow and turned toward the nearby house. Christ, it was cold.

"Come along before we both die of consumption."

"Come along where? Oh . . . no." Ridiculously, she dug in her heels. "I cannot enter the home of a bachelor."

Raoul didn't bother to argue. The woman had clearly lost any claim to sense. Instead, he swept her off her feet and headed up the snow-covered walk.

"Very well."

She stiffened in outrage, but trapped by the thick folds of her gown and wool cloak, she was incapable of struggling.

"What the devil are you doing?"

"You cannot enter the home of a bachelor, so I am kidnapping you for your own good." He glanced down at her scowl. "Although I suppose you have some ridiculous rule against that as well."

"Do not mock my concern. Gentlemen may be immune to the damage of malicious gossip, but women are always at the mercy of their reputation."

The words held no bitterness, but were spoken with the sort of quiet resolution of a woman determined to change the world. Even if it were only her small corner of the world.

His lips twitched. It was absurd, but his odd fascination with the spinster only intensified the more he knew of her.

"I would have thought a woman willing to establish her own household and take in ill-bred strays would not give a damn about the opinions of others."

"Perhaps I wouldn't if it were not for those ill-bred strays," she retorted, her eyes flashing a dark warning. "The boys have endured enough ugly scandal in their short lives, as I would think you of all people would understand. I will not make them suffer more."

"Pull in the claws, *ma belle,* there is no one about to know of your stay beneath my roof," he promised gently. "Unlike the Vicar, I had the sense to send the daily servants home an hour ago."

She remained stiff in his arms. "Surely you have your own servants?"

"My valet and groom, both of whom are paid a ludicrous sum for their loyalty and discretion."

She clenched her teeth, trying to hide her violent shivers as he climbed the shallow steps to the front terrace.

"Then you are grossly overpaying them. The rumors of your exploits are legendary even here in Cheshire."

"Ah, those rumors were not started by my servants." He chuckled. "Well, not until I specifically crafted the tales to best titillate society."

As he hoped, the confession was distraction enough to allow him to push open the door and step into the foyer without shrieks of outrage.

"You?"

"A man does not become a legend by mere chance."

She snorted. "Please do not share that secret morsel of information with my maid. Maggie would be crushed to discover your reputation as an insatiable rake was in any way exaggerated."

"And what of you, Miss Sarah?" Slowly he lowered

her to her feet, his hands swiftly dealing with the frozen ribbons so he could remove the cloak. It fell to the black-and-white tiled floor with a heavy squish. "Are you crushed?"

Instinctively, she wrapped her arms around her waist, no longer capable of battling the shivers that wracked her slender body.

"At the moment, I'm more frozen."

"Damn, you need to be near the fire."

Ignoring the hands that lifted to fend him off, Raoul once again swept her into his arms, carrying her through the door leading to the library.

Curling one hand into a fist, Sarah smacked him in the center of the chest.

"Mr. Charlebois."

His brows snapped together at her absurd indignation. It wasn't that he did not comprehend her fear of scandal. Or even that he didn't sympathize with her need to protect the boys.

It was just . . .

What?

Mon Dieu. He did not know, except that he wanted her to feel safe and . . . dammit, protected in his company. Not threatened as if he were some sort of ogre.

"My name is Raoul. And no one, not even in this godforsaken corner of England, would condemn a woman for seeking shelter from certain death." His jaw clenched. "Even if I am Beelzebub himself."

There was a stark silence as he carried her into the library and settled her on the leather chair closest to the fire. Then, kneeling before the chair, he tackled the frozen laces of her half boots.

Half-expecting to be smacked over the head as he

bent to his task, Raoul was unprepared for her soft words of apology.

"You are right."

"I am . . . ?" He glanced up, suspicious. "Is this a ruse?"

"No ruse." She settled back in the cushions with a wry smile. "I am being silly. Even if it is discovered that I was forced to seek shelter here, no one would believe you would attempt to take advantage of me."

He tugged off her boots, not nearly as comforted as he should be. "No?"

"Of course not. It is well known that you are notorious in your preference for only the most beautiful women." She shrugged. "Clearly, I should be safe enough."

He sat back on his heels, stunned by her words. Was it possible she was unaware of the disturbing awareness that plagued him?

"That is the most idiotic thing I have ever heard," he barked.

"What?"

"I can assure you that I have contemplated little else but seducing you over the past four days."

"Are you demented?" She frowned. "You were just attempting to convince me that I am safe beneath your roof."

"Yes."

"Yes, I am safe?"

He glared into her wary eyes. "Yes, I am demented, and it is entirely your fault."

"Well, I certainly believe you are not entirely right in the head," she muttered, twitching the skirt of her French gray gown to hide the tiny feet now covered with nothing more than damp stockings.

"Let us get this straight." With a fluid motion, Raoul

was on his feet. Leaning down, he planted his hands on the arm of the chair, effectively trapping her and bringing them nose to nose. "There will be no gossip, because no one will ever know you were here, and even if it does become known, the locals are far too fond of you to think the worst." He brushed his lips over the lush temptation of her mouth. "As for me . . ."

"Mr. Charlebois."

"Raoul."

She stubbornly turned her head to deny him her sweet lips. "Mr. Charlebois."

Raoul was unfazed. Deprived of her lips, Raoul nibbled a path over her chilled cheek.

"As for me, Miss Sarah, I might devote an unreasonable amount of time to considering the taste of your lips and the silkiness of your skin, but you are in no danger that I will force myself upon you." He briefly nuzzled the tiny hollow beneath her ear before he was abruptly straightening and moving to pour her a large measure of the cider. Returning to her side, he pressed the ceramic cup into her hand. "Drink this."

"What is it?"

"Nothing more alarming than warm cider." He settled on the carpet next to the chair, regarding her with a brooding gaze. It was a mistake to give in to these urges to touch her. Already his body was hard with unfulfilled hunger. Unfortunately, his hands were not currently taking commands from his brain, and they instinctively reached for one slender foot, pulling it into his lap so he could gently warm her frozen toes. "Did you think I concocted a devil's brew in the event an innocent young woman might pass this way?"

Sarah Jefferson met his gaze with a guarded

expression. For a moment, Raoul was certain she intended to pull away from his gentle massage. Then, with a faint shake of her head, she settled back in the leather seat and sipped at the hot cider.

"No doubt a character in one of your plays would have."

Stupidly pleased to continue the intimate caress, Raoul lifted a golden brow.

"I am shocked by the mere suggestion, Miss Jefferson," he lightly teased. "Surely you must know that I am never cast as the villain."

"Never?"

"Not on stage."

"And in life?"

"I am not entirely certain," he confessed ruefully. "Now that I am retired, I may have the opportunity to discover."

She frowned at him over the rim of her mug, her toes curling beneath his slow, firm strokes along the arch of her foot.

"Is this a game you are playing?"

"Game?"

"This pretense that you find a spinster attractive?"

He narrowed his eyes. "You believe I am merely pretending to desire you?"

"Are you not?"

"I believe you should be the judge of my sincerity, Miss Sarah."

Wise enough to sense the sudden danger in the air, Sarah hastily set aside her mug as he shifted to kneel directly before her. Not that it protected her from his determination to prove once and for all he wanted nothing more than to have her in his bed, her legs wrapped around his waist as he put an end to her maidenly innocence.

Allowing his fingers to trail up the back of her legs, Raoul tugged them as far apart as her skirts would allow, peering deep into her wide eyes.

"Mr. Charlebois," she breathed.

"Raoul."

"Mr. Charlebois."

Leaning forward, he buried his face in the curve of her neck, savoring the womanly spice of her scent.

"I swear, I will hear my name on your lips."

She shivered even as her hands lifted to land against his chest. "So that is it."

He pulled back to study her blushing face, his heart halting as he was struck anew by her warm, exotic beauty.

"I am frightened to ask."

"You consider me a challenge."

"I consider you a delicious distraction who refuses to leave me in peace, Miss Sarah Jefferson." He returned to his exploration of her neck, memorizing the precise curve before shifting his attention to the stubborn line of her jaw. She shivered, but this time it was not from the cold. His fingers slipped up the bend of her knees, his mouth nibbling a path over her beautiful countenance. "Eyes the precise color of a midnight sky." He skimmed down to her lush mouth. "Lips that beg for a man's kiss." He teased the edge of her mouth. "Such evocative inno-cence, combined with womanly provocation."

"I . . . oh . . ."

She sucked in a sharp breath as his fingers sketched aimless patterns on the soft skin of her inner thighs, nearing the ribbons that held up her prim stockings.

"Mr. Charlebois."

He traced the outline of her enchanting mouth with his tongue.

"Raoul."

"Mr. Charlebois." Her hands pressed against his chest with a sudden flare of panic. "Enough."

Ignoring the urgent protest of his body that was un-accustomed to being denied, Raoul pulled back and gently smoothed down her heavy skirts.

He wanted the woman. Desperately. But oddly, he discovered he needed her good opinion even more than her body.

Astonishing.

"Are you convinced?" he demanded, his voice thick.

"I am not entirely certain what I am." She lifted a not-quite-steady hand to shove back a raven curl that had strayed from her simple braid. "You are dangerously overwhelming for a rustic old maid."

Raoul settled back on his heels, inwardly admitting that Sarah was not the only one dangerously over-whelmed.

"Why have you never wed?" he abruptly demanded.

She shrugged. "I have never been in love, and I refuse to settle for anything less."

"You believe in love?"

"Of course I do. My parents were utterly devoted to one another. They taught me the importance of choos-ing a husband who could offer more than security." A wistful smile touched her lips. "My mother would say that it is not only the body that must be nourished, but the heart and soul as well."

There was a painful twinge in Raoul's heart. That was precisely the sort of romantic drivel that Dunnington would believe.

Foolish blighter.

"I suppose you intend to tell me that is why you took

in those two orphaned brats?" he drawled. "To nourish your heart?"

"And because they needed me."

His heart gave another twinge.

Envy?

No. That would be preposterous.

"And what of your soul?"

She retrieved her mug of cider, shifting deeper into the cushions of the chair.

"My painting fulfills my soul."

Raoul blinked in surprise. "You're an artist?"

"More of a dabbler, but my sketches are in enough demand to put food on the table and keep the boys in decent clothing. Not an easy task when they seem to sprout an inch or more over the breakfast table."

There was no mistaking her sense of pride. Not in her artistic talent. No, her pride was in her hard-won independence.

Understandable, of course, but not entirely pleasing to Raoul.

He scowled. "So you are content to remain a spinster?"

"Is that so shocking?" she challenged. "You, after all, appear content to remain a bachelor."

"But I am not."

"You are not a bachelor?"

"I am not content."

"You desire a wife?"

She appeared nearly as shocked as Raoul felt at his unexpected confession. What on earth possessed him to reveal his growing discontent with his lonely existence?

He hadn't even shared his dissatisfaction with Ian or Fredrick.

It was too late now, however, to take back his words.

"A wife, a lover, a . . ." He caught and held her gaze. "Companion."

Something flashed through her dark, beautiful eyes before she was hastily lowering her lashes.

"Truly you must keep these less than rakish traits to yourself, Mr. Charlebois."

"Or I shall disappoint Maggie Stone?"

"Precisely."

"Do you know, I cannot wait to meet this mysterious maid."

Sarah's lips twisted in a dry smile. "She would no doubt swoon the moment you walked into the room."

"Unlike her mistress, who did everything in her power to be rid of me?"

"Obviously I did not do nearly enough."

"So cruel, Miss Sarah." Unable to resist, Raoul reached out to wrap the stray raven lock around his finger. "What does a gentleman have to do to earn your trust?"

The tip of her tongue peeked out to dampen her lips. "I do not believe that it is my trust you truly desire."

He slowly shook his head. "Much to my astonishment, you would be wrong, *ma belle*."

Chapter 5

December 13
The Great House

Nico Dravali was frozen to the marrow by the time the cook at the Merriot Great House eventually noticed him huddled near the garden gate. At last opening the kitchen door, Mrs. Horton called for him to take shelter from the blizzard.

Silently cursing his long-ago decision to give up his life of crime to become an almost respectable valet to Raoul Charlebois, Nico scurried into the welcome warmth of the kitchen and took a seat at the ruthlessly scrubbed wooden table.

Covertly studying the cook as she briskly poured him a cup of hot tea, Nico judged her to be the bossy sort who ruled her kitchen with the command of a seasoned general. It was revealed in the authoritative angle of the broad shoulders beneath her brown woolen gown, and the grim hardness of her long, horsey countenance that was unfortunately emphasized by her habit of scraping back her silver hair in a tight knot.

"Here you are." The formidable woman set the steaming cup before Nico and folded her arms over her ample bosom. "Drink every drop. It will rid you of that nasty chill."

"Thank you, Mrs. Horton." Nico pretended to sip the overly sweet tea. His devotion to Raoul might include freezing his privates, but it did not extend to ruining his finely honed palate with nasty English tea. "So kind of you to show pity on a passing stranger."

"I know my Christian duty." A hint of speculation entered the brown eyes. "And it is not as if you are a complete stranger. Everyone knows you work for Mr. Charlebois."

Nico hid his smug expression as Mrs. Horton readily headed down the path he intended to take her. His investigations had already revealed that this woman had not only worked for the Merriots for the past thirty-five years, but that she was an incessant gossipmonger.

If there were any past scandals in Lord Merriot's past, then she was the person to reveal them.

"Ah yes, this is the home of his father, is it not?"

Nico flashed his most beguiling smile. He might never compete with his master when it came to felling women with a single glance, but he was not without his own share of charm, as was proven when Mrs. Horton took a seat at the table and reached for one of the ginger biscuits placed on a plate.

"It is."

Pretending he did not notice her obvious eagerness to indulge in a comfortable chat, Nico widened his dark eyes.

"Forgive me." He deliberately glanced toward the undercooks who were busily chopping and peeling on the far side of the spacious room. "Perhaps you prefer not to speak of Charlebois?"

The woman sniffed. "There are no doubt some who would as soon forget little Raoul, but I have never been the sort to blame the son for the sins of the father."

"Most compassionate of you."

"My conscience is clear, which is more than most can say."

Ah. Now that was promising.

He flashed another persuasive smile. "I must admit I'm curious about my master. Were you employed here when Charlebois was a lad?"

"Aye." The woman readily accepted his smooth lie. "Of course, I was only a scullery maid back then. Still, I will never forget the day that French nurse arrived at the door with the child clutched in her arms. Even then Raoul was as cute as a button."

Nico's lips twisted. "Yes, I can imagine he charmed the entire household."

"At first, both Lord and Lady Merriot seemed happy enough to have the boy beneath their roof. I always thought it was because they didn't have children of their own."

"Odd. Charlebois has always implied he was estranged from his family."

Mrs. Horton polished off the biscuit and reached for another. It was little wonder her figure was so stout.

"Well, that is true enough. Everything changed when he was . . . oh, he must have been three or four years of age. I blame it on that money his lordship inherited." A stark disapproval tightened her horse features.

"Suddenly they could think of nothing but impressing their grand London visitors. The house had to be made larger, and all the belongings were to be burned and replaced with new, expensive furnishings. If not for Mr. Jefferson taking a few of the pieces that had been in the Merriot family for generations, all would have been lost."

Nico pretended to sip the tea as he tucked away the tidbits of information.

"Lord Merriot inherited a large amount of money?"

"Too much, if you ask me."

"And it was then that they took a dislike at having a . . ." Nico bit back the word bastard. "An illegitimate son underfoot?"

"Aye, although to be fair, I suppose it could have been the two babies that Lady Merriot lost afore they could be properly born. Such a loss does make a woman bitter."

Nico shrugged, indifferent to Lady Merriot's misfortunes. Charlebois had revealed precious little about his past, but Nico did know that the woman had made his childhood a misery.

"Perhaps, although it's a common enough tragedy, and she did eventually produce a healthy heir."

"Aye, poor soul. Since Peter's death . . ." Her words trailed away with a tragic sigh.

"Yes?"

"The household has not been the same." The woman leaned forward in a conspiratorial manner. "To be honest, I believe Lord and Lady Merriot hold themselves to blame for the lad's death, although everyone knows it was naught more than an unfortunate accident."

Nico echoed her motion until their heads were close enough to share a whisper.

"Perhaps a guilty conscience?" he suggested.

The brown eyes widened in shock. "If you think they had anything to do with Peter's death, then . . ."

"No, no," Nico hastily denied his brief speculations. "I just meant that there are natives in India who believe that ill fortune is visited upon us because of our own bad behavior."

The cook thinned her lips, not seeming to notice Nico had happily butchered the Hindu faith for his own devious purpose.

"I do not hold with heathen beliefs."

"What good English woman would? Still, I am certain you will agree that God does punish us for our sins." He deliberately hesitated. "Perhaps Lord or Lady Merriot have some transgression in their past that now haunts their future."

The momentary wariness melted as Mrs. Horton was overcome by her delight in revealing her superior knowledge of the Merriot family.

"There were rumors that the previous Earl was a scoundrel who had wasted the family coffers at the gaming hells."

"And what of this Earl? Does he gamble?"

"No more than any nobleman," she grudgingly admitted. "He has always preferred to devote himself to hunting and entertaining his friends."

"And enjoying the delights of the French ladies, as Raoul is ample proof."

"Indeed." She clicked her tongue. "Shameful."

"I don't suppose you ever knew anything of the mother?"

"Certainly not."

"How thoughtless of me." He reached for a ginger biscuit, brushing her plump hand with the tips of his fingers. "I just assumed that the French nurse who brought Charlebois to England would have known the mother."

The woman fluttered, anxious to impress her handsome young guest.

"If she did, she would never breathe a word. The French are always so difficult, nothing ever suits them. And Francine . . . that was the nurse's name, well, let me just say that the entire staff was pleased when she moved to London to open her own seamstress shop."

Nico stilled. "When was this?"

Her brow wrinkled. "Oh, Raoul must have been six, maybe seven. Poor little mite cried for weeks after she left."

"A seamstress shop," he mused. "Quite ambitious for a French nurse. I wonder where she got the funds?"

"There are those that implied she was in truth Raoul's mother, and that the Earl paid her a sum to be rid of her, but I never held with such notions."

"Why not?"

"She was a rough, common sort of female."

"Not the sort to capture Lord Merriot's fancy?"

"Not the sort to have born a son such as Raoul Charlebois," Mrs. Horton corrected stoutly. "Why it's as plain as the nose on your face that his mother must have been a rare beauty. It is my opinion that she must have been a lady of quality."

The thought had occurred to Nico as well.

"You are most perceptive, Mrs. Horton," he murmured, watching the pleased blush touch her cheeks. "I wonder who she could have been?"

"That is a question best not asked beneath this roof."

Knowing the woman would never be able to keep

such a secret if she actually knew the truth, Nico inwardly grimaced. It seemed he had frozen his manly bits for nothing.

"Ah well, if the only scandal attached to the Merriot name is one long forgotten mistress, then they have accomplished more than most in society." He gave it one last effort. "The tales I could tell you of London."

"London is a den of iniquity. I've always said it." Mrs. Horton assumed a patronizing expression. "The Merriots might have been prideful and frivolous in the past, but they are decent folk at heart. I should never have remained here if I believed any different."

Nico glumly stuffed the biscuit in his mouth.

"Quite."

Two hours after her arrival at the Baxter lodge, Sarah forced herself to rise from the comfort of the wing chair, not surprised by the pang of regret she felt that the brief encounter with Raoul Charlebois must come to an end.

For all her protests at entering the home of a notorious rake, she had felt a tide of thrilling excitement from the moment Raoul had swept her into his arms and carried her over the threshold.

An excitement that had become breathless exhilaration beneath his skillful seduction, and then astonishingly . . . an intellectual fascination as he had remained settled at her feet, discussing everything from his opinion of Princess Charlotte's wedding to Prince Leopold of Saxe-Coburg-Saalfeld to the dangers of the recent Spa Field Riots.

Raoul was more than just a charming rogue.

He was quick-witted, well-informed, and capable of

listening to her opinions with an unwavering interest that she found far more enticing than all his golden male beauty.

He was also frighteningly capable of disguising his emotions.

A complex and dangerous man.

Just the sort a wise spinster avoided.

"I believe the snow has passed," she murmured, forcing herself to head toward the door with a brisk step. "I should be on my way."

"Wait . . . Sarah." With a smooth motion, Raoul Charlebois was at her side, catching her arm in a firm grip as they reached the black-and-white tiled foyer. "I will ensure you get home, but first I have need of your artistic expertise."

Forced to a halt, Sarah managed to stifle her shiver of pleasure at his touch.

She did not entirely understand his seeming pleasure in captivating a lonely spinster, but she suspected he was a gentleman who was compelled to flirt with anything in skirts.

She would be a fool to ever believe his interest was anything more.

"You are in the market for an etching?" she demanded.

"Perhaps later, but this afternoon I have been commanded to finish hanging the evergreen and ridiculous bows, since the snow forced Mrs. Dent and her daughter to leave early."

She glanced toward the stack of cut evergreen branches piled at the bottom of the wide staircase.

"It cannot wait until she returns?"

"Apparently not." He heaved a martyred sigh. "She offered a dozen different directions of why and how it was to be hung as she was headed out the door, but to be honest, I was so anxious to be rid of her giggling daughter, I paid little heed. Now I must depend on your kindness to ensure I do not make a complete hash of the decorations."

"A disaster, indeed," Sarah said dryly.

"My Christmas would be utterly ruined."

She rolled her eyes. "Has there ever been a female you could not charm?"

His impossibly handsome features hardened. "My mother obviously found little charm in me since I was sent away from her when I was just a baby, and of course, Lady Merriot considered me a plague and a pestilence that had invaded her home."

Sarah bit her lower lip. "I'm sorry."

"'*Oft expectation fails, and most oft there where most it promises*,'" he softly quoted Shakespeare, using her momentary distraction to tug her toward the staircase. Once there, he bent to pluck an evergreen branch and began threading it through the oak banister. "Tell me, Miss Sarah, what happened to Willie and Jimmy's parents?"

Sarah briefly wavered, knowing that if she had any sense, she would gather her cloak and return to her cottage.

As much as it might rub at her pride, Sarah was honest enough to admit she was not nearly as indifferent to this gentleman's charm as she should be.

Logically, she understood he was a rake who enjoyed toying with the hearts of women. And that only the worst sort of fool would encourage his fickle attentions. But logic had no control over the flutter of her heart, or the treacherous longing to spend just a few more stolen moments in his company.

Knowing that she was bound to regret her weakness, Sarah plucked a red velvet ribbon from the pile beside the evergreen.

"Their father was killed in a mining accident when they were just babes," she said, twining the ribbon over the evergreen and tying a large bow to attach it firmly to the banister. "I doubt either of them remembers him."

Raoul gathered more branches, holding them steady as Sarah tied them to the banister with the ribbon, slowly working her way up the stairs.

"And their mother?"

"Polly was barely more than a child herself when she married Bart Andrews. Certainly she was not mature enough to support herself and tend to two very spirited boys."

"Willie said she had done a . . . flit?"

"Yes." She nearly dropped the ribbon as he deliberately allowed his fingers to tangle with her own, his warm breath brushing her cheek as he stood far too close. "Although the boys would never admit as much, I suspect that Polly made a habit of leaving the boys home alone while she sought comfort at the local pub. One night she left with a groom from Wallingford and never returned."

Much to his credit, Raoul didn't offer the usual outrage at a mother who would abandon her children. Or the tedious predictions of the fate for boys who came from bad blood.

In fact, she could detect nothing more than curiosity in his steady gaze.

"How did they end up beneath your roof?"

"After Bart's death, I occasionally brought dinner for the boys." She knotted another bow. "One night when I arrived, I could tell something was wrong. Still, it took nearly a week before Willie would admit his mother was gone. I brought them to my cottage until I could discover a family willing to take them in."

"You never found one?"

"After the first few days, I stopped looking."

A wry smile touched his lips. "Somehow, I am not at all surprised."

She shrugged. "I never realized how empty my home had become until the boys filled it with their laughter."

He shifted to lean against the banister, his gaze unwavering as he studied her pale features.

"Not always laughter, I think."

She wound the ribbon around the last of the branches, a familiar warmth filling her heart.

After the death of her father, she had been determined to remain at the cottage, despite those who claimed it was improper for a young woman to establish her own household. She had her elderly nurse to offer her companionship, and her mother's herb garden to tend, and there was always her art to occupy her days. But, even then, she had known there was something missing.

When she had taken the boys into her home, that emptiness had disappeared.

Still, Raoul was right.

It had not been painless.

"No, not always laughter," she agreed softly. "In the beginning, the boys refused to unpack their few belongings and quite often would sleep on the floor rather than in the beds I had made for them. At first I assumed that it was because they were hoping their mother would return and take them home, but then I overheard Willie warning his brother that I was bound to get tired of them."

A strange smile touched his lips. "A child who is rejected by those who should love him never finds them easy to trust."

Her breath tangled in her throat, realizing just how intimately Raoul could sympathize with Willie and Jimmy. Barely aware she was moving, she reached up to lightly touch his cheek.

"No, but the tears and trials are a part of love, and I would not trade them for all the treasure in the world," she murmured.

"That is exactly what Dunnington used to say."

"Dunnington?"

Ignoring her confusion, Raoul covered her hand with his, pressing her palm against the smooth heat of his cheek as he studied her with a searching gaze.

"What will you do if their mother returns?"

She flinched, his words touching her deepest fear.

"I am not entirely certain. I have no legal claim to them, but . . ."

Easily sensing he had distressed her, Raoul gripped her fingers and carried them from his cheek to his lips, pressing a lingering kiss on her knuckles.

"It is highly doubtful she will ever return."

"Yes." She determinedly tilted her chin, banishing the dread that haunted her late at night. "If Polly truly wanted them, she would have never been gone for such a length of time."

There was an odd silence as Raoul continued to study her, rather as if he were examining a rare specimen. Then, threading her arm through his, he led her to the bottom of the stairs.

Reaching the foyer, he loosened his grip on her arm and bent over the box that had held the evergreen.

"Now this is an odd thing."

"What is it?"

Straightening, he held up a tiny sprig of greenery. "I believe it is known as mistletoe."

She snorted, trying to ignore the delicious anticipation that tingled through her body.

"I should have known you had some devious scheme in mind."

He prowled toward her, a wicked smile curving his lips. "You begin to understand me, *ma belle*."

"No." Her hands lifted to press against his chest as Raoul wrapped one arm around her waist and lifted the other over her head, dangling the mistletoe from his fingers. "I do not believe you have ever allowed anyone to truly understand you, Mr. Charlebois."

His head dipped downward, brushing a devastating path of pleasure down her cheek to the corner of her mouth.

"Raoul," he teased.

"Mr. Charlebois."

He chuckled at her stubborn refusal to give into his command, stealing a short, possessive kiss.

"Someday," he said against her lips.

"You are very confident."

His tongue tenderly outlined her lips. "Very determined."

"Why?"

"I am not entirely certain." He pulled back to regard her with a rueful expression. "You are beautiful, but I have known many beautiful women."

The pang that clenched her heart was not jealousy.

It was . . . pique. Nothing more than annoyance that he would feel the need to toss his vast experience in her face.

"I think we have already established that fact."

His lips twitched, as if he saw far more than she wanted.

"You are also intelligent, but I am not at all certain why that would stir my fantasies. Clever women are always so difficult."

"Because they have enough wits to avoid notorious rakes?"

He ignored her taunt, his gaze following the path of his fingers as they drifted down her neck and along the line of her bodice.

"It can only be this."

She tried to pretend she wasn't melting beneath his touch, her fingers clutching his lapels as her knees went weak.

"My cameo?" she husked, as he reached the brooch she used to fasten the lace tucked modestly into her neckline. "I assure you that while it is precious to me it . . . oh . . . heavens . . ."

Her words stuttered to a breathless halt as he replaced his fingers with his warm lips, moving over her exposed skin with slow, savoring strokes.

"Your heart, *ma belle*." He lingered over the frantic pulse at the base of her neck. "That generous, sweet, kind heart."

Chapter 6

Polishing off the last of the cured ham and coddled eggs, Raoul tossed aside his linen napkin and rose from the table he had requested be set beside the fire in the library. Raoul preferred eating in this room to the small but formal dining room; and he regarded his valet with a jaundiced gaze.

He wasn't particularly surprised that Nico had taken it upon himself to begin investigating Lord Merriot's past. The damnable man was loyal to a fault, but he was as overprotective as a mother hen.

"I should have suspected you could not trust me to question Mrs. Horton," he grumbled.

Nico leaned against the mantel, a dark, lean predator.

"It's not a matter of trust," he countered.

"No?"

"It's knowledge of human nature. Mrs. Horton might be eager to share the wicked foibles of Lord and Lady

Merriot with a fellow servant, but she would never speak ill of the family with one of its members."

Raoul's lips twisted. "I am a bastard, not a member of the Merriot family. Thank God."

"Your blood still runs blue."

Having spent a great deal of time among the blue bloods, Raoul found no comfort in Nico's assertion. Actually, Fredrick Colstone was the only nobleman he could stomach, and only because he'd been raised with the belief he was a bastard.

"Clearly the color of my blood is meaningless," he mocked. "The old man did not even bother to give me his name."

"True." Nico paused as he considered Raoul's words. "I presume that Charlebois is your mother's name?"

"So my father always claimed."

"You have reason to doubt him?"

Raoul wandered toward the window, surveying the landscape that was charmingly swathed in a layer of snow. Far different from the grimy slush that he'd left behind in London.

A pity he was not in Cheshire to simply admire the view.

"I have traveled throughout France on several occasions, and while I have discovered any number of those with the name of Charlebois, not one can claim knowledge of a female family member who was acquainted with Lord Merriot, let alone close enough to bear his bastard," he confessed, recalling his early attempts to discover his mother. At the time, he had dismissed his inability to discover something of the woman who had given him birth to the confusion and natural distrust that permeated France after the bloody revolution. Now he began to wonder if it was something more nefarious.

Nico absently toyed with a delicate figurine placed on the mantel, his expression brooding.

"It is odd that your mother has not made an effort to acquaint herself with such a renowned son."

"Or at least to acquaint herself with my fortune," Raoul added dryly.

"Precisely." Nico lifted his head to regard Raoul with a cynical gaze. "If it were known I had a few quid rattling in my pocket, I would have a half dozen relatives arriving on my doorstep."

"Perish the thought," Raoul retorted, not entirely teasing. The mere thought of a dozen of Nico's relatives running wild through the streets of London was enough to make any English native shudder. "Did Mrs. Horton speak of my mother?"

"Nothing more than her own fancy that she must have been an aristocrat."

"Why the devil would she believe such a thing?"

A slow smile curved Nico's lips. "Because no commoner could possibly have created such an exquisite angel."

Raoul laughed. "Angel bedamned. Still, I am pleased to say I bear no resemblance to my father."

"That is not entirely true. You both possess an appreciation for a lavish existence. The cook mentioned your father receiving a large inheritance. Do you know where it came from?"

Raoul frowned. In truth, he had never considered the matter. In those days, he had been far too occupied with the task of avoiding Lord and Lady Merriot's ill-concealed distaste for his presence to notice more than the hordes of workmen invading the house.

"Some relative who was thoughtful enough to pop off while they were still flush in the pocket, I suppose."

"Yes, but which relative?" Nico pressed. "After leaving your father's estate this morning, I nosed about the village."

Of course he had. Raoul resisted the temptation to ask if he was allowed to have any part in the search for his father's secret.

"I presume the nosing was accomplished at the pub?" he demanded instead.

Nico arched a raven brow, a wicked amusement smoldering in his dark eyes.

"It bloody well was not at the church. Such a frigid day demands a warm fire and cheap ale."

"And willing barmaids?"

"They are never unwelcome."

Raoul raised a hand in defeat. "So what did you discover?"

"Nothing."

"A day well spent, it would seem."

"What I mean is that no one knows the identity of the relative who was so generous as to leave his fortune to the Merriots," Nico clarified. "Your grandfather and his two brothers were prolific gamblers who all perished deeply in debt, while your various cousins were known as loose-screws who either drank themselves to an early grave or married into the merchant class and were shunned by your father."

The revelations were far from shocking to Raoul. He'd always sensed a weakness of character in his father. It was in his sharp, disdainful treatment of those he felt beneath him, and his habit of neglecting the local merchants' bills until they were forced to arrive at his doorstep, hat in hand, to plead for a measure of relief.

And, of course, there was his tangible dislike for his own son.

Still, it did beg the question of where such a vast inheritance would have come from.

"Perhaps the money belonged to Lady Merriot's family. Females cannot inherit entailed property, but it is not unheard of for some settlement to be set aside for them."

Nico shook his head. "From what I could discover, her father was the younger son of a minor nobleman who fled to Paris to escape his creditors, and stayed when he married the daughter of an English diplomat. In fact, there was a mighty dustup when your father arrived from his travels abroad with a near penniless bride. It was expected he would do his duty and wed a large dowry." Nico regarded him with a questioning gaze. "Do you remember anything as a child?"

Raoul shrugged. He had devoted the past years to forgetting his childhood beneath Lord Merriot's roof.

"I recall when the workmen descended on the Great House. *Mon Dieu,* you could not enter a room or walk through the gardens without tripping over the crews."

"Were the Merriots in mourning at the time?"

"No." Raoul stilled. *Sacrebleu.* Why had he never before considered his father's sudden windfall? "Quite the opposite. There was not a week that passed without a deluge of guests arriving. And of course, there were the inevitable journeys to London."

"Rather odd if they had lost a family member close enough to leave them such a tidy fortune. They should have been in black for at least a few weeks."

"I need to discover where that inheritance came from."

"I will . . ."

"Hold, Nico." Raoul swiftly interrupted. "This is a task perfectly suited to Ian Breckford. There are few who can match his understanding of finances. Besides, since taking over his uncle's investments, he has cultivated precisely the sort of connections among solicitors and bankers that will allow him to trace my father's wealth far easier than either of us can do."

Nico thinned his lips, but wisely didn't bother to argue. Even he had to concede that Ian possessed an uncanny skill when it came to matters of money.

"Then I shall investigate the French nurse," he announced. "She must have knowledge of the mysterious secret if someone was willing to finance her London shop. Such a thing would take considerable capital."

Raoul folded his arms over his chest. "Actually, I believe that I will request Fredrick to track down the elusive Francine. Older women tend to dote on him with nauseating delight."

Nico narrowed his gaze. "I see your devilish plot. You are determined to keep me stuck here in the wilds of Cheshire."

"You can't expect me to suffer alone?"

"You do not appear to be suffering." The all too shrewd gaze searched Raoul's countenance. "In fact, you look disgustingly pleased with yourself."

Raoul smiled wryly, his thoughts instinctively turning toward the womanly temptation of Miss Sarah Jefferson.

"Trust me, I suffered the entire night. And if I do not mistake matters, I will continue to suffer many more nights." He paused, startled to realize that despite his raging frustration, he was pleased with himself. Or rather, pleased with an erotic spinster who claimed far too much of his thoughts. Stupid when he had no assurance the woman would ever offer him more than a stolen kiss or two. And then there were those brats, Willie and Jimmy. Raoul gave a shake of his head. He was clearly well on his way to bedlam. "Besides, what would I do without my faithful valet?"

Nico rewarded this fine compliment with a roll of his eyes. "What is it you truly desire of me?"

"Discover what you can of Polly Andrews."

Nico stiffened at the unexpected command. "Does she have a connection to your father?"

"No, she is the mother of Willie and Jimmy. Miss Jefferson has been told that the woman disappeared with a groom and traveled to Wallingford, but I wish to know for certain."

"Good God, why?"

Raoul leveled a steady gaze at his companion. "Does it matter?"

"Wallingford?" Nico grimaced at the thought of traveling near twenty miles over bad roads in the frigid weather. Especially when the village promised little in the way of entertainment. "Why not just banish me to the gates of hell?"

"With your skills, it should only take a day to discover her whereabouts."

Nico was far from appeased. "And what should I do once I locate her? Haul her back here to take care of her brats?"

Raoul shook his head. "No. Just discover what you can of her. If she's wed, if she has a new family . . . if she is in need of funds."

Nico threw his hands in the air and headed for the door. "I am beginning to wonder if your retirement has made you batty."

"Just beginning?" Raoul muttered at his retreating servant before turning back to the snow-covered countryside.

Aimlessly drawing a pattern on the frosty pane with the tip of his finger, Raoul tried to concentrate on his purpose for coming to Cheshire. He would have to send messages to Ian and Fredrick without delay. They could be depended upon to discover the information he desired. And there were one or two locals he still intended to question.

His thoughts, however, soon turned traitor and instead of setting about his business, he remained at the window brooding on his peculiar behavior.

Why was he sending his valet to hunt down Polly Andrews?

Because of the haunting fear that had flared through Sarah's eyes at the mention of having the boys taken from her care?

Because the thought of Willie and Jimmy being wrenched from the stability of a loving home to be returned to an indifferent parent reminded him of his own fear as a child at being taken from Dunnington?

Because the rapscallions brought out that protective urge that he had felt toward Ian and Fredrick?

He was still standing at the window when the sound of raised voices had him crossing out of the library and into the foyer.

"*Sacrebleu,*" he muttered, studying the wide girth of his housekeeper's back as she attempted to bar the way of an unwelcomed visitor. "Is there a problem?"

The woman glanced over her shoulder, her chubby face surrounded by a frizz of red hair.

"Sorry, sir. It's the Andrews boys, thinking they can just arrive on the doorstep and be shown in like they be royalty. I told them . . ."

"It is fine, Mrs. Dent. I will see them," he said, firmly overriding her condemning words.

The woman sniffed, her estimation of Raoul clearly plummeting.

"It's not my place, sir, but you shouldn't encourage them. Miss Jefferson does her best, but them two are a handful."

Raoul swallowed the urge to tell the grating woman that he damned well preferred the company of the boys to her and her bird-witted daughter.

Nico would slice his throat if he ran off the only household servants they currently possessed.

"Do I smell something burning?" he inquired, his voice deceptively mild.

As expected, the woman gave a small shriek of alarm. "Oh lordy, my shepherd's pie."

He waited until Mrs. Dent had waddled off with surprising speed before turning to regard the two urchins grinning at him from the doorway.

Both were swaddled in heavy wool coats with knitted scarves wrapped around their heads. They also sported what appeared to be new boots that were currently covered in snow.

Miss Jefferson obviously had conceded defeat in attempting to keep two rambunctious boys locked in a cottage, and instead armed them to endure any weather.

His blood heated as the image of the raven-haired beauty flared through his mind, and it was only with effort that he managed to focus his concentration on his unexpected guests.

"Told you he was a right one, Jimmy," Willie said, elbowing his younger brother in the ribs.

"Hmmm." Raoul refused to be swayed by the flashing dimples and rosy cheeks, folding his arms over his chest. "Does Miss Jefferson know where you are?"

Willie cleared his throat. "We are on our way home from the vicarage now, sir, and I was thinking as we walked past the lodge that you are the perfect solution to a problem that's been nagging at me and Jimmy."

Raoul arched a brow. "I must admit I have always been much more likely to be considered the problem rather than the solution. I wonder if this means I am getting old?"

Jimmy regarded him with his big blue eyes. "If I say nay, will you offer your help?"

Raoul tilted back his head to laugh with genuine amusement. "Brat. Mrs. Dent was right, I should have allowed her to run you off." Knowing he had been outgunned by a pair of shameless imps, Raoul stepped back with a wave of his arm. "Come in and tell me what you want."

Leading his guests into the library, Raoul took spiteful pleasure in the trail of snow left in their wake. Mrs. Dent deserved to have her nose tweaked.

Raoul pointed the boys toward the low settee near the fireplace, and hid a smile as they both perched on the edge of the cushions, clearly discomforted by their surroundings. The Lodge might be modest to Raoul, but to two boys raised in a cramped cottage, it must seem a mansion.

With casual motions, he crossed to the breakfast table and collected the plate of jam tarts he'd left untouched.

"I have a vague recollection of being constantly hungry as a lad," he murmured, setting the plate between the boys. "Help yourself."

As hoped, the lads forgot their unease and swiftly demolished the tarts. Then, licking his fingers, Willie regarded his host with the expression of a true connoisseur.

"Good enough, but not so fine as Miss Sarah's tarts."

Raoul sucked in a deep breath as the vivid memory of Sarah, her cheeks dusted with flour, her luscious body wrapped in an apron, flared through his mind. She had tasted of gingerbread and he had ached to devour her.

He *still* ached to devour her.

"She does possess a magical touch in the kitchen," he murmured.

Thankfully unaware of his less than pure thoughts, Jimmy flashed a sudden grin.

"Miss Sarah says I'm allowed to believe in magic even if the Vicar frowns on it. She says the world is too beautiful not to be enchanted."

"Jimmy likes reading books about Camelot," Willie swiftly explained, almost as if afraid Raoul would mock the young boy's innocent belief.

"A young gentleman of discerning taste, I see," Raoul commended.

Jimmy frowned. "Discerning?"

"Exquisite."

"Oh." Jimmy paused. "Do you believe in magic, sir?"

A faint smile touched his lips. "I'm beginning to. Now, perhaps you should tell me what has brought you to my doorstep."

Willie exchanged a swift glance with his brother before squaring his shoulders. "Well sir, Christmas is coming and Jimmy and me were wanting a present for Miss Sarah."

"Ah. Are you in need of a small loan?"

"Nay, we've been doing chores for the Vicar and saved our wages," Willie proudly announced. "We can pay."

"Then how can I be of service?"

"We seen a set of paints when Miss Sarah took us to Chester to buy shoes . . ."

"They were the fancy sort that real artists use," Jimmy interrupted, only to be elbowed by his brother.

"Anyways, they would be the perfect gift, but we can't figure a way to get to Chester," Willie continued, his brow furrowed. "Leastways, not without Miss Sarah knowing where we're going. She's mighty particular about keeping track of us."

"My opinion of Miss Sarah's good sense rises with every passing moment."

"We was hoping if we gave you the money, you could purchase the paints for us afore Christmas."

Jimmy dug in his coat pocket and pulled out a tattered piece of paper.

"Look, we wrote down the name of the store and everything."

Taking the offered scrap, Raoul read the neatly printed name.

"Spencer's Fine Emporium."

"Just a block from that big cathedral," Willie directed.

"You can't miss it," Jimmy added.

Raoul lifted his head to meet their pleading glances. "That does not seem an excessive request."

Willie breathed an exaggerated sigh. "Then you'll do it?"

Raoul chuckled. "Yes, you scamp, I will collect your

precious paints and even have them wrapped with a tidy bow."

"Thank you, sir. I'll bring the money to you . . ."

"Perhaps it would be best if I call at the cottage," Raoul overrode Willie's offer, not making the least effort to resist temptation. "Miss Sarah might question why you would wish to come to the Lodge."

"Aye, she would." Willie sadly shook his head. "And she is near impossible to gull."

Raoul regarded the young man with a severe gaze. "A true gentleman does not *gull* a lady."

The boys pondered a moment, clearly not entirely pleased with the sage piece of advice.

"Not even when it's just to keep her from fretting?" Jimmy demanded.

"Especially if it is to keep her from fretting, since a lady always manages to uncover any mischief, no matter how clever a gentleman might believe he is being. And then, of course . . ."

"There's bloody hell to pay," Willie muttered glumly.

Raoul knew precisely how he felt.

"Exactly."

Chapter 7

Raoul considered himself a gentleman of remarkably good sense.

Despite his undoubted success upon the stage, not to mention his near adoration among London society, he had never allowed his head to be turned. He, better than anyone, understood that his life of glittering fame was no more than an empty illusion. Only a fool would allow his well-crafted deception to fog his wits.

His good sense, however, seemed in dire jeopardy as he shrugged on a natty blue coat cut by Shultz that was perfectly matched to the blue and ivory striped waistcoat, and tied his cravat in an Oriental style.

By no stretch of the imagination could he claim his intention to travel to Miss Jefferson's cottage furthered his attempts to discover the truth of his legacy. Nor could he pretend that this was simply a careless desire to help

Willie and Jimmy. Not when he'd spent an agonizing hour deciding which coat best suited him.

Finally, he gave a shake of his head, and wrapping himself in his box coat and shoving a beaver hat on his golden curls, he headed to the stables to have his groom saddle Hercules.

He might not understand his provoking fascination with Miss Sarah Jefferson and her two rapscallions, but there was no battling it.

Avoiding the main thoroughfare, Raoul chose a rarely used path, hoping to keep his visit to Sarah's cottage as discreet as possible. It would not be utterly scandalous to briefly call upon Sarah, so long as her maid and children were in attendance. Still, he preferred to avoid making her the source of gossip. And no matter what he did, even taking ale at the local pub managed to be a source of speculation.

He had traveled some distance when his attention was caught by a run-down cottage with a roof badly in need of patching and a dozen chickens scratching at the snow. On the point of passing, he suddenly whistled, bringing Hercules to a halt.

Such a disreputable excuse for a home could only belong to one man in the neighborhood.

Perhaps he could use this journey to accomplish something beyond making a fool of himself.

Ignoring the chaffing need to continue on his path, Raoul vaulted from his saddle and, leading Hercules into the overgrown garden, tapped the horse lightly on the leg. Instantly, his obedient mount lifted his hoof, his head lowering as if in acute discomfort.

Raoul had never been able to deduce why anyone

would train a horse with such a trick, but he couldn't deny it had come in handy a time or two.

He had only a few minutes to pretend to inspect Hercules's fetlock when there was the sound of a door slamming. A small, baldhead man with a ferret face and pointed nose marched toward him, wrapping a threadbare cloak around his scrawny body.

"Here now, this here be private land," the man barked, glowering at Raoul.

"Forgive my intrusion, but my horse has come up lame." Raoul straightened, his most charming smile curving his lips. "Ah . . . Mr. Drabble, is it not?"

The pale blue eyes narrowed with suspicion. "Aye."

"Perhaps you do not recall me . . ."

"A course I remember you. Not like I would forget Merriot's bastard." He grimaced, his gaze flicking dismissively over Raoul's elegant attire. "Not with the entire county forever jawing about your grand acting career."

"You have my utmost sympathy. I cannot imagine a more tedious subject."

The brewing belligerence faltered at Raoul's mild retort. "Aye well, I never did have a bone to pick with you. Always a good enough lad. Not that I have any use for actors," he was swift to add, as if worried that Raoul might take his words as a compliment. "Frippery business. A man should be expected to do a respectable day's work to earn his coin."

"Then it is a fortunate thing I have quit the stage."

"Gads, I have heard of nothing else these past days. As if I give a grout if you choose to prance about a stage or become another one of them worthless libertines who litter London."

Raoul wisely hid his smile. Although his memories

of the man were sketchy at best, he did recall more than one angry confrontation between this man and Lord Merriot. One that nearly came to blows when Drabble arrived at the Great House with the complaint that the various workmen were disturbing his pig.

"No, I shouldn't think it would matter a wit, although I must protest at being considered a worthless libertine," he retorted. "I intend to devote the next few months to the writing of my memories."

"Christ." Turning his head, Drabble spit near his worn boots, clearly revealing his opinion of Raoul's memoir.

More amused than offended, Raoul allowed his eyes to widen, as if struck by a sudden thought.

"Do you know, it occurs to me that you would be of service."

"Me? Bah. What would I know of you beyond the fact that you were a snotty nosed brat who barely had two words to say for yourself?"

"Actually, my interest is in my father's past," Raoul smoothly assured him. "My publisher is convinced that the readers will wish to know something of the man who fathered me. Unfortunately, the Earl has refused to be involved in what he considers a repulsive scheme."

The mere mention of the Earl was enough to bring a militant gleam to the pale blue eyes, proving the ancient hostilities were far from buried.

Perfect.

"Oh, he does, does he? Not surprising," the man growled. "Always was too high in the instep, thinking himself better than his fellow man, even when he didn't have two shillings to rub together."

"You've known him for several years, have you not?"

"Since we were both grubby lads and I gave him a

black eye for pinching my favorite fishing pole. I near got thrashed to an inch of my life by my pa for having dared strike the old Earl's precious son."

Raoul frowned. Could Drabble be mistaken? Why the devil would his father steal a fishing pole from a penniless boy when he no doubt had a dozen of his own?

"I always knew there was bad blood between the two of you, but I didn't realize it extended back quite so far."

Drabble snorted. "It wasn't the fishing pole or even the thrashing I got that's made for bad blood."

"No?"

Lifting his hand, the older man pointed a gnarled finger directly into Raoul's face.

"That blighter accused my brother of stealing his watch and had him transported."

Raoul jerked in surprise. He knew his father could be a cold, callous jackass, but to have a young man transported . . .

"*Mon Dieu.*"

Mistaking Raoul's astonishment for condemnation of his brother, Drabble yanked his brows together.

"Frank was as honest as the day was long. He would never have taken nothing that didn't belong to him."

"Then why would my father accuse him?"

"Frank was an under-gardener at the Great House. One night they caught him sneaking through the back parlor."

"As much as I loathe having a man transported for anything but the most serious crimes, that does seem rather suspicious. I presume he didn't reside at the house?"

"Nay, but Francine did."

Raoul's vague curiosity altered to acute interest.

The mention of Francine twice in one day could be

mere coincidence, but Raoul felt a strange premonition creep down his spine.

"My nurse?"

"Frank and her were stepping out," Drabble clarified. "He was only there to be with her."

"Did Frank have any notion why Lord Merriot would accuse him of stealing his watch?"

"Nary a one." Drabble's face hardened with his long-nurtured resentment. "So far as Frank knew, the Earl didn't so much as say a word to him the three years he worked at the estate."

"Did my father know that Frank was courting Francine?"

"It weren't no secret. The two were planning to wed." Drabble clenched his hand into a fist. "Vindictive rotter had Frank hauled away while she pleaded on her knees for him to have mercy."

Raoul had no argument with Drabble's estimation of his father's character, but he was more interested in the reason for Lord Merriot's ruthless treatment of Frank.

Was it just the act of a nobleman who was outraged at having a thief in his home? Or was it an attempt to be rid of a young man who had such a close connection to Francine?

A young man who perhaps had shared intimate secrets with his French lover?

"My memories of my nurse are spotty at best, but I do recall her leaving," he murmured, becoming increasingly certain his father must have paid Francine an enormous sum to leave the Great House. And to leave him. "She traveled to . . . London, did she not?"

"That was the rumors."

There was nothing in the old man's voice to suggest he knew anything about her flight to the city.

"Did my father treat any other servants with such cruelty?"

"Not that I heard tale of." Drabble snorted. "Course, most people in these here parts are frightened to speak ill of such a powerful family. Hell, most of them would kiss the Earl's arse if he asked it of them."

Raoul's lips twisted, intimately familiar with the repulsive fawning accorded the Merriots by the locals.

"One can hardly blame them. There are few families in the neighborhood who do not depend upon the Merriots for their livelihood."

"Cowards, the lot of them."

"You, however, are obviously made of sterner stuff." Raoul determinedly steered the conversation back in the direction that he desired. "I commend your courage."

Drabble narrowed his gaze. "Trotting it a bit hard, Charlebois. What is it you're a wanting?"

"It occurs to me that beyond the mere details of my father's past, the sales of my memoir will be greatly enhanced by a few . . . disreputable stories. There is nothing London society adores more than scandal."

The older man nodded sagely. "Ah, wanting to make a few pounds off the old swell, are you?"

"It would be the only thing I ever received from my father," Raoul said grimly. "Unfortunately, I haven't been able to discover even a hint of gossip. I can only presume Lord and Lady Merriot have lived the lives of near saints."

"Not bloody likely."

"You know of a scandal?"

"Beyond ruining my brother?"

"A grievous act certainly, but do you know of any others?"

A sly glint entered the pale blue eyes. "I heard tale that he was seen in London in a certain establishment just off Fleet Street. Course that was years ago and it was all hushed up."

It took Raoul a moment to realize what the elder man was implying.

"It is not that unusual for a nobleman to hock a few belongings to pay his most pressing bills," he at last retorted. "And from what little I can discover, my father was in dire need of funds until he came into his inheritance."

"Aye, but this occurred after his good stroke of fortune, which is why it was so easily dismissed as a hum."

Raoul frowned. That did seem odd. Why would a gentleman who had come into a vast inheritance need to sell off his valuables.

"After, you say?"

Drabble leaned forward. "For my part I always wondered if his high and mighty lordship had become a common thief."

Raoul choked back a laugh of disbelief. "A thief?"

"He stole my fishing pole as cool as you please," Drabble pointed out. "What's to halt him from pinching a few pretty baubles from his rich friends?"

"Surely his guests would eventually become suspicious if their valuables were forever disappearing when they visited the Great House?"

"Not if he were to place the blame on his servants." Drabble's eyes glittered, clearly warming to his outlandish tale. "Perhaps he was afraid others were beginning to realize something was amiss, and made a show of catching poor Frank filching from the house."

For a brief moment of insanity, Raoul actually considered the notion.

It would explain his father's sudden wealth, his eagerness to have a hapless servant transported, his presence near Fleet Street, and even his willingness to be extorted of twenty thousand pounds by Dunnington.

Then, he gave a sharp shake of his head.

Sacrebleu. This was not one of his plays.

No matter what their desperation, peers of the realm did not become jewel thieves.

Besides, his father didn't have the backbone to set upon such a daring path.

"I am not certain my readers will be prepared to believe such a . . . colorful tale," he at last admitted.

"They'd readily believe it if I was the one accused."

Well, Raoul couldn't argue with that logic.

"And therein lays the difference between being an aristocrat or one of the great unwashed masses."

"You have that right and tight."

Realizing that he had drained this particular well dry, Raoul reached into his coat pocket and pulled out a handful of coins.

"If you happen to think of anything else, I hope you will call on me at the Lodge." He held out the small bounty. "Allow me to compensate for your time. I know you must be a busy man."

"Thank you kindly." The coins were tucked away with remarkable speed. "Difficult to believe you can be related to Merriot."

"Nearly impossible." He gave a discreet tap on Hercules's flank, and the horse promptly lowered his leg and tossed his head with a display of impatience. "Ah, it seems that Hercules has recovered. Good day, Drabble."

* * *

Seated in her favorite seat beside the parlor fireplace, Sarah stitched a rip in Jimmy's shirt, sternly keeping her thoughts from wandering.

As tempting as it might be to dwell upon her latest encounter with Raoul Charlebois, she was wise enough to resist. A pity really. She couldn't deny that she would enjoy recalling the skill of his caresses and the scent of his warm, male skin.

She might be a virgin, but she had been kissed more than once. Certainly enough to recognize the touch of an expert. What better means of keeping a lonely spinster warm on such a chill afternoon?

Unfortunately, as much as she might secretly have enjoyed Raoul's brief, tantalizing seduction, she had been honest when she told him that she couldn't risk any hint of scandal being attached to her.

Sarah lifted her head, her gaze instinctively seeking out the slender form of Willie who stood across the small parlor.

A familiar warmth stirred in her heart.

"Willie, you have been standing at the window for a near a half hour," she murmured. "Whatever are you staring at?"

The lad jerked, as if caught in some mischief, before he turned his head to grin at her with charming innocence.

"I'm thinking the snow is piled mighty high. Do you think Father Christmas will be able to find us?"

"I do not have a doubt in the world." Setting aside the shirt, Sarah rose to her feet and crossed to her young charge. In the past three years, she'd come to know Willie. Although he was like any other boy of his age, quick to fall into scrapes and full of high spirits, he was also fiercely protective of his brother and, despite Sarah's best efforts, inclined to harbor fears that he and Jimmy might be taken from their newfound home. Reaching out, she absently brushed a hand through his tumbled locks. "Now tell me what is truly on your mind."

Without warning, Sarah felt Willie stiffen, his nose pressed to the frosty panes.

"Look, it's that Mr. Charlebois. I think he's coming here." Slipping past a startled Sarah, Willie darted toward the nearby entryway, bellowing for his brother who was upstairs finishing his day's schoolwork. "Jimmy."

"Please do not shout, Willie," Sarah pleaded, her brows knitting as Willie hastily tugged on his coat and scarf. "Where are you going?"

Reaching into his coat pocket, he pulled out a shriveled piece of fruit.

"I've been saving this here apple for Hercules."

"But, my dear . . ."

Her words were cut short as Willie slammed the front door behind him and Jimmy clamored loudly down the stairs, skidding to a halt in front of the parlor window.

"Mr. Charlebois is here."

"Yes, I am certain the entire county must know of his arrival by now," she muttered, her eyes narrowed with a growing suspicion. "The question is, *why* is he here?"

Jimmy ignored her pointed inquiry, his gaze trained on the gentleman leading his horse through the gate. Not that Sarah could blame him. Raoul Charlebois was a riveting sight.

Not just his flawless countenance, or the white gold curls, or the magnificent body shown to advantage in his caped coat. His beauty was the stuff of legends. No, it was the smile of genuine pleasure that touched his lips as Willie ran toward him that made her breath tangle in her throat.

He possessed a near magical ability to make another feel as if they were the most fascinating person in the world.

A dangerous talent for the unwary.

Sarah watched as Raoul bent his head to listen intently to Willie, the two seemingly involved in a private conversation that once again stirred Sarah's curiosity. What the devil was the man doing here?

"Simon swears that he is a famous actor." Jimmy broke into her thoughts. "One of the most famous in all of England."

"Yes. I believe he is hailed as London's leading man."

"He isn't nearly so toplofty as you would think he would be, is he Miss Sarah?"

A wistful smile touched her lips. "He does possess a remarkable charm."

Jimmy tilted his head to regard her with a hint of surprise, perhaps sensing her conflicted emotions.

"Do you not like him?"

She swiftly shook off the odd sensations gripping her, and reached out to ruffle Jimmy's hair. The young boy was far too sensitive to her every mood.

"We are barely acquainted, but I do not doubt that I find him as enchanting as most of England seems to."

Reassured, Jimmy turned back to the window. "He's coming in."

"So I see." Before she could halt herself, Sarah reached up to smooth the curls that had escaped from her simple braid. "Perhaps you could run and ask Maggie to put the kettle on, poppet."

"Yes, ma'am."

Jimmy darted toward the kitchen, leaving Sarah a few moments to gather her composure. Ridiculous that she would need to do so, but there it was.

She was still standing near the window when Raoul entered the tiny cottage, removing his outerwear before stepping into the parlor, followed closely by his young companion.

Performing an elegant bow, he straightened to flash her a smile that promised all sorts of wicked pleasure.

"Good afternoon, Miss Jefferson. I hope I don't intrude?"

Her heart slammed painfully against her ribs. His presence seemed to fill her tiny parlor, his tantalizing scent already teasing at her nose.

"Not at all . . ." Her polite greeting trailed away as Raoul closed his eyes and tilted his head back. "Is there a problem?"

He opened his eyes to regard her with a warm gaze. "Your cottage always smells like . . ."

"What?"

"Home."

He, of course, couldn't have said anything to please her more. She had done everything in her power to make this small cottage a home for the boys.

As he must well know.

"Thank you." Her expression revealed that she was aware of his deliberate attempt to charm her. "I trust your hanging of the evergreen met with Mrs. Dent's approval?"

Undisturbed, Raoul allowed his smile to widen.

"She was frankly astonished that I managed so well. In truth, I have greatly risen in her esteem."

"Have you?"

"Indeed. I have gone from a frippery lobcock to a cunning rogue."

"Ah, a great improvement."

"I have hopes of eventually reaching a pompous sapskull."

"It is important to hold onto your dreams."

"So I have been told," his voice dropped, becoming low, intimate.

Her heart gave another of those discomforting flops. He was weaving a spell between them that was near tangible. Definitely time for a distraction.

She found it as she glanced toward the silent Willie. His expression was far too innocent. A certain warning that some plot was afoot.

Turning back to Raoul, she regarded him with a hint of suspicion, vaguely aware that Jimmy had returned to the room.

"Is there a particular reason for your visit?"

"Can't a bloke just happen by?" Willie demanded.

Her gaze never wavered, holding Raoul's twinkling blue gaze. "I am beginning to wonder."

"Actually it was something you said that brought me to your doorstep," Raoul replied, his expression equaling Willie's in faux innocence.

"And what is that?"

"You mentioned that the boys are planning to perform charades at your Christmas party."

Jimmy moved to Raoul's side, regarding him with a hint of adulation.

"We wrote them ourselves and everything."

He tapped the end of Jimmy's nose, clearly at ease with young boys, despite being a bachelor.

"I have decided to assist you."

"You, sir?" Jimmy breathed in wonder.

"I have developed some skill over the years."

"Aye, but . . ."

"I can at least look over the script and give you some assistance with your staging," he assured the enthralled Jimmy.

"Do you mean it, sir?" Willie demanded, all too familiar with empty promises. "You ain't . . . I mean, you aren't bamming us, are you?"

Raoul met the boy's searching gaze with a somber expression. "I never jest about my work, Master Willie."

Sarah frowned, as baffled by this gentleman's offer as the boys.

"That is very generous, Mr. Charlebois," she said slowly. "But may I inquire as to why you would be willing to assist with a simple charade?"

He turned to her, his expression unreadable. "Let us just say I am diligent in upholding the dubious reputation of the English theater."

"Hmmm."

He arched a brow at her disbelieving tone. "And you did mention that it is for the local orphanage."

"And what interest would you have in an orphanage?"

"I never forget that it is a place that I could easily have been raised," he said, his lips twisting. "I always lend my support in causes that help children."

Her breath caught.

She was becoming adjusted to his assault on her senses. Perhaps even to relish the tiny tingles of excitement that raced through her body.

But she was unprepared for the hint of vulnerability

she had just glimpsed in his eyes. Or his ready kindness to the boys.

It was one thing to lust after a man. After all, what woman in her right mind wouldn't? He was dazzling. But, it was quite another to actually . . . like him.

"May he help, Miss Sarah?" Jimmy pleaded.

Sarah hesitated. A part of her warned it was dangerous to encourage this gentleman. Especially if he thought to use the boys to gain entrance to her bed.

Then she swiftly dismissed the unpleasant notion.

Mr. Raoul Charlebois had no need to play such foolish tricks on women. Besides, not even an idiot could fail to notice how his features gentled whenever he glanced at Willie or Jimmy.

She wasn't about to steal this rare treat for the boys because of some vague unease.

"Do you promise to be on your best behavior and mind your manners?"

Jimmy brushed his finger over his chest. "The very best, cross my heart."

"Me too," Willie added.

"Very well."

Willie released a war cry before grabbing his brother by the arm and dragging him toward the door.

"Come on, Jimmy, let's get the script."

Chapter 8

Acutely aware of the woman standing just a few steps away, Raoul watched her expression of fond indulgence shift to one of guarded curiosity as she turned her midnight gaze in his direction.

He had no reasonable explanation for the compulsion that brought him to the cottage. Or the strange sense of contentment that was spreading through him merely by being surrounded by Sarah and the boisterous lads.

He only knew that of all the lavish mansions and sprawling country estates he'd visited, none could compare to this simple cottage.

The silence stretched before Sarah at last cleared her throat.

"Will you have a seat?"

Raoul glanced toward the satinwood settee that had clearly seen better days. His brow lifted as he realized why he had been struck by a sense of familiarity the first time he had entered the cottage.

"I recognize this," he muttered, his hand running over the worn blue and silver striped satin.

"Yes, most of the furniture came from the Great House," she admitted. "My father was always a frugal man and when he discovered your father intended to burn a large portion of his old furnishings, he retrieved them. He brought a few pieces here, along with a pile of old paintings I've stored in my workroom, and the rest he gave to those who were in need."

Of course his father would never consider the notion of donating the furnishings, rather than burning them like a pile of rubbish.

"I am happy to know that there are a few men of sense in Cheshire."

"If there are any pieces you desire . . ."

"*Mon Dieu,* no."

Her eyes widened at his harsh tone, then without warning, she tilted back her head and laughed.

Raoul stilled, his heart halting at the rich, full-bodied sound that filled the room.

He was accustomed to the artful laughs of society women, or the simpering giggles of debutantes. They were nothing but pale shadows in comparison.

Just as the women themselves were pale shadows in comparison to Sarah.

She was vibrantly, unashamedly full of life.

And he was . . . captivated.

"No, I do not suppose you do," she said, her dark eyes twinkling with amusement. "I doubt it would complement the furnishings in your fine London mansion."

"To be perfectly honest, I have not paid enough attention to my furnishings to know what might complement them."

"Are you jesting?"

"Not at all."

"I know gentlemen care little for such things, but surely you are familiar with your own home?"

"It is not a home, *ma petite*. It is merely a place I go when I wish to be alone."

Her amusement faded. "How sad."

He moved to brush a stray curl from her cheek, drawn to her warmth like a moth to the flame.

"I never thought so." His thumb brushed the edge of her mouth. "I had my career, endless acquaintances, two very dear friends, and all the entertainment that London has to offer."

A faint color touched her face, but she made no move to pull away.

"It does sound like an existence most people would envy."

"But not you?"

"I prefer a more simple life."

He smiled deep into her eyes. "It does have its charm."

Her tongue peeked out to dampen her dry lips, unwittingly sending a jolt of need through his body.

"You said you had never thought your life sad, implying that you have had a change of heart."

He paused, his gaze sweeping over her beautiful face. A dozen flip comments flitted through his mind, but he could not force them past his lips.

The lies he could weave so skillfully evaporated beneath her innocent gaze.

"I recently lost the man who I considered my true father."

Genuine sympathy softened her expression. "Oh, I am sorry. I can understand how that can make you question what is important in your life. A father is . . ." She struggled for the proper words. "Like an anchor. When he is gone, you feel adrift."

"Adrift." He considered the past year of aimless apathy that had plagued him. Slowly he nodded his head. "Yes."

Without warning, her hand lifted to touch his face. Her touch was gentle, but it was enough to make his gut twist with awareness.

"You will always miss him, but the days do get easier to bear."

He regarded her with a sense of baffled wonder. Since he had left the schoolroom, women had been dazzled by his looks, his easy charm, and his innate ability to know precisely how to please them.

Not one had ever seen him as a man like any other. A man who might have fears and uncertainties that keep him awake at night.

Not until Miss Sarah Jefferson.

"You are unlike any other woman I have ever known."

"That I well believe." Her hand dropped, leaving him with a feeling of loss. "I have little in common with ladies of society. Or even actresses, for that matter."

"It was meant as a compliment."

"Yes, I know." Her smile was wry. "You are very good at them. No doubt you have had a lot of practice."

He arched a brow, oddly offended. "You think me a rake?"

"Are you not?"

"I have enjoyed a few discreet affairs, but most of the rumors surrounding my conquests are grossly exaggerated." His thumb brushed her bottom lip. "I prefer quality to quantity."

"Conquests." She met his gaze squarely, but she

couldn't disguise the rapid pulse beating at the base of her throat. She was as susceptible to the raw passion that simmered between them as he was. "Yes, that does seem to be an appropriate description."

He chuckled. "A direct hit. Did your father teach you to fence?"

"No, but I am quite handy with a pistol."

"I shall try to avoid a duel," he murmured, his head lowering to brush his lips over her lush mouth. She tasted of womanly spice, making his body clench with yearning. "At least with pistols."

For a breathless moment, her lips softened, inviting him to deepen his kiss, then, with a soft gasp, she was abruptly stepping away from his touch, her cheeks flushed with a delightful confusion.

She smoothed her hands down the skirt of her buttercup-yellow gown.

"How long do you intend to remain in the neighborhood?"

He briefly wrestled with the overwhelming urge to yank her into his arms and kiss her until she moaned her pleasure. She wanted him. She *belonged* to him. And he would be damned if he allowed her to pretend otherwise.

Thankfully, common sense overruled his purely male impulse.

Any moment, the two boys would be rushing back into the room. He would do nothing to disrupt their sense of contentment. Not even if his thwarted need was becoming downright painful.

"My plans are not yet fixed," he said, allowing her to drift further away, at last coming to a rest near the stone fireplace.

She regarded him with an all-too-knowing gaze. "Because you are still adrift?"

"I suppose that is part of it," he admitted.

"And the other part?"

"Fascination."

"I cannot imagine anything fascinating to be found in such a dull community."

"Then perhaps you should glance in a mirror."

Her gaze narrowed. "Mr. Charlebois."

"Yes, Miss Jefferson?"

"I do not believe for a moment I am the reason you remain in Cheshire."

"Dine with me at the Lodge tonight, and I will prove my sincerity."

He heard her breath catch, but her expression revealed nothing but faint disapproval at his low, husky invitation.

"Do not be daft. I cannot dine in the home of a bachelor."

"Then I will visit you. Once the boys are abed . . ."

"Certainly not."

"Even if I promise to be on my best behavior?"

"That is what frightens me."

Caught off guard by the tart retort, Raoul tilted back his head, and laughed with genuine amusement. Then, allowing his gaze to drink in her dark, exotic beauty, he slowly shook his head.

"If I were a true gentleman, I would put you from my mind."

Something flashed through her eyes before she was tilting her chin.

"Indeed, you would."

He smiled wryly, knowing there wasn't the least hope

he could follow the urges of his conscience. The woman had stirred a need he had to ease before he went mad.

"Thankfully, I have never been burdened with such tedious rules."

"You do not consider yourself a gentleman?"

"A man is born to such a position."

She frowned at his flippant tone. "I prefer to judge others on the content of their heart, not their position in society."

"As I said . . ." His gaze drifted down to the modest neckline. "Fascinating."

"We got it!" Willie's shout echoed through the cottage, along with the clatter of footsteps on the stairs. "Mr. Charlebois, we got it!"

Raoul swallowed a groan. "I want it."

It was not until dinner had been cleared away and the boys sent upstairs to prepare for bed that Sarah was at last able to return to her mending.

Not that she seemed to be accomplishing much work, she ruefully acknowledged.

So far, she had spent more time staring into the fire than tending to her work, despite the fact her broodings weren't doing a bit of good.

She still had no notion as to why a gentleman who was one of the most sought-after men in all of England would be interested in a poor spinster. Or why he would devote an entire afternoon to entertaining two abandoned boys with their Christmas charades.

What she did know was that while Raoul Charlebois might claim to find her fascinating in the hopes of seducing her, she truly did find him the most intriguing man she had ever encountered.

Who was Raoul?

Was there truly a lonely vulnerable man beneath all that golden beauty and charm? Or was that just another disguise?

The sound of approaching footsteps intruded into her thoughts, and lifting her head, Sarah swallowed a sigh as she recognized the knowing glitter in the brown eyes of her maid.

A few years older than Sarah, Maggie Stone was pleasingly plump, with honey-brown curls and pretty features. She was fiercely devoted to the boys and a great help to Sarah around the small cottage, but she did tend to treat Sarah with a familiarity that few employers would tolerate.

Not that Sarah minded. At least, not usually.

Tonight, however, she already sensed where the conversation was headed.

"Right kind of Mr. Charlebois to help the boys with their charades," the woman predictably murmured, pulling on her heavy cloak.

Sarah lowered her head, more to hide her expression than to concentrate on her mending. Maggie knew her too well.

"Very kind."

"And so good with the scamps. Who'd have thought such a gentleman would have a real knack for handling little ones."

"He assures me he is no gentleman."

Maggie sniffed, obviously as susceptible as every other female to Raoul's allure.

"I suppose the nobs would not count him as one, but

to my mind, his manners are a good sight better than those who consider themselves his superior."

Sarah's lips twitched. "And, of course, it does not hurt that he is so devilishly handsome."

"Aye, he is that." Maggie heaved an appreciative sigh. "Like one of them Greek gods."

"Apollo," Sarah breathed, all too easily conjuring Raoul's golden beauty.

"Beg pardon?"

"Never mind."

There was a pause before Maggie cleared her throat and at last said what was upon her mind.

"Do you know, Miss Sarah, I believe Mr. Charlebois has taken a fancy to you."

Sarah's heart fluttered, a heat stealing through her body. "Hardly flattering. I would say he takes a fancy to anything in skirts."

"Not everything," Maggie stoutly denied. "I met up with Mrs. Dent in the village, and she says that Mr. Charlebois has behaved with perfect propriety to her daughter, who is maid at the Lodge. And she claims he hasn't had one female there, despite the local tarts who have done all but toss themselves at his feet."

Sarah tried to ignore the flare of satisfaction that warmed her heart. Foolishness.

"Well, he has only been here a few days," she retorted.

"I know a thing or two about men, and when they're staring at a woman like Mr. Charlebois is staring at you, they have no taste for other females. Mark my words."

Sarah at last lifted her head, meeting the maid's expectant gaze. "It does not matter in the least how he looks at me, Maggie. I have two boys who depend on me, and I will not disappoint them."

Maggie's expression fell. "A pity. How often is such a man likely to come to the village?"

Sarah shivered at the mere thought of endless temptation. "Thankfully, never."

"A wise woman takes opportunity when it comes a knocking."

"A wise woman recognizes the difference between opportunity and foolish risk."

Maggie clicked her tongue. "You talk like an old maid."

"No doubt because that is exactly what I am."

"Nonsense."

"I do have a favor to ask of you." Sarah firmly turned the conversation away from Raoul Charlebois.

Maggie was easily distracted. "Of course, what do you need?"

"I must travel to Chester."

"More paintings to sell?"

"Yes, as well as shopping for the boys. I hope to purchase their Christmas presents," she explained. "Can I leave them in your care?"

"No need to even ask." Maggie waved her hand. "I am always willing to lend a hand with them lads. When will you be leaving?"

"The first of next week, so long as we do not endure another snow storm. I will travel by stage on Monday morning and return Tuesday evening. If you will stay here with the boys, then I needn't worry they will be up to mischief."

The brown eyes sparkled with amusement. "Don't you be fretting. I can mind them."

Sarah had absolute faith in her maid. The woman loved the boys, but she had a firm enough hand to prevent any trouble.

"Thank you, Maggie," she said, a relieved smile curving her lips. "I truly do not know what I would do without you."

"Fah." A blush of pleasure flooded Maggie's face as she headed to the door. "Now, do not allow those boys to keep you up the entire night reading them stories."

"Good night, Maggie."

Night had fallen by the time Raoul left the village. After leaving the cottage, he had been unable to bear the thought of returning to the empty Lodge. Not after hours spent being entertained by Willie and Jimmy's antics, his heart warmed by Sarah's full throated laughter.

It had been far too long since he had enjoyed such simple pleasures. Not since he'd left Dunnington's to make his way on the stage.

He had forgotten the sheer contentment of being surrounded by a loving family.

It had only been when Sarah had firmly sent the boys to the kitchen to wash up for dinner that he had forced himself to accept he had lingered far longer than was reasonably proper.

Sacrebleu. He had felt like a stray dog begging to be allowed to remain in the warmth of the cottage for just a bit longer.

Pathetic.

What the devil had happened to the sophisticated, dashing gentleman who could cause a traffic jam just by stepping out of a building?

Trying to ignore the tiny ache that he very much feared was loneliness, Raoul turned Hercules toward the village. He had better things to do than sit about the

Lodge and brood on his unreasonable fascination with Sarah and her orphans.

Not that his time in the village had been productive, he wryly acknowledged.

As usual, his presence in the small pub had caused a flurry of excitement. Even after he had collected his ale and made his way to the back of the common room, he could not escape the rabid curiosity of the gathering crowd.

Unable to discreetly question any of the guests, he had been forced to content himself with telling ribald stories of his days in London, disguising his impatience until he could reasonably take his leave.

Gathering Hercules, he shivered against the brutal wind and set out for the Lodge.

He could only hope the notes he had sent to Ian and Fredrick would arrive swiftly. He had paid Mrs. Dent's oldest son a handsome sum to ride to London with the messages with all speed. Perhaps they would have more luck than he. Certainly they couldn't do any worse.

In truth, his journey to Cheshire had not gone at all like he had anticipated.

Not only had he failed to realize the difficulty his fame would make his efforts to dig through his father's past, but he most certainly hadn't expected to be distracted by a dark-eyed beauty and two charming scamps.

A shiver raced down his spine. Whether from the frigid night air or the thought of Sarah Jefferson was impossible to determine.

Or perhaps it was a premonition.

Barely paying heed to the darkness shrouded about him, Raoul was caught sadly off guard when two men burst through the hedge and darted straight toward him.

Muttering a curse, he struggled not to be thrown as Hercules reared at the unexpected attack. Damn. Why hadn't he been paying more attention? He had allowed his isolated surroundings to lull him into lowering his guard, and now he was paying for his stupidity.

Busy trying to regain control of his mount, Raoul was unable to retrieve the pistol he had tucked in the pocket of his coat. Unfortunately, Hercules had been well and truly spooked, and ignoring Raoul's urgings to gallop on, the skittish horse was more determined to strike out against the rushing men.

"Bloody horse," one of the attackers rasped, dodging a hoof aimed at his head. "Grab his leg."

The other man darted forward, only to be met with a kick from Raoul. "I'm trying." He muttered a curse as Raoul's boot connected with his shoulder, but with grim determination, he plowed forward and wrapped his beefy hands around Raoul's upper calf.

With one sharp yank, he had Raoul jerked out of his saddle and lying flat on his back on the frozen path.

The force of his landing exploded the air from his lungs, and Raoul struggled to breathe. What the hell was going on? Even the most ruthless highwayman contented himself with holding his prey at gunpoint while he relieved the poor fool of his valuables. Why risk injury when you could remain at a distance and complete your business?

The ridiculous thoughts floated through his mind as he felt a vicious kick to his side and another to the side of his head.

"We don't like yer sort around here," a rough voice growled between kicks. "Return to London or the next time we'll slice yer throat."

Despite the ringing in his head, Raoul suddenly realized that these weren't common bandits. They hadn't so much as glanced at the heavy gold ring on his finger or the ruby stickpin tucked in his cravat.

No, they were obviously here to frighten him from Cheshire, and there was only one person who wanted him gone.

"Tell my father that nothing in hell will make me leave," he gritted, the words barely leaving his lips before another kick to his head sent him tumbling into a welcome darkness.

Chapter 9

Raoul was uncertain how long he lay unconscious. He suspected it was only a few minutes, but it was enough to leave him stiff and shivering from the cold.

Forcing himself to his feet, he groaned at the pain that wracked his body. His head throbbed, his ribs felt as if they had been kicked by a mule, and his spine was still protesting its violent impact with the hard ground. On the bright side, Hercules remained patiently waiting in the middle of the road, and there was no sign of his assailants.

Managing to limp to his horse, Raoul hefted himself into the saddle and continued the short distance to the Lodge. On this occasion, he had his pistol drawn and was prepared to shoot at the first hint of trouble.

Nothing stirred as he rounded the Lodge and left Hercules in the hands of his stoic groom, avoiding the man's curious gaze as he turned to make his way into the looming house. Later he would reveal his humiliating defeat. For tonight he simply wanted to crawl into his bed and plot the best means for revenge.

A fine notion that was unfortunately ruined when he entered the kitchen to discover Nico consuming what was left of the shepherd's pie.

Mon Dieu. He hadn't expected his valet to return before tomorrow. Now he knew there was no hope of being allowed to deal with his attackers without interference. Nico had assigned himself as Raoul's protector, regardless of the fact Raoul was quite capable of taking care of himself. The servant would take this assault as a personal insult.

On cue, Nico rose to his feet, his dark eyes narrowing as he took in Raoul's disheveled appearance and pronounced limp.

"*Christo,*" he breathed, hurrying to Raoul's side. "What happened?"

"Would you believe I was thrown?"

"I'd as soon believe that my father has given up his thieving ways."

Raoul smiled wryly, allowing Nico to wrap an arm around his waist and lead him out of the kitchen.

"Perish the thought."

"You were attacked."

"Yes."

"Who did it?"

"A couple of ruffians." Raoul grunted, as much from the painful memory of his stupidity as his lingering aches. "*Mon Dieu.* I am an idiot."

Steering Raoul through the foyer and toward the stairs, Nico stabbed him with a dark gaze.

"In that we are in perfect agreement."

Raoul ignored the insult. It was taking every ounce of his willpower to remain upright as he slowly climbed the staircase. Sweat beading his forehead, teeth clenched, he forced one foot in front of the other.

"I allowed myself to believe the country lanes were less dangerous than the streets of London," he gritted. "I did not even get a shot off."

"At least tell me you landed a few blows to the bastards?"

"Nothing more than a pathetic kick. They leaped from the hedge without warning, and before I could draw my pistol, I found myself on the ground with a boot in my ribs."

Nico scowled. "Highwaymen?"

Raoul hissed a breath of relief as they reached the top of the steps. Only a few more feet to his bedchamber.

"If they are, they're the worst outlaws in the entire kingdom."

Nico shifted to open the door. "Why?"

"They didn't bother to relieve me of so much as a quid. Even after they knocked me unconscious."

With a curse, Nico halted Raoul beside the four-poster bed and efficiently began stripping away Raoul's rumpled attire.

"Then why did they attack you?"

"I suspect they were paid to frighten me back to London. Either that, or they possess an unreasonable dislike for my latest interpretation of Othello."

Nico knelt to tug off Raoul's boots, his expression tight with fury.

"Your father."

Raoul shook his head. He still found it nearly impossible to accept. Lord Merriot might be a cruel, petty man who assumed that the world should cater to his every whim, but this . . .

It was one thing to have your father dislike you, it was quite another to have him threaten your life.

Still, there was no other reasonable explanation.

"I knew he would be displeased by my presence in Cheshire, but I never thought he would stoop to hiring common thugs to run me off," he muttered, his tone bitter.

Straightening, Nico finished undressing Raoul and gingerly helped him into the bed.

"It's not displeasure that makes a man act so desperate."

"No." Raoul sighed in relief as he sank into the feather mattress. "It's fear."

Nico folded his arms over his chest and regarded Raoul with a somber gaze.

"There is a secret your father can't afford to have exposed."

Raoul snorted. "Maybe not, but he doesn't need to send out his curs to threaten me. I have discovered precisely nothing thus far."

"No, but your father must be aware you are nothing if not stubborn. You will never halt once you have fixed upon a goal."

Raoul's lips twisted, his head throbbing in time with his heartbeat.

"I am firm in purpose, not stubborn."

"Firm in purpose enough to get yourself put in an early grave."

"Don't worry. I intend to ensure that my father understands the dangers of threatening me."

Nico looked far from impressed. "Describe your attackers."

"No, *mon ami,*" Raoul rasped. "They are mine."

For a moment, Nico struggled against the urge to

argue, then clearly sensing Raoul would not yield, he heaved a frustrated sigh.

"At least allow me to fetch the surgeon. Your skull is too thick to harm, but your ribs are not quite so impervious."

"Absolutely not." Raoul swallowed as his slight move sent a searing pain through his ribs. "I will not have the entire neighborhood chattering. It will only make it more difficult to continue my search."

Nico narrowed his gaze. "Stubborn."

"Not so stubborn that I will refuse your assistance in pouring me a glass of brandy."

Muttering beneath his breath about the lunacy of Englishmen and the obstinacy of one particular Englishman, Nico crossed the room to pour out a large measure of the brandy kept on the mantel of the black marble fireplace.

He returned to the bed, and shoved the glass into Raoul's hand.

"It won't cure your wounds, but I suppose it might ease the pain."

Raoul gratefully drained the brandy, sighing as the warmth spread through his chilled body. With the covers pulled over his aching body, he was relieved to note his shivers had eased.

Setting aside the empty glass, he frowned as Nico headed toward the door.

"Where are you going?"

"I have a small errand to attend to."

"Nico . . ."

Pausing, Nico allowed a faint grin to touch his lean, dark face.

"Ease your battered brain. I will leave the villains in your hands."

Raoul narrowed his gaze. It wasn't that he didn't trust Nico's pledge. But the wily man had his own way of interpreting his promise.

"You haven't told me what you discovered in Wallingford."

Nico shrugged. "That can wait until the morrow."

"You found Polly?"

"Yes, and that is all I will say on the matter."

"And you claim me stubborn."

"Lay there and try not to do yourself more damage. I'll return shortly."

Sitting beside the parlor fireplace, Sarah sipped at her tea and lost herself in the novel that Maggie had brought from the village.

She loved the boys and could not imagine her life without them, but they could never be considered peaceful companions. She had learned to savor the hour after the boys had been tucked in their beds, when the cottage was bathed in silence.

Lost in the adventures of a daring heroine and the determined seducer who she pictured as a golden-haired Apollo with eyes as blue as a summer sky, Sarah nearly tumbled from her chair when there was a soft knock on her door.

For goodness' sake, who would call at this late hour?

Setting aside the book, she tried to still her pounding heart. Surely a criminal would not have politely knocked at the door?

Still, she remained seated for a long moment,

considering the wisdom of simply ignoring the intruder. Surely whoever was out there would eventually give up and go away?

As if to squash her brief hope, another knock echoed through the cottage, this one much louder. With an exasperated sigh, Sarah rose to her feet and crossed to the door. The last thing she wanted was the boys disturbed.

"Who is there?" she demanded, her voice sharp.

"Nico. I'm Mr. Charlebois's valet."

Sarah frowned, her lingering fear altering to confusion. "What do you want?"

"There's been an accident."

"Good lord." Hastily unlocking the door, Sarah yanked it open and waved her hand toward the dark-haired man. "Please come in."

The stranger stepped over the threshold and if Sarah hadn't been so rattled, she might have smiled at the sight of his lean, dark countenance and gorgeous brown eyes. Maggie had caught sight of the servant in the village, and had dreamily described him to Sarah as a dashing foreigner who looked more pirate than valet.

Nico lingered near the door, his gaze running a brief but thorough survey over her heavy dressing gown and hair she had pulled into a simple braid.

It wasn't the usual male appraisal. In truth, Sarah felt as if she had been put on a set of scales and weighed for her worth.

"Thank you," he murmured.

"What has occurred?"

"Charlebois was . . ." There was the faintest hesitation. "Thrown from his horse on his return to the Lodge."

"Thrown?" Sarah's brows jerked together as she recalled Raoul riding up to the cottage. Never in her life had she seen a horse and rider in such obvious harmony. "I do not believe it."

"Even the finest rider can take a tumble."

"Yes, but . . ." Realizing she was wasting precious time, Sarah gave a shake of her head. "Never mind. How badly is he injured?"

"He has taken a blow to the head, and his ribs are injured. I can't say if they're broken. In any case, he's in a great deal of pain. I heard in the village you were skilled with herbs."

A shocking relief raced through Sarah, making her knees weak. Raoul was hurt, but at least he wasn't . . .

No, she could not even bear to consider the other.

"Not so skilled as my mother, but I do have several remedies that I keep handy for those in need."

"Will you bring them to the Lodge?"

She blinked at the abrupt request. "But . . . surely Mr. Charlebois would prefer a trained surgeon? I assure you Mr. Dalton is far more qualified than myself in dealing with such injuries."

"Charlebois has refused to call for him."

"But why?"

"A gentleman has no desire to have it widely known he was tossed like a greenhorn."

"You believe I would be any more discreet?"

He regarded her with a steady gaze. "I do."

"Hmmm."

"Will you come?"

Much to her surprise, Sarah felt herself wavering. Every bit of logic told her to inform the man in no uncertain terms that she would not be hauled to an unwed gentleman's home in the middle of the night. Not even if most villagers would accept she was only there in the role of a healer.

But another part desperately wanted to rush to Raoul's side. Not only to offer what humble assistance she could, but to simply reassure herself that Raoul was not seriously injured.

Why it was so vital that he be well was a question she would dwell on later. For now, she had enough troubles to occupy her mind.

"I'm sorry, but the boys are already asleep and I cannot leave them here alone."

"Understandable." Nico nodded toward the open door. "I brought Pickens with me."

Sarah peered through the darkness, able to make out a large man standing next to the elegant carriage.

"Pickens?"

"Charlebois's groom. He rarely has a word to say for himself, but he is quite dependable and the oldest of seven children. He can watch your boys until you return."

Her refusal trembled on her lips, but could not be uttered.

Blast it all. She would never be able to sleep. Not until she was assured that Raoul was on the mend.

How foolish was that?

Foolish, but undeniable.

She heaved a sigh, more aggravated at herself than the poor servant who had come to fetch her.

"Allow me to gather a few items."

Nico's expression never altered, but she sensed his coiled tension ease.

"Thank you."

"Do not thank me yet," she muttered, turning on her heel to enter the kitchen and collect her supplies.

It took another few minutes to pull on her heaviest boots and wool cloak. No doubt she should have changed from her dressing gown, but she was in a hurry to reach the Lodge and in truth, the robe that buttoned to her neck and was fashioned from white cambric was far more modest than many of her dresses.

Still, it felt odd to be led from the cottage by the impatient Nico without the familiar discomfort of her shift and corset.

Pickens gave a nod of his head as they passed and made his way to the cottage. Sarah was able to make out heavy features with a surprisingly sweet expression, but it was not his appearance of a gentle bear that made her trust him without a qualm.

She knew Raoul well enough to know he would never hire anyone who would harm a child.

Permitting Nico to hand her into the interior of the carriage, she impatiently allowed him to wrap her in the waiting blanket before he was shutting the door and climbing onto the high seat to set the carriage into motion. In some distant part of her mind she recognized the biting chill in the air and the sway of the carriage over the rough path, but her thoughts were centered on reaching Raoul.

At last they pulled into the circle drive and halted before the covered portico. Sarah untangled herself from the blanket and climbed out of the carriage before Nico could assist her.

The dark, unnerving gaze flicked over her, then he turned and led her toward the nearby door. Together they entered the silent house, Nico pausing to help her out of her heavy cloak before leading her up the stairs.

Oddly, Sarah felt no embarrassment as she prepared to enter a gentleman's private chambers. Not even attired in nothing more than her dressing gown. Instead, she clutched her leather satchel and fought back the urge to dash up the stairs like a schoolgirl.

Reaching the landing, Nico waved a slender hand toward the open doorway.

"This way."

A rich, familiar voice floated through the air. "Nico?"

"I have returned, lord and master."

There was a sound of impatience. "If I was truly your lord and master, you would not have disappeared after leaving the brandy decanter . . ." The words broke off in shock as Nico stepped through the doorway, closely followed by Sarah. "*Sacrebleu.*"

"I brought you something much better than brandy," Nico announced as Sarah took a swift glance about the bedchamber.

She took note of the blue and ivory drapes, the satin wall panels, and solid walnut furnishings that matched the large, four-poster bed. There were only modest ornaments to soften the impression of stark masculinity. Even the few oil paintings hung on the wall were scenes of hunting or rugged landscapes.

Her gaze skimmed over her surroundings, giving her the opportunity to brace herself before at last turning her attention to the man sprawled across the bed.

Even prepared, however, she couldn't halt her heart from skipping a beat as she caught the full view of Raoul Charlebois.

Good . . . lord.

When he was fully attired, Raoul was an elegant, breathtaking gentleman of society. A man with a smooth charm and clever wit who could melt the heart of the most discerning female.

Now he was half-reclined on the pillows, with his golden curls tousled and a hint of stubble darkening the line of his jaw. More disturbing, the blankets that covered his body had fallen to expose the hard expanse of his upper chest.

Her breath caught, and a strange sensation fluttered in the pit of her stomach.

The sophistication had been ripped aside and she was suddenly confronted with the raw masculinity he kept disguised.

With his lashes half-lowered, Raoul allowed his blue gaze to glide down her body, the smoldering heat nearly tangible despite her voluminous gown.

"You have, indeed," he murmured, his gaze lifting to study Sarah's flushed cheeks. "Remind me to give you an increase in pay."

Gathering her composure, she tilted her chin. "I am here because your servant claims you are too foolish to call for the local surgeon."

Nico cleared his throat. "I had to reveal to her as how Hercules gave you a toss, and you were too embarrassed to have it known throughout the village."

A golden brow arched as Raoul shot a swift glance toward his servant.

"Thank you, *mon ami*."

His dry tone warned Sarah that there was far more to Raoul's injuries than a simple tumble from the saddle.

"Always happy to be of service," Nico drawled.

"Perhaps you could be of service by making a pot of tea? I am certain Miss Jefferson must be frozen to the bone to have been out in such weather," Raoul retorted, wincing in obvious discomfort as he shifted on the pillows.

Abruptly noting the lines bracketing his mouth and the shadows beneath the brilliant blue eyes, Sarah moved briskly to the side of the bed, perching on the edge of the mattress and opening her small satchel. It did not appear as if Raoul was on his last leg, but he most certainly was in pain.

"I am quite well, thank you, but I could use hot water and a sturdy mug to steep my herbs. Mrs. Dent will no doubt have left a kettle near the fire." She set her mixture of herbs on the nearby table, along with her various salves. "Oh, and I will need some strips of clean linen if they can be found."

Nico gave a short dip of his head. "I will return in a moment."

Waiting until Nico slid from the room, Sarah turned her attention toward the man stretched out beside her.

"Now, Mr. Charlebois, do you intend to tell me what really happened?"

"Perhaps." A strained smile touched his lips. "Someday."

"Someday?" Her eyes narrowed. "I begin to wonder what brings you to Cheshire, Mr. Charlebois."

"Raoul," he countered, softly.

She bit back her demand to know the truth. For all his efforts to disguise his misery, she could sense he was hurting. Now was not the time to badger him for answers.

"Show me where you are injured," she instead commanded.

"This is not at all nec . . ." His words broke off as she ignored his ridiculous words and simply leaned forward to run her fingers through his hair, exploring his scalp until she discovered the two distinct lumps that had already formed. "*Mon Dieu*."

Although not formally trained, Sarah had been tending to injuries since she was sixteen. She had discovered that many wounds did far better to heal on their own, so long as they were not infected.

"Painful, no doubt, but not fatal," she murmured.

"They are a great deal less painful when you are not poking at them."

Leaning back, she regarded him with the same patient expression she used when the boys were being petulant.

"I believe Nico also mentioned that your ribs were injured."

"Yes."

"May I see?"

There was a pause before a wicked smile curved his lips. "If you insist."

With a slow, deliberate motion, Raoul tugged at the covers, drawing them down to his waist.

Unable to help herself, Sarah sucked in a sharp breath, her eyes captivated by the smooth torso that literally begged for her touch.

Oh . . . my.

Chapter 10

Despite his lingering pain, Raoul was smugly pleased by the stunned expression on Sarah's face.

He wanted her to react to his naked chest. He wanted her heart thundering and her blood racing with the same biting need that had clutched him since she'd walked through the door wearing nothing more than her dressing gown.

It only seemed fair.

"Is something the matter, Sarah?" he teased, his voice thick with his raw awareness.

She wetted her dry lips, then with obvious effort, she sucked in a deep breath.

"Of course something is the matter. Unlike many women you might be acquainted with, I am not at all accustomed to being alone with half-naked gentlemen."

His lips twisted as he briefly wondered what her reaction would be if she knew that he was more than half naked. Then, catching sight of the uncertainty shimmering in her dark eyes, he felt an unexpected pang of remorse.

Damn. It had been so long since he had been in the company of a truly innocent woman, he forgot how unnerving it must be to find herself alone with a gentleman in his bedchamber.

His expression softened as the unexpected need to protect this woman overcame his more basic instincts.

"Then return to your cottage, *ma petite*," he urged. "I cannot think what possessed Nico to drag you out in such cold."

Her shoulders squared, as if she were struggling against her own better judgment. And perhaps she was.

"First I intend to put salve on those bruises, and to mix a tonic that will assist you in sleeping."

His brows snapped together. "Laudanum?"

"No, it is no more than a mixture of chamomile and lavender, with just a bit of lemon balm. It is quite harmless, I assure you."

His repugnance was replaced with a faint amusement at her defensive tone.

"I have complete faith in your abilities, *ma belle*."

Before she could respond, Nico returned carrying a large tray that he set on the table beside the bed.

"The hot water you requested and some strips of linen, although if Mrs. Dent should wonder what happened to her apron, I refuse to take the blame."

Sarah tilted back her head to flash Nico one of her devastating smiles. The seasoned rogue blinked, as if stunned by the blinding beauty.

"Thank you."

"That will be all, Nico," Raoul growled, not entirely pleased by his servant's lingering gaze.

With a mocking bow, Nico headed toward the door.

"I'll return below stairs. We wouldn't want any unexpected visitors."

Nico stepped out of the room, deliberately closing the door behind his retreating form. Thankfully, Sarah was too busy mixing a handful of dry herbs in the mug of hot water to notice.

Leaving the herbs to soak, Sarah returned her attention to him, although she was careful to ensure that her gaze never dipped below his chin.

"Nico seems to be a most unusual valet."

"You have no notion."

"Was he in the theater?"

"No, he comes straight from the stews."

That clearly surprised her. "But you trust him?"

"With my life."

She pulled a ceramic pot from her leather satchel. "You are fortunate to have such a loyal servant."

"Some days I feel more fortunate than others . . ." Raoul sucked in a shocked breath, unprepared for her soft touch as she soothed the salve onto the bruises spreading over his ribs.

Her fingers stilled. "I'm sorry, did I hurt you?"

Raoul clutched the blankets bunched about his waist. "*Ma belle,* you have been torturing me for days."

Realizing his discomfort had nothing to do with his wounds, Sarah sent him a chiding frown and continued with her gentle ministrations.

"This salve should ease the stiffness, although the bruising is too deep to completely avoid a measure of discomfort over the next few days. I suppose it is too much to hope that you will remain in bed until you are properly healed?"

"Only if you give me sufficient inducement to linger."

She shook her head. "If you are well enough to flirt then you are well enough to lift yourself so I can wrap the linens around you."

Pressing his upper torso off the pillows, Raoul hid his flare of pain as he deliberately leaned close to inhale her cinnamon sweetness.

"I am well enough to indulge in any number of activities," he whispered close to her ear, unable to resist temptation.

Doing her best to ignore his blatant invitation, Sarah efficiently wrapped the linen around his waist, tying it off with a knot.

"There, that should keep the salve . . ." She sucked in a sharp breath as his lips brushed over the curve of her ear. "Mr. Charlebois."

"Yes, Miss Jefferson?"

"You should not."

He teased the hollow below her ear, his earlier determination to behave as a gentleman dissolving into a forgotten wisp of sanity.

"I am well aware I should not," he growled. "Unfortunately, I cannot seem to help myself."

"You . . ." She shivered as he trailed his tongue down the curve of her neck. "Oh."

"Sarah." Forgetting his aches and pains, Raoul grabbed her face in his hands and studied her with a sense of bemusement. "I do not comprehend what you have done to me, but I have no defense against you. I am utterly at your mercy."

Her breath came in quick pants between her parted lips. "I have done nothing."

"No?" Shifting, Raoul took her hand and pressed it

to the blanket, directly over his hard erection. "I would say you have done more than you bargained for."

"I should return to the boys."

"Please . . . Sarah," Raoul murmured, not above pleading as he planted desperate kisses along the line of her jaw.

"What?"

"Just a few moments. I beg of you."

With a gentle insistence, he urged her down on the mattress beside him, careful to keep his touch light enough that she would know she could pull away at any moment.

Typically, she had no concern for her own welfare. Instead, her eyes widened as he leaned over her, his expression hard with a stark longing.

"You must be careful. Your injuries . . ."

"Are nothing compared to my aching need for you," he husked, lowering his head to press a soft kiss on her lip. "Mmmmm. You have been baking gingerbread again."

She trembled, but she made no effort to push him away. "It is the boys' favorite."

"I am growing fond of it myself."

To prove his point, Raoul returned his attention to her lips, nibbling and teasing until they at last parted in silent invitation.

Raoul groaned, his hands trembling as they reached to tug at the buttons holding the dressing gown together. *Mon Dieu.* He felt as if he were once again an untried youth, so overwhelmed by the sensations jolting through his body that he could barely breathe.

Deepening his kiss, Raoul allowed her exotic taste to fill his senses, his fingers dealing with the last of the buttons so he could pull back the dressing gown to reveal the splendor of her body.

He lifted his head, his heart stuttering to a halt as his gaze drifted down her body.

In the candlelight, her skin glowed with a rich sheen, her curves so soft and lush he had to swallow a low moan of appreciation.

Returning his gaze to her face, Raoul was startled by her uncertain expression. As if she did not realize just how stunningly beautiful she truly was.

"Perfect," he whispered, his hand moving to cup a full breast. "So perfect."

She shivered at his touch, her eyes darkening with a pleasure she couldn't disguise.

"I am far from perfect," she breathed, her hands tentatively lifting to stroke over his chest.

Raoul growled deep in his throat, his muscles quivering beneath her soft exploration. Blessed saints. How could such a simple touch send him up in flames?

Lost in the spell she was unwittingly weaving, Raoul dipped his head to capture the tip of her breast between his lips. Her gasp of shock echoed through the room, but even as Raoul stiffened at the thought that he may have frightened her, she was arching her back in silent encouragement.

He was swift to oblige.

Pleasuring her with his tongue and teeth, Raoul allowed his hand to skim down the curve of her waist, pushing the fabric of her dressing gown out of his path. His erection throbbed at the sound of her soft moans and the restless stirring of her body beneath his fingers. Sarah might be innocent, but she was also a woman who had denied her passions for too long. Her need was a tangible force that wrapped around him and stole any hope of coherent thought.

Instead, he allowed himself to be caught in the gathering storm.

Shifting his hand to gently tug apart her legs, Raoul turned his attention to her other breast, his erection rubbing against her hip. He was aching with the desire to be within her, but for tonight it was enough to teach Sarah the pleasures to be discovered in his arms.

Her hands slid to his shoulders, her nails biting into his flesh with the sweetest pain.

"This is . . . I never . . . Mr. Charlebois."

"Sssh, *ma belle,*" he murmured, nibbling a path of kisses up her throat until he at last reached her mouth. "Trust me."

He didn't give her an opportunity to respond, covering her lips with a kiss of blatant hunger.

Not that she seemed to be in any mood to argue. Indeed, she met the thrust of his tongue with her own, pulling him ever closer as his fingers stroked her inner thigh, heading higher with each sweeping motion.

For a maddening moment, Raoul felt her stiffen at his intimate touch and he forced his fingers to still. It might damn well kill him to halt, but he would rather endure a lifetime of frustration than risk frightening her.

Time seemed to stand still before she slowly relaxed and her hips lifted in an unconscious plea for relief.

Raoul shuddered, scattering desperate kisses over her flushed face as he slipped a finger through the damp heat between her legs. Sarah whimpered, her body trembling as he discovered her precise point of pleasure.

Stroking her with a slow, growingly insistent pace, Raoul found his own hips rocking forward, his body desperate for release. A groan was wrenched from his throat as he lifted his head to study the woman writhing beside him.

Mon Dieu. She was beautiful.

A handful of raven curls had escaped from her braid to frame her face, her eyes dark with smoldering passion, her lips parted.

In this moment she was the vision of female desire.

And he was utterly captivated.

Shifting his finger to sink into the damp heat of her body, Raoul gritted his teeth and continued to thrust his erection against her hip, relieved that the covers would disguise his climax from Sarah. Tonight he did not want anything to distract her from reaching her own completion.

With a soft gasp, Sarah lifted her hips off the bed, her eyes squeezing shut as her body tensed. Raoul increased his pace, allowing her soft gasps to judge the moment that she reached her peak.

Raoul's own climax slammed into him the same moment her lips parted, and swooping his head down, he swallowed her startled cry of bliss.

Wrapping his arms around her shivering body, Raoul felt the shuddering pleasure continue to race through him, the sensations intense enough to send a sharp alarm through his heart.

This was supposed to be . . . what?

A momentary distraction?

A brief, maddening fascination?

Either was acceptable.

What wasn't acceptable was the voice whispering in the back of his head that warned him his entire life had just been irrevocably altered.

Against his will, he recalled Fredrick's words at Ian's wedding.

"Run if you will, Charlebois, but destiny is waiting for you."

Unnerved by the direction of his thoughts, Raoul shifted onto his elbow and ran a gentle hand over Sarah's flushed cheek.

He might not comprehend his strange sense of premonition, but for the moment he had far more pleasurable matters to ponder.

"Sarah." His glow of contentment faltered as she refused to lift her lashes and meet his searching gaze. "Look at me."

Rather than obeying his soft command, Sarah jerked her robe together and with shaking hands began refastening the long row of buttons.

"It must be very late. I need to return home."

He paused, his brows drawing together. "Nico will take you in the carriage, but not until I am certain you are well."

Finishing up her self-imposed task, Sarah struggled to break from his arms.

"Why would I not be?"

Raoul refused to release her. Not until she would look him in the eye and admit the truth.

"Neither of us can deny that what just occurred was anything less than earth-shattering."

"I do not comprehend how it could have been earth-shattering for you," she muttered.

"Why not?"

"I am not the first woman you've had in your bed."

Ah. Was she jealous? The thought was oddly satisfying. He brushed a kiss over the top of her head. "Perhaps not the first, but by far the most memorable," he whispered. "You are teaching me that there is a vast difference between desiring a woman and *needing* a very particular woman."

She tensed, her gaze at last lifting. "How do you do that?"

"What?"

"Always say precisely what a person wants to hear. Is it a talent that comes with your acting skills?"

Raoul flinched, untangling himself so he could glare down at her with genuine outrage.

Sacrebleu. Why did she not just slap him? It would be less painful.

"You think I am playing a role?"

Before he could react, Sarah slipped from the bed, her guarded gaze never wavering from his hard expression.

"I think you are so accustomed to hiding behind a mask you have forgotten who you truly are." Her second blow neatly delivered, she hurried toward the door. "Good night, Mr. Charlebois, do not forget to drink your tonic."

December 16
Baxter Lodge

The night proved to be long, painful, and filled with the sort of unpleasant soul-searching that Raoul avoided like the plague.

At last he could bear his broodings no longer, and ignoring his lingering aches, he forced himself from the bed and prepared for the day.

Not that he could toss aside his aggravating thoughts as easily as he could toss aside the covers.

Even as he pulled on his buff breeches and a claret jacket, he found his mind churning with the memory of Miss Sarah Jefferson.

The woman was obviously demented.

What other explanation could there be for her to so willingly offer her body to his touch one moment, and in the next, to treat him as if he were a coldhearted calculating rake?

Or perhaps he was the demented one, he ruefully conceded.

After all, there was no reason to drive himself batty over Sarah Jefferson.

He had come to Cheshire to discover the secret in his father's past, not to fall victim to a pair of midnight eyes. And more importantly, as soon as he had the truth, he would be returning to London and the life awaiting him there.

What did he care if Sarah had bolted from his bed as if he carried the plague?

Abruptly sensing that he was no longer alone, Raoul turned to discover Nico standing near the open door.

His less than cheerful mood was not improved by the hint of mocking amusement in his servant's eyes.

"I might have known you wouldn't have the sense to stay in bed," Nico drawled, leaning his shoulder against the door jam.

Raoul grunted, noting that Nico appeared even more the cutthroat this morning in his rough linen smock and buckskins. Clearly Nico had been indulging his love for intrigue.

"And have Mrs. Dent up here fussing?" Raoul shuddered, then winced as his ribs gave a throb of protest. "I'd as soon be back in the hands of those idiot ruffians."

"Speaking of ruffians."

Raoul narrowed his gaze. "Did I imagine your promise to allow me to deal with my attackers?"

Nico's amusement deepened. "You are in a foul mood for a gentleman who spent a considerable amount of time alone with the female who has captured his fancy."

"Nico."

"At least do not tell me you wasted the perfect opportunity I handed to you?"

"Miss Jefferson is a lady," Raoul snapped, his temper flaring. "I will not have her discussed as if she were a common trollop."

"Obviously the blows to your head did more damage than I first suspected."

Raoul took a warning step forward, indifferent to the knowledge he was revealing far more than he desired.

"Do not press this, *mon ami*."

Nico straightened, his amusement replaced by a shrewd curiosity.

"No need for violence. At least not toward me."

Well, that was true enough. If he wanted a victim to bear the brunt of his frustration, he had any number of choices.

Beginning with his coward of a father.

Sucking in a deep breath, Raoul reined in his churning emotions.

"Tell me what you have discovered."

Nico lifted his hands in a gesture of peace. "I did nothing more than keep a watch on the Great House."

"And?"

"At the break of dawn, two men met with your father behind the stables."

Raoul's sharp laugh was without humor. "I didn't know my father was capable of leaving his bed before noon."

"Paying off cutthroats is a rather delicate business that is best done before the house begins to stir."

"So I have discovered." Ignoring the stupid flare of betrayal that clenched his heart, Raoul forced himself to concentrate on more important matters. "Were you close enough to overhear the conversation?"

Thankfully Nico knew him well enough to realize that he would reject any suggestion of sympathy.

"No, I didn't want to risk exposing my presence. I did, however, manage to follow your assailants back to their den."

"Den?"

"I will not dignify the pile of rubble as a home." He pulled a scrap of parchment from his pocket. "I drew you a map, so you should be able to track them down easily enough. Unless, of course, you lose your bearings in the snow."

Raoul heaved a sigh as he plucked the paper from her servant's fingers. He should have known Nico was aware that he could not leave the Lodge, no matter what his intent, without finding himself at Sarah's small cottage.

"My bearings are all quite sound."

Nico arched a brow. "If you say so."

"Enough," he growled. "Tell me what you discovered of Polly Andrews."

Nico shrugged, taking the abrupt change of conversation in stride.

"She wasn't difficult to locate. I discovered her in the first pub I entered."

"She was working there?"

"Not precisely."

It took a moment for Raoul to realize that Willie and Jimmy's mother had been reduced to selling her body.

Not an unusual tale, unfortunately. Women had few options when forced to support themselves.

His sympathy for Polly Andrews, however, did not alter his belief that it was imperative that the boys remain in the custody of Sarah Jefferson.

Why he gave a damn . . . well, that was a question that didn't bear scrutiny.

"Did you speak with her?"

"I did my best. Unfortunately she was drunk as a louse before I arrived."

"Did you learn anything?"

"From what I could gather from her ramblings, she was abandoned by her lover after he had foisted a child on her. She has taken to desperate measures to support herself and the babe."

"So she has no intention of returning for the children she abandoned?"

Nico grimaced. "Not unless she could find some profit in it."

"That is what I feared." Raoul's expression was hard. "If she knew how attached Miss Jefferson has become to those boys, she would do everything in her power to bilk her."

"She would be even more eager to play the long lost mother if she knew there was an extremely wealthy gentleman involved," Nico drawled.

Since the precise thought had crossed his mind, Raoul ignored the less than subtle warning. In truth, he was becoming astonishingly accomplished at ignoring any number of things.

Instead, he concentrated his thoughts on Willie and Jimmy, who would be the ultimate victims if they were taken from the home they had grown to love.

"Do you think she could be convinced to give up her rights?"

"For the proper price."

"Then I must consider what the proper price is for two young boys."

Nico gave a slow shake of his head. "I would say that the blow to your head rattled your wits, but they've been scrambled since we came to Cheshire."

Raoul's lips twisted. "And I would argue if you were not so painfully right."

"We could pack our bags and return to London. Your father would be satisfied and call off his dogs. And you could turn your thoughts to enjoying your retirement."

"Tempting," Raoul retorted, even as he knew that nothing in hell would drag him from Cheshire. "But my father has thrown down the gauntlet. You do not imagine I will call craven at such a blatant challenge?"

"Gauntlet? Very Shakespearean of you."

Raoul stiffened at his servant's unwitting words. "Nico."

"Yes?"

"Do you think I am always performing?"

"I think you are adept at being whatever others want you to be," Nico carefully admitted.

Raoul frowned, regretting he had even asked.

"I see."

"It is a handy talent. You would have made a fortune in trade."

"Nice to know." Hearing the sounds of Mrs. Dent's approaching footsteps, Raoul reached out to grip his servant's shoulder. "Thank you, *mon ami*. As always, your assistance has been invaluable."

"Just how invaluable?"

Raoul chuckled. "I will return before dinner."

Nico's smile faded. "Charlebois, take care," he warned. "Those men looked to be desperate. They won't be pleased by your visit."

"Don't fear. On this occasion, surprise will be on my side."

Chapter 11

Being in the worthy sort of community that attended church services with dutiful, if not overly devout dedication, Raoul was able to traverse the snowy lanes without concern of being seen.

Of course, he was not reckless enough to come within sight of his father's estate. Unlike his neighbors, Lord Merriot possessed the opinion that members of nobility were destined for heaven without the tedious need to sit on a hard pew.

Besides, taking the path to the Great House would lead him past Sarah's cottage.

The very last thing he needed was to be distracted on this morning.

Following Nico's map, Raoul at last halted Hercules in a small copse of trees, and crossed the narrow path to the cottage that was nearly hidden behind a tangle of overgrown hedges.

He stepped through the broken gate and grimaced at the derelict building. *Sacrebleu*. It was little wonder that Nico had dismissed it as a den. Although Raoul had doubts that even an animal would choose to nest in among the crumbling stones and rotted thatching.

Keeping in the shadows of the hedge, Raoul carefully made his way to the door that hung precariously from its hinges.

His assailants might live in squalor, but that did not make them any less dangerous.

As Nico had pointed out, desperate men were never to be taken lightly. Especially when they felt cornered.

Pausing near the door, Raoul pulled his loaded gun from his pocket and drew in a deep, steadying breath. Then, using the toe of his boot, he gently pushed open the door.

He instinctively winced as the stench of fried fish and unwashed bodies billowed through the air.

Damn. The men clearly possessed an aversion to soap and clean water.

Ignoring the urge to gag, Raoul stepped through the doorway, not surprised to find his two attackers seated at a small table near the fireplace, both so intent on the card game they were playing that neither noticed they were no longer alone.

Determined he would not be caught off guard again, Raoul swept a swift gaze around the cramped, filthy room, ensuring there were no other villains lurking in the shadows. Only then did he shift his attention to the men at the table.

His lips twitched as he took note of their hulking size dwarfing the room, and the hard expression on their beefy countenances. At least he could take comfort in knowing his attackers were not spotty-faced lads half his size.

Lifting his arm to point the gun directly at the head of the nearest villain, Raoul loudly cleared his throat.

"Is this a private game, or can anyone play?" he drawled, watching with some amusement as the men surged to their feet, knocking the table aside and sending cards and coins flying through the air. "Easy, gentlemen," he growled as they both bunched their muscles as if preparing to charge. "My finger is a bit unsteady this morning. I suggest you do not so much as twitch."

"Damn." The largest of the two idiots shoved his fingers through the thick thatch of brown hair. "How did ye find us?"

Keeping his arm steady, Raoul curled his lips in disgust. "I followed the stench. I believe we have some unfinished business."

The younger of the two swallowed the lump in his throat. "Yer not here to kill us?"

"That all depends."

"On what?" idiot one demanded.

"On whether or not I'm satisfied with your answers."

"What answers?"

"We will get to that in a moment. First I want you gentlemen to stand against the wall and keep your hands where I can see them." The two exchanged a worried glance, as if considering something stupid. Raoul stepped forward, his pistol glinting in the firelight. "Now."

"Fine." The larger man, who was clearly the leader of the two, shoved his companion until they were both pressed against the far wall. Then, lifting his hands, he regarded Raoul with a petulant expression. "We done it."

"Give me your names."

There was a pause, then with a glance at the gun, the leader muttered a vile curse.

"I be Tom Simmons and this here is me brother, George. Why do ye want to know?"

"I always prefer to be introduced to a man and look him in the eyes before I shoot him. So much more civilized than leaping from the hedge to ambush a poor soul." His eyes narrowed. "Only cowards employ such tactics."

An ugly flush crept up George's thick neck. Like his brother, he was dressed in rough wool clothing that should have been condemned to the fire years ago.

"Here now . . ."

"Shut up, George," Tom commanded, giving his brother a punch to the arm before returning his wary attention to Raoul. "Tell us what you want."

"I want to know how much Lord Merriot paid you to threaten me."

Shock rippled over both men's faces.

"The Earl?" Tom licked his lips, a hint of desperation edging his voice. "What dealings would we have with the likes of him? Me and George are simple folk."

Raoul took another step forward. "Wrong answer."

"Wait," Tom rasped, sweat trickling from his brow despite the biting chill in the air. "What makes ye think Lord Merriot is involved?"

"Do you claim he wasn't?" Raoul drawled. "Perhaps the scurrilous attack was your and your brother's notion?"

"No . . . I mean . . ." Tom floundered, his tiny mind obviously incapable of functioning with a gun pointed at it. "Mayhaps there was someone who paid us to frighten you away, but it wasn't Lord Merriot."

"Then who sent you?"

"I don't know his name. A London bloke, I think. Gave us the money and disappeared."

Raoul snorted. The two were as worthless at lying as they were at housekeeping.

"How terribly convenient. A pity I don't believe a word coming out of your mouth." A cruel expression hardened his features. "Perhaps you have forgotten what happens when I am not satisfied with your answers."

George made a strangled sound, his fear a tangible force in the air. "We can't tell you. He'll have us killed."

"And I intend to kill you if you do not tell me. A devilish dilemma, is it not?"

There was a tense pause, then hunching his shoulders in defeat, Tom glared at his captor.

"Fine. It were the Earl who hired us."

So . . . there it was.

His suspicions were confirmed.

Lord Merriot had gone from being a callous, incompetent father to a violent madman willing to do whatever necessary to keep his secrets hidden.

Welcome home, Raoul Charlebois.

"How did he find you?" Raoul gritted. "Not to be insulting, but I cannot imagine that he often rubs elbows with any of your acquaintances."

"Not bloody likely," George muttered.

"Then how?"

It was Tom who explained. "My cousin works in the stables. When his lordship approached him about hiring some men to tend to a . . ."

"Delicate, that's what he said," George helpfully supplied. "A delicate problem."

Tom flashed him an annoyed frown. "My cousin knew we were just the men for the job."

"Did you meet with him?" Raoul demanded.

"Aye," Tom admitted. "Two days ago behind the stables, and then again this morning to get our pay."

"What did he say? Exactly."

"I can't remember exactly."

Raoul gave a tiny wave of his gun. "Try very, very hard."

Tom swiped the sweat from his forehead with the back of his hand.

"He said that his bastard had returned to the neighborhood, and that it was upsetting Lady Merriot."

Raoul gave a sharp bark of laughter. Lady Merriot had barely been capable of looking at him when he was young. Obviously, the years had not stirred her maternal affection.

"Yes, I can imagine."

"And then he said as how he would be willing to pay to have you roughed up a bit so you would leave the Lodge," George broke in, anxious to prove his cooperation. "He also told us to keep our gobs shut about the business."

Roughed up a bit?

Well, that was a nice way of ordering your own son to be beaten senseless.

"He gave you no other reason for wanting me to leave?"

Tom furrowed his brow as he struggled to recall. "He said he couldn't . . . what was the word . . ." He snapped his fingers. "Afford, aye, that was it. Says as he couldn't afford you lingering in Cheshire. That we was to scare you good."

Afford? Raoul stilled, his thoughts churning. Did his father's words imply that his presence in Cheshire threatened him financially rather than socially?

But how was that possible?

As a bastard, he had no claim to his father's estates, or his fortune.

Unless he feared that Raoul would blackmail him as Dunnington had done?

"An odd choice of words," he muttered.

As if worried he had said something wrong, Tom pressed a hand to his chest.

"That's what he said, swear on me mother's grave."

Frustrated, Raoul gave a shake of head. These men were mere pawns. Actors on a stage, following Lord Merriot's directions.

They did not have the answers he sought.

Of course, that did not mean he intended to allow them to walk away unscathed, he grimly acknowledged.

"Allow your poor mother to rest in peace and let us return to my original question."

"I . . ." Tom glanced toward the nearby door, as if judging whether or not he could make a bolt for it. With a deliberate motion, Raoul took a step closer to the cringing George, his pistol pointed directly between his crossed eyes. Realizing that Raoul held the upper hand, Tom heaved a sigh. "What was that?"

"How much were you paid to leave me knocked senseless on that frozen path?"

A cunning expression touched Tom's beefy countenance. "We each got two shilling."

"Careful, Tom," Raoul warned, a lethal edge to his voice. "The lives of you and your brother are hanging in the balance."

Tom briefly weighed the worth of his brother against keeping his ill-gotten gains before muttering a curse.

"Fine. He gave each of us five Crowns."

Raoul held out his free hand. "Give it over."

"Have ye lost yer bloody mind," George squawked. "We did the work that was asked of us. We deserve that money . . ." His words ended in a small scream as Raoul pressed the pistol to his forehead. "Hellfire."

Still growling and sputtering at the unfairness of life, Tom dug the silver coins from his pocket and shoved them into Raoul's waiting hand.

Never allowing the gun to waver, Raoul backed slowly toward the door, his expression warning he was quite willing to pull the trigger.

"Since you two have so kindly cooperated, I'm going to give you a piece of advice," he paused, a hard smile curving his lips. "While I am not one to hold a grudge, I possess two loyal servants who are not so forgiving. And since they both have the opinion that any injury to me is a personal insult to them, I would wager they will be eager to spill the blood of those responsible. Pickens would no doubt be willing to limit his revenge to a sound thumping, but Nico . . . he prefers a knife to the back."

With a mocking bow, Raoul stepped through the doorway. "Good day, gentlemen. A pleasure doing business with you."

Despite the vast army of servants that Lord Merriot felt necessary to support his luxurious lifestyle, Raoul had little difficulty slipping through a side door and making his way to his father's private study.

As a child, he had memorized the best means to travel through the spiderweb of rooms and corridors without attracting attention. A skill that he used today to bypass the sleepy footmen and various maids who scurried about the house.

Entering the elegant room that had always been kept strictly off-limits to Raoul, he briefly glanced over the satinwood furnishings and ivory satin panels. Across the room, a white marble fireplace was intricately carved with a wide mantel that held his father's collection of enamel snuffboxes, and a miniature portrait of Peter as a child.

Not surprisingly, he had never been requested to sit for a portrait. At least not by his father.

Which suited him just fine, he thought with a small grimace.

Perhaps it was simply because Lord Merriot had proven to be a treacherous bastard, but the entire house seemed to reek of a slow, relentless decay.

Shaking off the strange sense of bleak gloom that seemed to permeate the air, Raoul swiftly moved to the desk situated near the long bank of windows and riffled through the various papers and ledger books, searching for anything that might appear out of place.

He discovered two letters that were swiftly dismissed, along with a small leather-bound journal that was filled with his father's tight handwriting, rather than his steward's more fluid strokes, but proved to be no more interesting than a list of various supplies needed from the village.

Then, convinced he had found all that was to be discovered in the desk, he moved to the shelves of books, searching for anything that might be hidden among the leather-bound tomes.

Finding nothing of interest, Raoul was at the point of searching the walls for a hidden safe, when the sound of footsteps had him spinning around as the door was thrust open.

Lord Merriot entered the study, momentarily unaware that his private sanctuary had been invaded. Remaining silent, Raoul watched his father move with slow, heavy steps toward the desk, the once handsome countenance lined with a strange weariness.

Or perhaps not so strange, Raoul cynically acknowledged, the festering sense of betrayal clenching his heart.

His father was accustomed to sleeping until luncheon. It must be draining to force himself from his bed at the crack of dawn to pay off his henchmen.

Folding his arms over his chest, Raoul leaned against the bookshelf and smoothed his expression. His ability to conceal his innermost emotions might annoy Sarah Jefferson, but it did come in handy when dealing with a homicidal relative.

"Good afternoon, Father," he drawled. "I've been waiting for you."

Jerking in surprise, Lord Merriot swung around, his face a sickly shade of gray.

"For God's sake, Raoul, you nearly gave me heart failure."

Raoul snorted. "To have heart failure, one would have to presume you have a heart. And we both know that is absurd, do we not?"

"How the devil did you get in here?"

Raoul arched a brow. "Are you not more curious as to *why* I am here?"

"Should I be?"

"Yes, Father, you most certainly should be." He deliberately paused, petty enough to enjoy watching the older man squirm beneath his steady gaze. "You see, I just had the most intriguing conversation with the Simmons brothers."

The Earl's brown eyes darkened with genuine fear as he realized Raoul had discovered his attackers.

"I haven't the least notion who you are referring to," he attempted to bluff.

"Perhaps this will refresh your memory."

Reaching into his pocket, Raoul pulled out the coins he had taken from the Simmons brothers, and tossed them at his father's feet.

Merriot stumbled backward, as if he feared the coins were cursed.

"What is that?"

"The money you paid the brothers to ambush me outside the Lodge, supposedly in the hopes of frightening me out of Cheshire."

"Outlandish," the Earl barked, reverting as always to intimidation when he felt threatened. "How dare you accuse me of such . . ."

"Cut the line, Father. You were seen this morning behind the stables paying your henchmen for thrashing your own son," Raoul interrupted, his voice harsh.

"You are spying on me? How dare you?"

"At least I did not hire cutthroats to beat you like a stray dog." Raoul clenched his jaw, unable to halt the question that had plagued him since he was attacked. "Did it occur to you that I might have died on that icy path? Or was that what you hoped for? Perhaps you desired to be rid of your bastard without getting your hands dirty?"

He did not truly expect an honest answer. Certainly not from this man who had been willing to risk his own son's life to keep his secrets. So, it was no surprise when Lord Merriot turned his back and walked jerkily toward the fireplace.

"I want you out of my house."

"Believe me, there is nothing I want more. Unfortunately for both of us, I have no intention of leaving until you have answered a few questions."

Without hesitation, the Earl reached to tug on the rope near the mantel.

"If you will not leave of your own accord, then I will have you thrown from the estate."

"So brave as long as you have others to enforce your will," Raoul mocked, his hands curled into fists as he resisted the urge to cross the floor and knock the blustering sod on his ass. "But you are a coward at heart, are you not, Father?"

"I have nothing to say to you."

"Why did you pay Dunnington twenty thousand pounds?"

"How . . ." With a hiss, Merriot turned to meet Raoul's unwavering stare, a hectic flush staining his cheeks. "You are mistaken. I paid Dunnington for your schooling, nothing more. And a sad waste of money that was."

Raoul clicked his tongue. "A coward and a liar. I begin to wonder if you have any redeeming qualities, Father."

"I took you in when I could have allowed you to be . . ." The words were sharply cut off, as if his father had nearly revealed more than he desired.

"Be what?"

"Left on the streets."

It was not what his father had intended to say. He would bet his life on it.

"If you expect my appreciation for making my childhood a misery, then you are even more a fool than I thought," he retorted.

A bitter regret twisted the older man's expression. "I wish I had refused you beneath my roof. You have brought nothing but ill fortune since you stepped over the threshold."

Even accustomed to his father's callous disregard, Raoul was shocked by the outrageous accusation.

"I have brought you ill fortune?" he rasped. "I did nothing but try to earn your affection, and when that proved impossible, I disappeared from your life."

"If you had not come to England, I would never have been tempted."

"Tempted?" Raoul's eyes narrowed. "Tempted by what?"

Clearly regretting his impetuous words, Lord Merriot moved toward the door and yanked it open.

"Leave this alone, Raoul. It is too late to change the past."

"Perhaps I cannot change the past, but I am no longer a helpless child. You will not be allowed to destroy my future."

Hearing the approaching footsteps that heralded the arrival of the servants, Raoul moved to stand directly before his father, his expression hard with warning. "If it is a question of who survives, Father, do not think for a moment I will not protect myself. By whatever means necessary."

Chapter 12

Luncheon had passed and Sarah was settled in the stone workroom attached to the back of the cottage when the sound of Delilah's low growls warned that someone was approaching.

It would be Mr. Charlebois, of course.

She had known from the moment she had crawled from her sleepless bed that he would come in search of her.

Not because she was naïve enough to believe that their intimate encounter meant more to the infamous rake than a brief distraction. For her it might have been a night that would be forever branded into her memory, but Raoul had no doubt enjoyed such trysts on countless occasions.

No, she simply had enough hours in the long night to realize that Raoul was not a man who often had his will crossed. The mere fact that she was struggling to resist his potent charm was enough to stir his predatory nature.

A pity, really.

If she were not in a position where her fragile reputation was of such importance, she would have been more than willing to give in to temptation.

Last eve, Raoul had taught her that she was sacrificing more than just male companionship in her life as a spinster. Even now her body ached for the bold touch that had sent her up in flames.

With a shiver, she continued stroking the charcoal stick over the stretched canvas. Now was not the time to consider the pleasure Raoul so willingly offered.

The door that connected the cottage to the workroom was pushed open and without turning her head, Sarah greeted her visitor.

"Good afternoon, Mr. Charlebois."

There was the heavy sound of footsteps, then her visitor was looming beside her, his arms folded over his chest, a heavy scowl marring his perfect features.

"Where is your maid?" he snapped.

Sarah arched a brow at the less than gracious greeting, pretending her heart had not slammed into her ribs at the sight of his magnificent body revealed by his tailored claret jacket, and buff breeches that clung to long legs. Or that she was not suddenly wishing she was wearing something besides the shabby green gown, with her hair pulled into a simple braid.

"Maggie took the boys to the village to visit with the Vicar's son. Why?"

"Because, Miss Jefferson, a young woman left alone in an isolated cottage should at least possess the sense to keep her door locked," he gritted.

"Delilah," she called softly, smiling faintly as the large dog at her feet offered a low, threatening growl. "Down, girl," she soothed, patting the dog's head. "If that is all, Mr. Charlebois? I do have work to finish."

His lips tightened, as if he were not entirely satisfied, but clearly realizing that Sarah would not be bullied, he instead turned his attention to her sketch of a snowy garden, with one child pulling another on a sled.

Shifting so that he was leaning over her shoulder, he bent his head to whisper directly into her ear.

"Beautiful."

She sucked in a sharp breath and then wished she hadn't when his warm male scent invaded her senses.

"Thank you."

"Sarah."

She jerked her head to the side as his lips brushed the tip of her ear, sending jolts of excitement through her entire body.

"Mr. Charlebois . . ."

"We need to speak," he interrupted, moving to regard her flushed countenance with a somber expression.

"No." Her hand trembled as she set aside the charcoal. When she was alone, it was easy enough to be sensible, but with Raoul standing there in all his glorious beauty . . . well, being sensible was the last thing on her mind. "You need to be about whatever mysterious business has brought you to Cheshire, and I need to complete my etching before tomorrow."

He caught back the words trembling on his lips, seemingly struck by a sudden thought

"Why Monday?"

"It truly is none of your business."

He flicked a careless finger over her cheek. "You know you will never be rid of me until you have answered my question."

"You . . ." She heaved an aggravated sigh. "Fine. I am traveling to Chester tomorrow to sell my etchings and finish my Christmas shopping for the boys."

His gaze was intent. "You intend to travel alone?"

"I will travel on the stage and spend the night at the local hotel before traveling back." Her tone was edged with warning. "It is a journey I have made on several occasions and one, I might add, I do not have to ask your permission to embark upon."

His lips twitched in amusement, an oddly arrested expression on his handsome countenance.

"It may be difficult to believe, but I did not come here to argue with you."

Disconcerted by his unwavering gaze, Sarah unnecessarily smoothed her skirt. "Then why did you come?"

"That, *ma belle*, is a question that eludes any reasonable explanation."

Her gaze lifted at his strange response, for the first time noting the shadows beneath his brilliant blue eyes.

"You are pale," she said, her brief annoyance swiftly replaced by concern. "I warned you to remain abed until you were properly healed."

"I did offer to remain in bed if you would stay there with me," he murmured, a wicked smile touching his lips.

Her stomach fluttered at the realization of just how much she wanted to be in that bed before she hastily returned her thoughts to more immediate matters.

"I do not know why you must be so stubborn. You are doing harm to no one but yourself."

"Actually you are mistaken, I have managed to do harm to at least three others this morning," he drawled.

She frowned, oddly disturbed by the thought he had put himself at risk.

"Are you jesting?"

"Not at all."

"Why would you wish to harm anyone?"

"It was not my intent until they set upon me last eve." His features hardened with fury. "I am a reasonable gentleman, but I do not tolerate being attacked without offering some retaliation."

Her eyes widened. "I knew you were not thrown."

"I am flattered to think your opinion of my skills in the saddle is so high."

Sarah was not amused. He might be flippant at being assaulted, but the mere thought was enough to clench her heart with horror.

"Do not be flattered," she muttered. "I was more convinced that Hercules was far too well trained to give you a toss. Willie has assured me that he has never encountered such a perfectly behaved beast, and he is never wrong when it comes to animals."

He chuckled. "Are you certain your father never trained you to duel?"

She refused to be distracted. "Why were you attacked?"

"My father paid two cutthroats to frighten me away."

"Good heavens. Why would Lord Merriot do such a thing?"

He hesitated a long moment, his expression enigmatic. "Because he fears I have come home to uncover a secret he has kept hidden for decades."

Sarah gave a slow shake of her head. Her father had been utterly devoted to her. It was difficult to even imagine how a man could wish to harm his own child, no matter what the cause.

It was little wonder that Raoul instinctively hid his emotions behind glib charm. Lord Merriot must have taught him at an early age that others could not be trusted.

Had she not found Willie and Jimmy equally wary when they first moved into her cottage?

Her heart twisted with a pity she was wise enough to keep hidden.

"Is he wrong?" she demanded softly.

"No."

"So what is this terrible secret?"

"I haven't the least notion."

She studied him with a hint of puzzlement. "You know there is a secret, but not what it is?"

"Precisely."

"That makes no sense."

"I know there is a secret because Dunnington, the tutor who raised me in London, left me a legacy of twenty thousand pounds along with a brief message that revealed the money had been extorted from Lord Merriot."

She blinked. Good lord. It all sounded like some plot from a melodrama. Only the bitter smile that twisted Raoul's mouth assured her that it was all painfully real.

"Your tutor blackmailed your father?"

"You cannot be more shocked than I was," he retorted. "I have never known a more honorable man than Dunnington. Still, I am convinced his actions were solely to ensure my future. He understood my father would never offer me the support most sons could expect from their family."

"Twenty thousand pounds."

"Perhaps you will look more kindly at me now you know I am a gentleman of such worth," he teased.

She waved away the ridiculous words. He was not a gentleman who would ever need wealth to entice a woman. *Any* woman.

"It is a great deal of money to pay to a tutor."

"It is." The bitterness deepened. "Which proves that whatever sin Lord Merriot is hiding must be worthy of such a considerable sum."

"You did not know of this legacy until your tutor died?"

"Dunnington did not offer so much as a hint."

"How odd."

He shrugged. "No more odd than revealing he had blackmailed my father without offering an explanation of what hidden secret he had discovered, or how he stumbled across the information in the first place."

"Actually, that part I understand perfectly," she said without thought.

He stilled, his eyes narrowed. "You do?"

"He presumably swore a pledge not to reveal the secret when he requested the money, do you not think?" she pointed out, rather surprised when he appeared struck by her words. "If he is the man of honor you believed him to be, then he could not go back on his word."

"*Mon Dieu*," he muttered, his lips twisting. "I never considered the matter in such a light."

She paused, her stomach still queasy at the mere thought that anyone, let alone Lord Merriot, would wish this man harm.

"Well, at least I now know what keeps you in Cheshire," she muttered.

His eyes darkened, his finger brushing over her lips. "If you think it is only my father's secret that keeps me here, you would be wrong."

Delicious warmth cascaded through her body, the

workroom with its barren stone walls and flagstone floor suddenly seeming far smaller and more . . .

Intimate.

She jerked from his touch as if she had been branded.

"Have you made any progress in your search?" she demanded, her voice annoyingly breathless.

A smile touched his lips, as if pleased by her revealing reaction.

"I am fairly confident that it has something to do with my arrival from France."

"Why?" She frowned. "He claimed you as his son, did he not?"

The smile faded, and was replaced by lurking bitterness. "Yes, but shortly before I was sent to Dunnington in London, my father went to great effort and expense to rid the Great House of my French nurse, as well as her lover. It seems likely they knew something he did not want bandied about."

Sarah hid her lack of confidence in his logic. In truth, she did not find the fact that Lord Merriot had dismissed two of his servants as particularly suspicious. He was well known to be a difficult and demanding employer.

"Could you not simply ask your nurse for the truth?" she instead demanded.

"I have a friend searching for her. Once she is located, I will question her."

"Until then, you intend to remain in the neighborhood?"

He lifted a brow at her question. "Of course."

"Even if it is dangerous?"

He stepped closer, his eyes darkening. "Are you concerned for my welfare, Miss Jefferson?"

Well, of course she was concerned, she acknowledged with a flare of aggravation. Had she not seen the brutal bruises left by his attackers?

"Only a fool would deliberately stick his head in a viper's nest."

He reached to cup her cheek in his hand, his gaze skimming over her upturned countenance.

"In truth, I am far more terrified of the bewitchment you have so easily woven about me than of any danger my father might pose."

Sliding off the stool, Sarah retreated until her back hit the stone wall.

A mistake she instantly realized as he prowled toward her, placing his hands on the wall on either side of her shoulders to effectively trap her.

"Mr. Charlebois," she breathed. "You cannot . . ."

Raoul proved that he could.

And could do it well.

Sarah's eyes fluttered shut as he lowered his head and kissed her with a blatant hunger. She told herself that it was shock that had her grasping his arms as if they were a lifeline. And why her lips parted to invite the thrust of his tongue.

Although the dazzling pleasure that speared through her body did not feel like shock.

Good lord, she felt as if she were being devoured. And nothing had ever been so wonderful.

Tilting back her head, Sarah allowed Raoul to deepen the kiss, a restless ache blooming in the pit of her stomach. She instinctively arched to press against his hard muscles, needing to be closer.

She shivered as she felt the growing evidence of his arousal.

A brazen part of her longed to lower her hand and explore his erection just as intimately as he had explored her the night before. To discover what could make him moan. And sigh. And become so desperate with need that he would shove up her skirts and take her right there against the wall.

Dazed by her brazen thoughts, it took Sarah a moment to recognize the sound of childish laughter that echoed through the closed door.

She stiffened even as Raoul spoke against her tender mouth. "Ah, I believe I recognize the sound of hungry children in search of gingerbread." His tongue stroked over her lower lip. "No, not gingerbread. Cinnamon and apples." Lifting his head, he regarded her with a smoldering heat. "Tarts?"

Gathering her dazed thoughts along with her breath, Sarah belatedly pushed her hands against his wide chest.

"Mr. Charlebois, you must halt this . . ."

"Blundering attempts at seduction?" he smoothly supplied. "I am sorry, *ma belle*, but that is impossible." With a sigh, he stepped back and briefly closed his eyes, as if struggling for his own composure. Then, lifting his lashes, he sucked in a deep breath. "Unfortunately, my once perfect timing appears to have vanished along with my career."

With a dip of his head, Raoul turned to make his way to the door. "Return to your work, Miss Jefferson, I promised to assist the boys with costumes for their charade."

Left on her own, Sarah listened to Willie and Jimmy's shouts of pleasure as Raoul joined them, as well as his answering laugh. There was a rumble of conversation, and while the door prevented her from making out the words, it was obvious they were thoroughly enjoying each others' company.

It was not until the chill from the wall began to seep through the back of her woolen gown that Sarah roused herself from the strange sense of bewilderment, and forced herself back onto the stool.

Good lord.

She had been an idiot to believe she was prepared to meet with Raoul and treat him with the cool composure she had practiced the entire morning. He had only to walk through the door for her heart to race and her palms to sweat.

And when he had kissed her . . . well, she had gone up in flames.

Flames that continued to smolder and plague her with a restless need.

Most unnerving, however, was the ache of sympathy clutching her heart.

Raoul might pretend he felt nothing but fury at his father's contemptible behavior, but she had all too easily sensed the wounds that festered deep in his soul. He had been betrayed by the one man who should have loved him the most. The thought touched her with a frightening intensity.

It was one thing to be overwhelmed with lust.

That, at least, was easy enough to comprehend.

This . . . aching need to soothe his pain was far, far more dangerous.

Grimacing, Sarah reached for her charcoal, not at all surprised to discover her hand was shaking.

The ground was, after all, shifting beneath her feet.

* * *

December 18
Chester

It was a weary but satisfied Sarah who stood aside as the two maids poured the last of the hot water into the tub set beside the blazing fireplace.

She had arrived in Chester before luncheon and after delivering her etchings to the gallery that sold them on commission, she had devoted the day to strolling through the half-timbered shops that hung over the small cobbled streets, purchasing the various household items she needed before turning her attention to the small Christmas presents she could afford for the boys.

All in all, she spent more than she had intended, but she was pleased with her efforts, and at last made her way to the small but comfortable hotel. She had requested a bath in her chamber, preferring the thought of warming her chilled body to filling the empty ache in her stomach.

Gathering the empty buckets, the younger maid scurried from the room, leaving the elder servant to halt before Sarah with a warm smile.

"There you are, miss, nice and hot, just as you requested. Will there be anything else?"

"No, I thank you."

"I could have a dinner tray sent up," the woman pressed, her motherly tone matching her round countenance, her gray hair pulled into a simple bun. "The common rooms are no place for a lady."

Sarah pulled a coin from her reticule and pressed it in

the servant's hand. "That will not be necessary. I had a late tea."

Slipping the coin into the pocket of her voluminous apron, the woman waved a hand toward the rope hanging near the fireplace.

"If you change your mind, just ring the bell."

"I will."

"And lock the door," the servant warned as she stepped into the hall. "Our guests are decent folk, but the tap room is always filled with those men who believe a female without protection is inviting their attention."

"I will take the greatest care, I assure you," Sarah promised, waiting for the maid to walk down the hall before she closed and bolted the door.

Once alone, she swiftly shed her travel-worn clothing and sank into the waiting tub.

She moaned in relief as the hot water soaked away the lingering chill and eased her cramped muscles. Allowing her head to rest against the rim of the tub, she took in her surroundings, absently noting the narrow bed and the scruffy wardrobe that matched a low table, set with a candle and pitcher of water. It was hardly fit for royalty, but Sarah appreciated the rare sense of peace.

For the moment, there were no boys squabbling over who had the larger slice of bread, and no Maggie chiding her to attend some function or another in the village. And best of all, no Raoul Charlebois with his devastating smile and wounded eyes.

Perhaps if she spent the night reminding herself of all the reasons becoming involved with such a gentleman was nothing less than a disaster, she could manage to keep him at a proper distance.

The water had cooled by the time she had scrubbed

away the dust from the day, and climbing from the tub, she rubbed herself dry with a towel and pulled on her night rail.

It was too early for bed, but she was not foolish enough to stray from her room. Instead, she stood before the fire and held her hands toward the flames.

She was still standing there when a soft tap brought her out of her broodings. With a jerk of surprise, she glanced to the side, for the first time noting a door that connected her chamber to the adjoining room.

"What the devil?" she muttered, cautiously moving toward the door.

There was another rap, this one more insistent.

"Sarah."

Reaching the door, Sarah froze in shock.

Raoul. Even through the thick wood there was no mistaking his low rich tone. Or the shivers of desire it sent down her spine.

"Mr. Charlebois?"

"Open the door," he commanded.

She struggled to think through the fog of disbelief clouding her mind.

"I most certainly will not. What are you doing in Chester?"

"You are not the only one with business to attend to."

"Business?"

There was a short pause. "I was charged with a most important commission that I was obliged to discharge before Christmas."

She pressed a hand to her chest, wishing that it was outrage that was making her heart race. Instead, she very much feared that it was exhilaration.

"I do not believe you."

"It is the truth, I assure you."

"So you claim it is nothing more than a coincidence that you traveled to Chester on the precise same day as myself, and happened to have a room that adjoins my own?"

She heard his chuckle at her blunt challenge. "My business in Chester was genuine, although I will admit my decision to conduct it today was no coincidence."

"And your room?"

"I made certain that it would connect with yours."

Sucking in a sharp breath, Sarah took an instinctive step backward.

"You go too far, sir."

"Do I?" There was the sound of metal scraping against metal. "Then I suppose I might as well go even further."

"What are you doing?" she stupidly demanded, already knowing the answer as the door was thrust open to reveal Raoul casually leaning against the door jam.

"Going too far, *ma belle*," he murmured, his eyes dark with a dangerous heat as he allowed his gaze to drift over her linen night rail and the dark curls she had left free to cascade down her back.

A matching heat shimmered through Sarah as she did her own share of staring.

Like her, Raoul had removed his traveling attire and had changed into a brocade dressing gown that was loosely tied at his waist. Her mouth went dry at the glimpse of his smooth, broad chest, and the powerful legs that were lightly dusted with golden hair. Even his feet were perfect.

Apollo, indeed.

Sarah licked her lips, at last lifting her gaze to study

Raoul's satisfied expression. He was pleased to know his golden beauty disturbed her.

She tilted her chin. "You have a key to my room?"

"I rarely leave anything to chance." He shrugged. "Besides, it could be said that the key belongs to my room. The lock is, after all, on my side."

"You are . . ."

His brow arched. "Yes?"

"Impossible."

Ignoring the insult, Raoul moved smoothly forward and before Sarah could react he had wrapped an arm around her shoulder and steered her toward the doorway.

"And you must be starving," he said, smiling down at her startled expression. "I ordered dinner."

Sarah did not bother to struggle. It was not that she feared Raoul would physically force her to join him. He was not a gentleman who needed to overpower a woman to seduce her.

No. She did not struggle because she did not want to.

Already the delectable aroma of food was clenching her hollow stomach and reminding her that it had been hours since her late tea. And in truth, a very large part of her wanted to give into temptation.

Temptation for dinner.

For . . . Raoul.

Not that she was conceding absolute defeat.

Not when she feared this man was a threat to more than her innocence.

"You are rather certain of your own charms."

"No," he denied, urging her toward the small table set in the center of his much larger chamber. "Just convinced that for all your splendid care of Willie and Jimmy, you are far less dedicated to your own needs."

Her gaze briefly skimmed over the delicately papered walls that matched the curtains as well as the drapery around the four-poster bed. Hastily, she returned her gaze to the nearby table.

"That is ridiculous," she muttered.

"Did I mistake the matter?" he drawled, halting to pull out one of the wooden chairs. "Perhaps you have already ordered your dinner?"

She glared at him as she took her seat. "Obviously you overheard me tell the maid I did not care for a tray."

He leaned down to brush his lips over the top of her head before rounding the table and smoothly sliding into his own chair.

"Which offered me a perfect opportunity to lure you to my room."

"As I said. Impossible."

"And near the point of starvation." He reached across the table to unfold one of the linen napkins, and held it out to her with a teasing smile. "Surely you would not be cruel enough to condemn me to eating my dinner in solitude?"

She jerked the napkin from his waiting fingers and shoved it onto her lap.

"I do not doubt you would only have to step out the door to have all the companionship you might desire."

He studied her with a disturbing intensity. "But I want no other but you, *ma belle*."

Chapter 13

Raoul studied her from beneath half-lowered lids, the air suddenly prickling with awareness. Then as she shifted uneasily, he grimaced ruefully and leaned back in his seat.

"I trust your transactions were successful?"

Sarah swallowed the strange lump that had formed in her throat. "I believe so."

"You cannot keep me in suspense," he teased, his slender fingers aimlessly toying with a silver fork. "What delights did you come across for Father Christmas to bring for the boys?"

"I was fortunate enough to discover a set of tin soldiers for Willie, and a book of fairy tales that I believe Jimmy will enjoy."

"Fine treats, indeed."

She shrugged. "They are simple gifts, but the boys have so little . . ."

Without warning, he reached to grasp the hand she had laid on the table.

"Sarah, possessing a home, and having your love is

by far the greatest gift that Willie and Jimmy could ever receive," he interrupted, his voice harsh with sincerity. "Trust me, I know the meaning of such things."

"Yes, I suppose you do," she said softly.

"Sarah . . ."

Her heart felt as if it was melting, and with a burst of panic, Sarah was tugging her hand free to begin pulling the covers off the various dishes.

"Roasted duck. Salmon. Mushrooms in cream sauce. Asparagus. Buttered potatoes. Fresh strawberries." Her eyes widened as Raoul politely filled her plate and then his own with the bounty. "Good heavens, did the cook believe you were entertaining an entire regiment?"

He handed her a plate and poured the waiting wine into her glass. "I merely requested a few of her finer dishes."

Unable to resist, Sarah dug into the meal with undisguised hunger. Raoul had already guessed she was starving, and the food was delicious. Why pretend otherwise?

"Ah," she said, taking a sip of the wine. "Another victim of your smile. It is a wonder she did not insist on spoon-feeding you."

Seemingly pleased by her refusal to pick at her dinner as if she were a bird, Raoul set about enjoying his meal.

"If my smile is as fatal as you pretend it to be, I would not have to plot and scheme merely to share dinner with you, *ma belle*."

"Not all women are in the position to fulfill your whims, Mr. Charlebois."

The words had left her lips before she could halt them, and she stiffened as his eyes slowly narrowed.

"Whims?" he murmured, his voice husky. "You believe my interest in you is merely a whim?"

"Is it not?"

He polished off the last of the duck. "No matter what I say, you will merely dismiss it as shallow flattery, so I shall have to prove my sincerity by other means."

She frowned. "And what means would those be?"

"A clever general never reveals his battle plans." He reached for a platter and held it toward her. "Strawberry?"

Warily, she reached to take one of the offered treats. "Thank you."

Raoul settled back in his seat, sipping his wine. "Have you considered the future for the boys?"

She blinked at the abrupt question, wondering if he were trying to lull her off guard.

"Of course I have." She nibbled at the strawberry, savoring the tart juice that filled her senses. It had been years since she had enjoyed such a delicious feast. "To be honest, it has been preying on my mind since I took them in."

"And what are your conclusions?"

"I believe that Willie could be happy working as a groom or in the local stables. He possesses an uncanny skill with animals. But Jimmy . . ." Her words trailed off as she pushed aside her empty plate.

"Tell me."

"No doubt I am prejudiced, but I believe his intellect is quite superior, and his curiosity never sated," she discovered herself admitting, oddly relieved to share her anxiety about the future. "If he could be properly schooled, I believe he would have his choice of respectable professions."

"Schooling is an expensive luxury for most."

"Yes. And there is the awkward fact that I am not truly his mother. I am not certain I possess the right to send him from his home to a school."

He gave a slow nod, thankfully not dismissing her concern with some vague platitude.

"A pity that Dunnington is not still here," he instead murmured, his expression wistful. "He possessed a true genius for teaching. Even for those students who had no desire to learn, as Ian is ample proof."

"Ian?"

"One of my fellow bastards and my closest friend, along with Fredrick."

Sarah studied the beautiful male features, sensing that she was being offered a rare glimpse into Raoul's innermost feelings.

"The school has been closed?"

He drained the last of his wine, appearing heartbreakingly vulnerable in the flickering firelight.

"It was never a formal institute, more a house filled with young boys and a gentleman who loved them."

"You miss it," she said, softly.

"I do. Which I suppose explains why I . . ."

She leaned forward. "What?"

For a moment, she feared he might retreat behind his polished charm, but then, with a sigh, he met her questioning gaze.

"I bought the house."

"Oh." That was not what she had expected. "Do you intend to live there?"

"No."

"Then why did you purchase it?"

He set aside his glass. "At the time, I simply could not bear to think of it standing empty. It had always been so full of life."

"And now?"

His eyes became distant. "Now I am considering the

notion of returning it to what it once was, assuming I can find a suitable candidate to take Dunnington's place."

"You intend to start a school?"

"It is of yet nothing more than a vague hope." He gave a shake of his head, an odd smile lurking about his lips. "It's strange."

"What is?"

"You are the first person I have told," he admitted, watching the various emotions flicker over her countenance. "Have I shocked you?"

She could not deny that the thought of this exquisite gentleman who had made his fame among London society fussing over a pack of grubby schoolboys was difficult to imagine.

"I must admit that I am astonished."

His expression hardened, as if her words had struck a nerve. "I am not the utter feckless fribble you assume me to be."

Good lord, she *had* hurt him. Instinctively, she reached across the table to touch his hand.

"I do not think you a feckless fribble," she denied.

"Ah, no," he mocked. "You accused me of always performing upon a stage."

She hesitated, sensing she was standing at the edge of a precipice. For all Raoul's arrogance, there was a part of him that was still that small boy who expected to be treated with disdain.

All she had to do was allow him to believe that she lacked any respect for him as a person, and he would retreat from her forever.

The thought was dismissed as soon as it fluttered through her mind.

She might be terrified of her reaction to Raoul

Charlebois, but she was not such a coward that she would deliberately injure him. At least, not again.

His father had done enough damage.

"What I believe is that you have been taught to disguise your emotions, and that your trust is not easily won," she said, holding his gaze. "I also believe that you possess a genuine concern for those children who are not born into wealth. If you do begin a school, I have absolute confidence you will alter the lives of any child fortunate enough to become a student. That is a true legacy."

"Sarah." He turned his hand so he was grasping her fingers, then rising to his feet, he tugged her out of her seat. For a long moment he simply searched her upturned face, as if seeking some truth etched on her features. At last, a small smile curved his lips. "I never thought this was possible."

Sarah trembled beneath the force of his searing gaze. "What?"

"That there could be a woman who could see something other than the infamous Raoul Charlebois."

"It would be better if I did not."

"Why?"

Beyond pretense, she heaved a sigh. "You make me desire things I cannot have."

She heard his breath catch at her blunt honesty, his hand lifting to explore the sensitive lines of her face.

"Why deny yourself?"

She struggled to recall all the fine reasons for resisting the sensations that scorched through her body.

"Because I must think of the boys," she at last managed to rasp.

Taking care not to startle her, Raoul shifted to wrap

his arms around her waist, tugging her against the hard width of his chest.

"The boys are not here, *ma belle*." His head lowered to nuzzle her temple. "We are completely alone, with no one to know what we do."

No one to know, temptation whispered in her ear. Or perhaps it was the devil.

Home was miles away, and the boys in the care of Maggie Stone. Why should she not for once grasp the pleasure that was offered?

As if sensing her weakening resistance, Raoul allowed his hands to skim up the curve of her back, urging her ever closer to his rigid muscles.

Sarah lifted her hands, but rather than pushing him away, she found them slipping beneath the lapels of his robe, finding the satin smoothness of his skin.

"Convenience does not necessarily make it a wise choice," she muttered, ruining her pretense of sanity as her hands explored the rippling muscles beneath Raoul's heated skin.

He chuckled as he stroked his lips along the line of her ear.

"Wisdom is no doubt a fine thing, but I have always thought it highly overrated," he assured her, his lips finding the tender hollow beneath her ear. "Great art is created with the senses, not the mind."

Her head tilted back of its own accord, allowing him access to the tender curve of her neck. Raoul was swift to take advantage, his mouth leaving a trail of fire as he followed the line of collarbone.

"You consider this great art?" she husked.

"I consider *you* great art, *ma belle*," he said, his voice rough as he abruptly scooped her off her feet and carried her to the bed. With care, he lowered her onto the blankets, his eyes darkening as they slid over her flushed face and the tumble of her raven hair. "Nothing less than a masterpiece."

A distant alarm whispered in the back of her mind. Surely she should be uncertain? Or nervous? Or at least, mildly apprehensive?

Instead, any reasonable hesitation was lost beneath the rising tide of restless anticipation.

Her mind might comprehend that she was plunging into danger, but her body had been desperately longing for this moment since Raoul had tutored her in the ecstasy to be discovered in his touch.

"You are being ridiculous," she breathed, well aware that this man had known some of the most beautiful women in England. "I am nothing more than passable."

"Art is always in the eye of the beholder," he husked in low tones. "And to me, you are as exquisite as the Mona Lisa."

She smiled faintly. "I fear you must be blind."

"Blind?" He offered a wicked chuckle as he shifted to tug at the ribbons that held up her night rail. "I assure you, *ma belle*, my eyes have never seen more clearly." Gently he pushed the gown downward, his breath catching as he skimmed his gaze over her exposed body. "Nor have they ever been so pleased with what they see."

She shivered, ridiculously thrilled at the knowledge he thought her beautiful.

"I am not accustomed to allowing so much to be on display," she murmured, a faint blush touching her cheeks as he finished tugging off the night rail and dropping it on the floor.

"Do not be afraid, Sarah. I swear that I will do nothing

that you do not desire," he promised, lowering his head to close his lips around the tip of a nipple.

Afraid? Good heavens, she was going up in flames. Unable to halt her response, she parted her lips and moaned as his tongue teased the hardened nub, the caress sending a sharp excitement trembling through her body.

Instinctively her hands lifted to shove her fingers in his thick, golden curls, her back arching in silent encouragement.

His own hands were busy wreaking havoc as they moved over her trembling body, as if seeking to memorize each line and curve.

"I cannot think clearly enough to be afraid," she muttered, her voice thick with need.

"Then we are well suited," he groaned, yanking off his robe to reveal the powerful beauty of his naked body. "I have not had a coherent thought since the moment you lured me into your cottage."

"I did not lure you," she denied, sucking in a shocked breath as his mouth trailed a path of kisses down her stomach, the brush of his lips inflaming her senses and creating a strange dampness between her legs.

Sarah, you are lost, she acknowledged, easily allowing him to spread her legs so he could explore a path over her hip and down her inner thigh.

And more frightening, she did not have the sense to care.

She wanted to shiver as his body burrowed between her parted legs. She wanted her heart lodged in her throat as his warm breath brushed over her sensitive skin. She wanted to feel her lower muscles clench in sweet anticipation.

"Lovely, Sarah," he moaned softly, his fingers gripping her hips. "You lured me as surely as a siren."

She stirred restlessly beneath his tender caresses, needing something more.

"I did nothing but allow you into my home," she inanely argued, her mind incapable of rational thought.

"Now you will never be rid of me," he murmured, gently parting her folds to stroke his tongue into her damp heat.

Sarah's soft cry echoed through the room as her fingers yanked at his hair. He laughed softly, continuing his intimate caress, his hands shifting to hold her legs open as her hips lifted off the mattress.

Good . . . heavens.

She had never dreamed that she would ever allow a man to touch her with such intimacy, or that far from being shocked by his bold caresses, she would be terrified he might halt.

Sanity was for tomorrow.

For tonight, she intended to grasp this fleeting moment of passion.

As if sensing she had accustomed herself to his touch, Raoul shifted his head just enough to discover her center of pleasure. Gently he suckled and stroked the tender nub, his hands holding her hips steady as she writhed beneath the delectable assault.

"Mr. Charlebois," she gasped, then without warning her entire body stiffened, and with a rasping cry she reached her climax.

Lost in the bliss that quaked through her, Sarah was barely aware of Raoul pressing himself upward. Not until his lips brushed over her parted lips and his hips settled between her legs.

Sarah lifted her oddly heavy lashes to discover Raoul poised above her, his expression tight, a slash of color staining his cheekbones.

"Sarah, you must be certain . . ."

"I am certain," she interrupted, her heart turning over at the painful uncertainty that shimmered in his eyes. The mere fact that he was concerned she might have regrets only steadied her conviction that this was right. Her hands smoothed over his shoulders, urging his head downward. "Quite certain."

His teeth ground together, his breath rasping loudly through the air.

"So be it, *ma belle*," he gritted, tilting his hips until the tip of his erection pressed against her moist opening. "We shall both put our future in the hands of destiny."

She might have wondered at his mysterious words if the sensation of his cock slowly pressing into her had not stolen her every thought.

Instinctively, her nails dug into the skin of his shoulders, her heart halting as she felt herself being stretched to the point of near pain.

"Mr. Charlebois," she breathed.

He gave a choked laugh, his shoulders trembling beneath her fingers at the effort of holding his passion in check.

"Do you not think you could bring yourself to call me Raoul, *ma belle*?"

Even if she desired to comply with his request, Sarah found her throat closing as he pressed ever deeper, her tightness clamping about his erection with astonishing pleasure. Oh . . . yes. Despite the burning sensation, there was a growing pleasure as he slowly, carefully began to rock his hips.

Breathless, Sarah savored the feel of him moving inside her, her gaze mesmerized by his golden beauty in the smoldering firelight.

Perhaps he was a god, she fuzzily accepted. *Apollo come down from Mount Olympus to pleasure this willing mortal.*

With a groan, Raoul buried his face in her hair and greedily inhaled her scent.

"Nothing has ever felt so good," he whispered in her ear. "Never."

Her arms wrapped about him, holding on tight as he reached down to tease her back to full arousal. Her eyes squeezed shut, her legs wrapping around his hips as his pace quickened.

With astonishing speed, the tension once again built within her, spreading like warm honey from the center of her body to the very tips of her toes.

Lifting himself onto his hands, Raoul thrust ever deeper, his lips covering hers in a kiss of sheer possession as they shattered together in searing pleasure.

Chapter 14

Wrapping Sarah tightly in his arms, Raoul tugged the rumpled blankets over their naked bodies and buried his face in her hair.

He breathed deeply her womanly spice, savoring the utter contentment that flowed through his body. He was accustomed to finding pleasure in a woman's arms, even amusement, on occasion. But this sense of sated peace was a new experience. And as heady as the finest bottle of brandy.

It was also nothing less than a miracle, considering that the past hour had forever altered his life.

No, that was not precisely true.

He had known the moment he had left the Lodge to travel to Chester that his decision would be irrevocable. No gentleman, not even a bastard, would deliberately seek out a proper maiden with the firm intention of seducing her without knowing the cost.

Still, it did seem that he should feel a measure of unease at the realization that his future was now eternally bound to this woman, rather than this giddy sense of self-satisfaction.

It was little wonder that both Fredrick and Ian had laughed when he assured them that he was immune to fate.

Feeling Sarah stir in his arms, Raoul pulled back far enough to study her face, his heart slamming against his ribs.

He did not think he would ever become accustomed to her dark, striking beauty.

"I begin to believe there is a Father Christmas after all," he murmured, his fingers trailing down the length of her jaw.

She blinked in confusion. "Father Christmas?"

He slowly smiled. Cocooned in the soft feather bed, with only the fire to light the small chamber, Raoul felt as if they were completely alone in the world.

It was a sensation he could happily hold on to for an eternity.

"You are the finest present a man could ever hope to receive."

Her lashes fluttered downward, hiding her expressive eyes. "Hardly an original present for you."

Raoul gently outlined her lips, refusing to be goaded. "Now that is where you are wrong, *ma belle*. I cannot claim your innocence, but I can assure you that you are the most original woman I have ever encountered. And what passed between us . . ." He paused, surprised to discover a nervous flutter in the center of his gut. "It has altered my life."

Her gaze snapped upward. "Mr. Charlebois."

"Raoul."

She licked her lips, a pulse at the base of her throat beating at a frantic pace.

"I . . ."

"Yes?"

"I hope you are not considering anything foolish."

His brows lowered, easily sensing this was not going as he had planned. Of course, that was hardly an unusual sensation in his dealings with this woman.

"I seem to be doing that with increasing frequency since coming to Cheshire," he said dryly. "So perhaps you should be more specific as to which foolishness you are referring to."

Her wariness only deepened. "What happened between us was as much my choice as yours."

His fingers shifted to trail through the raven curls that were spread across the pillow. The texture was soft and silky beneath his touch. Much like her creamy skin.

A ready heat tingled through his body, hardening his muscles.

"Actually, I would say that neither of us had a choice," he husked. "It was inevitable from the moment I caught sight of you." His lips twisted. "Of course, there are those who might point out that I did my best to nudge destiny in the proper direction."

She shook her head, her hands lifting to press against his chest.

"My point is that this changes nothing."

Raoul's jaw tightened as he warred against his rising temper. Was the woman being deliberately obtuse? He had just taken her innocence. Did she think him the sort of cad who seduced virgins and then walked away?

"On the contrary, Miss Sarah Jefferson. This changes everything." He deliberately paused. "For the both of us."

"No." Genuine panic flared through her dark eyes. "Do not."

"Sarah . . ."

"Please," she pleaded, her voice thick. "I do not want any changes."

"You believe we can ignore what has happened between us?" he growled, frustrated.

"I did not say we must ignore one another . . ."

"Good, because I can assure you that is an impossible task."

Her expression settled in stubborn lines. "But, once I return home, I must consider the boys. This can be nothing more than a brief interlude."

"Interlude?"

"Yes."

Raoul glared down at her for a long moment. He wanted to growl and snap and demand. He wanted to force her to accept that she had effectively sealed her fate the moment she had entered his bed.

Unfortunately, he was beginning to know this woman too well.

She was not yet prepared to accept the truth, and the least hint that he was attempting to compel her would only make her dig in her heels so deep, he would never get them unstuck.

Not that he had any intention of conceding defeat, he grimly acknowledged.

In truth, he was more convinced than ever that this woman was destined to be his wife.

The mother of his children.

Strangely aroused by the mere thought of this woman heavy with his child, Raoul lowered his head, trailing his lips down the curve of her neck.

Matters might not be proceeding along the simple path he had expected, but he did not doubt his ultimate success.

And there was no reason he could not enjoy the journey.

Thoroughly.

Nuzzling a path of kisses down her collarbone, he shifted his hand to cup her breast, his thumb teasing the nipple to a hard bud.

"Then it seems we must make the most of our"—he smiled as she moaned in pleasure—"interlude."

December 19
Chester

If Raoul hoped that Sarah would come to her senses by morning, he was doomed to disappointment.

After a short but fierce battle of wills, in which Sarah had refused every reasonable request for him to see her home in the comfort of his carriage, he had been forced to watch her walk from the inn with nothing more satisfying than a brief kiss.

Thwarted but resolute, Raoul had settled for hiring one of the inn's grooms to follow the stagecoach at a discreet distance, ensuring that she made it to her cottage without incident, and kept her damnable pride intact.

Then deciding that he might as well take advantage of his presence in Chester, he sought out a local solicitor, ignoring the gentleman's suspicions as he concluded his business. Once he had the papers he sought, he collected his carriage for the cold journey to Wallingford.

He reached the village in good time, but it took

longer than he expected to conclude his dealings, and ignoring his biting need to be near Sarah, he forced himself to remain at the small inn rather than daring the icy lanes in the dark.

He was not about to risk his neck now that he could actually envision a future that was filled with possibility.

The delay, however, did nothing for his temper that was already rubbed raw by Sarah's panicked flight from Chester.

Leaving the carriage in the care of Pickens, Raoul entered the Lodge by a side door that led directly to the library. A wry smile touched his lips as he caught sight of Nico seated beside the fire, a decanter of brandy situated on a table beside him.

His loyal servant knew him well enough to suspect he would prefer to slip into the house unnoted by Mrs. Dent, or her giggling daughter.

"So the prodigal son returns," Nico drawled, pouring a glass of brandy before rising to his feet and crossing to press it into Raoul's hand. "I trust your journey was successful?"

Raoul drained the glass in one swallow, sighing as the fiery liquid spread through his veins.

"Not nearly so successful as it should have been," he muttered, setting aside the glass to remove his outer garments. "Do you know, there was a time when I actually believed I understood women?"

Nico snorted. "Which only proves you are a fool. There is no man who can claim to comprehend the workings of the female mind."

Raoul was far from comforted. "There are those more stubborn than others."

Nico paused, his dark, lean features unreadable. "You

would never respect a woman who did not have a mind of her own, and the ability to stand up to your will. You comprehend better than most the emptiness of blind devotion."

The man was correct, of course.

Over the years, Raoul had grown increasingly disenchanted with those women who were so anxious to please him that they became no more than pretty accessories that dangled from his arm.

Still, there was a vast difference between blind devotion and bloody single-minded obstinacy.

"I have no worry of that." He shoved his fingers through his hair. "The woman nearly ran screaming from the room when I attempted to discuss a future together."

"Future." Nico scowled. "Together?"

"Yes." Raoul met his companion's gaze without apology. "Whether she is willing to admit it or not."

Nico muttered a curse, glaring toward the nearby window. "I should never have allowed you to leave London. Too much fresh air would rattle the wits of any man."

"My wits may be rattled, but I know what I want." A blaze of pleasure warmed his heart as he recalled holding a sleeping Sarah in his arms. "And what I want is Miss Jefferson."

"You have known other women, many far more sophisticated than Miss Jefferson. Why her?"

"I am not entirely certain. I only know that the thought of a future without her is unacceptable."

"What if she will not have you?"

Raoul did not hesitate. "Then I will remain here until I convince her."

Nico tossed his hands up in defeat. "Fresh air. There is nothing more dangerous."

With a chuckle, Raoul strolled toward the fire, stirring a log with the tip of his boot.

"Did you keep a watch on my father?"

"Of course."

"Was there anything of interest?"

Nico joined him beside the fireplace, the flames dancing over his ruthless features.

"He appears to have dug in like a frightened badger. From all accounts, he rarely leaves his study unless the brandy decanter runs empty, while Lady Merriot refuses to budge from her bed."

Raoul nodded with grim satisfaction. He was petty enough to enjoy the thought of his father cowering in his study, terrified his bastard son was on the precipice of ruining his life.

He was not, however, stupid.

Lord Merriot might be shallow and self-absorbed, but he was also a powerful peer of the realm who had already proven his wiliness to sink to any depths to destroy Raoul.

"That does not make him any less dangerous."

"No," Nico readily agreed, his expression somber. "A rabid dog will eventually bite."

"Which makes it all the more imperative I discover the truth."

"Perhaps these will assist you." Reaching beneath his plain woolen coat, Nico pulled out two folded sheets of parchment from his pocket.

"From London?" Raoul demanded, reaching to pluck the messages from his companion's fingers.

"One arrived yesterday, the other this morning."

"Ah." Raoul unfolded the first, swiftly reading through the neatly printed words. "Fredrick has discovered the shop owned by my former nurse. Francine's Fashionable Accessories in Pall Mall."

"Did he speak with her?"

Raoul read on, his brows drawing together in resignation. "From what he could discover, the woman claims to have come straight from Paris with no mention of ever having been in Cheshire. She also denies any knowledge of Lord Merriot. Fredrick was reluctant to press her for fear she might become suspicious." He shook his head. "*Mon Dieu.* I shall have to travel to London to speak with her myself."

"Or you could send me."

Raoul lifted his head to meet his companion's dark, lethal gaze. He grimaced at the thought of loosening the one-time cutthroat on a hapless old woman.

"It is not that I do not trust your ability to question Francine, I only hesitate at your methods."

Nico smiled, unperturbed by Raoul's reluctance. "You fear I may put her on the rack?"

"Your tactics are usually more subtle, although no less dangerous. She is no good to me if she decides to bolt, or dies of heart failure."

"You can trust me, my friend."

Raoul slowly nodded, unable to deny the temptation to send Nico in his stead.

Nico would have no need to confront Francine directly to discover whatever information he desired. His connection in the underworld ensured he had eyes and ears in the most unlikely places.

Besides, the mere thought of leaving Sarah . . .

He clenched his jaw against the sharp pain that clenched his heart.

"I would never doubt you, Nico," he forced himself to mutter. "But this task is mine."

"Is that not why you hire servants?" Nico smoothly demanded. "To take care of such tasks?"

Raoul gave a sharp laugh as his servant neatly outmaneuvered him. "Why did I ever think I desired a valet with intelligence?"

Nico shrugged. "Because you have no tolerance for stupidity."

Raoul grimaced and unfolded the second message. "Perhaps I should read Ian's note before we make our plans."

Unlike Fredrick, Ian's handwriting was a florid scrawl that was nearly impossible to decipher.

"Well?" Nico at last prompted. "Did he discover anything of worth?"

"I am not entirely certain." Raoul struggled to make sense of the message. "He managed to discover that Merriot did come into a great deal of money several years ago."

"That tells us precisely nothing."

Raoul's voice hardened as he realized the risk Ian had taken. "Not in itself, but Ian has managed to have a glimpse at my father's private ledgers that are kept in the office of his Man of Business."

Predictably Nico smiled at the thought of Ian sneaking into the private office, no doubt in the dead of night.

"I have always liked Breckford."

"You should. The two of you are terrifyingly similar."

Nico's smile widened. "What did he find?"

Raoul dismissed his annoyance at Ian having risked

his respectable position as an investor, and instead concentrated on what he had managed to uncover.

"The bulk of his supposed inheritance was in actual money rather than bank notes, as well as a large collection of rare art that was sold to private collectors."

Nico snorted. "Since my only inheritance was a back-handed slap from my mother before she cocked up her toes, you might as well be speaking Greek. Is something wrong?"

"More odd," Raoul conceded, his thoughts shifting through the various implications before coming to the only logical conclusion. "Most inheritances are passed on through lands or entailed property. And any art would have brought more money at a public auction." He lifted his head to meet Nico's puzzled gaze. "Of course, a public auction would include a listing of the art work as well as the buyers."

"*Christo,*" Nico breathed.

Raoul nodded. "My father has ensured that no one can discover where his inheritance came from."

"More than odd."

"There is more." Raoul returned his attention to the message. "Ian managed to track down a broker who admits that he sold several fine jewels for Lord Merriot. All of them removed from their previous settings." He crushed the paper in his hand, recalling his conversation with Drabble and the man's crazed accusations against Lord Merriot. "Damn. Perhaps Drabble was not the raving lunatic that I presumed him to be."

Nico shook his head. "Not even the best thief could have stolen so much without creating a stir."

Raoul grudgingly agreed. A gentleman might be capable of stealing a few coins, or even one or two pieces of jewelry, but to filch large works of art would be nearly impossible.

"Always more questions with no answers," he growled.

"Lord Merriot cannot hide behind smoke and mirrors forever." Nico placed a comforting hand on his shoulder. "Allow me to travel to London to speak with your nurse."

Raoul gave a slow dip of his head. Even if he were not reluctant to leave Cheshire, he had to acknowledge that Nico could conduct an investigation far more discreetly than himself. There were times when his fame was nothing more than a nuisance.

"Very well, but take care, *mon ami.*"

Nico headed for the door, clearly anxious to be on his way. "I am not the one in danger."

"Do not be so certain," Raoul growled, knowing his servant too well to believe he would not risk his fool neck.

"I will watch my back, you worry about your own." Nico paused at the door. "And do not leave the house without Pickens."

Raoul rolled his eyes. "You are worse than a nagging wife."

Nico arched a brow. "You might as well become accustomed to it, eh, Charlebois?"

The servant disappeared before Raoul could answer the taunt. Not that it mattered. What could he say?

He did intend to take a wife.

The sooner the better.

With a shake of his head, Raoul left the library and climbed the stairs to his chamber. He was relieved to discover that Mrs. Dent had brought up a pitcher of hot water, and stripping off his clothes, he washed away the dust from the road.

He was becoming soft, he ruefully acknowledged,

noting the aches in his lower back from jolting over the rough paths. Or perhaps he was just growing old.

In either case, he knew he could think of nothing that would please him more than to spend the rest of the day seated next to a warm fire with Sarah at his side, listening to Willie and Jimmy filling the air with laughter.

Unless, of course, it was spending the afternoon with Sarah tucked in his bed.

Shivering at the mere thought, Raoul crossed to the wardrobe and chose a moss-green jacket that he matched with a striped waistcoat and black breeches. Then, tying a simple knot in his cravat, he returned to the library and gathered his outer garments.

His stomach rumbled at the smell of baking bread that filled the Lodge, but ignoring his hunger, he left by the door he had entered and returned to the stables.

Pickens made no comment as he saddled Hercules, but even as Raoul hauled himself into the saddle, the groom was leading his own horse from the stall.

Clearly Nico had convinced his fellow servant that Raoul was in dire peril. Raoul rolled his eyes, but made no effort to try and dissuade his silent companion.

Pickens could be as stubborn as a mule, and in truth, Raoul was not stupid enough to ignore the danger. If his father was truly desperate, he would not hesitate to see Raoul dead.

Still, he could not help grimacing as he urged Hercules along the frozen lanes, Pickens trailing behind him. How often had he and his friends mocked those ridiculous dandies who could not step out their front doors without a dozen servants to dance attendance upon them?

Nearing Sarah's cottage, Raoul turned in his saddle

to order Pickens back to the Lodge, assuring the doggedly obstinate man that he would not step foot from the cottage until the groom returned at nightfall.

He watched the groom ride away, ruefully hoping that Sarah did not turn him away at the door.

Continuing the short distance to the walled back garden, Raoul slid from the saddle and led Hercules toward the tall hedge that would keep him sheltered from the bitter wind. Then, following the sound of voices, he discovered Willie and Jimmy piling firewood near the back door.

At the sound of his approach, both boys turned, their faces lighting with a gratifying pleasure as they raced through the snow toward him.

"Did you get 'em?" Willie demanded as they skidded to a halt.

"I did." Raoul held up a slender hand as Willie's lips parted. "And before you ask, I have the box properly wrapped and safely hidden at the Lodge. I will bring them to you the day before Christmas."

Willie squared his shoulders. "And we sent enough money, sir?"

"More than enough," Raoul smoothly lied, reaching beneath his coat to pull out a few small coins. "These are yours."

A frown of suspicion marred Willie's brow as he slowly tucked the coins in his pocket, but before he could ask any awkward questions, Jimmy tugged on Raoul's sleeve.

"Miss Sarah says we can hang the evergreen tomorrow," he said, his eyes sparkling with excitement. "Then she says we get to sing carols and have hot cider."

"And plum cake," Willie added, his thoughts easily distracted by the promised treats.

"A fine day's entertainment."

"Did you hang mistletoe when you were a boy, Mr. Charlebois?" Jimmy demanded.

Raoul paused, scouring his mind for a memory of past Christmases. Vaguely he recalled standing on a stool to play with a sprig of holly.

"No doubt the maids decorated the nursery when I was a very young child, but my father did not possess Miss Sarah's appreciation for Christmas traditions." His lips twisted in a humorless smile. "Or for young boys like yourselves."

"Aye." Willie hunched his shoulders. "Not all folks care for boys."

"Mum called us filthy brats," Jimmy added. "Even after I scrubbed behind my ears."

Raoul crouched downward, looking the young boy straight in the eye. Suddenly, he realized that beneath Jimmy's brittle happiness was a hint of fear.

"Never you mind that, I have been called far worse," he said, his voice rough with suppressed emotion. "Besides, you are with Miss Sarah now, and she loves you whether you always remember to scrub behind your ears or not."

Jimmy bit his lower lip. "You don't think she might get tired of us?"

Raoul grasped one of his tiny hands. "Never."

"That's what I keep trying to tell him," Willie said, his expression troubled.

"What is it?" Raoul squeezed Jimmy's fingers. "You can trust me."

When Jimmy refused to speak, Willie at last revealed the truth.

"Jimmy overheard Mrs. Kohl tell the Vicar that we have bad blood, and that Miss Sarah should send us to the orphanage afore we kill her in her sleep."

"We would never do such a thing," Jimmy denied anxiously.

Raoul muttered a curse before he could rein in his fury. Damn the evil bitch. She could not have done more damage if she had taken a dagger and stuck it directly in the young boy's heart.

He better than anyone understood how words could fester and scar as deeply as any weapon.

"Of course you would not. Mrs. Kohl is obviously a repulsive mawworm who takes delight in spewing vile to any who will listen."

"But what if Miss Sarah believes . . ."

"Listen to me, Master Jimmy," Raoul firmly interrupted. "You are an extraordinary young man who is worthy of holding your head high, no matter what anyone might say." He turned his head to study Willie's carefully guarded expression. "And you, Master Willie, may be certain that your talent with horses will not go unnoticed. Soon enough, gentlemen will be pleading to have you in their employ." Straightening, he included the both of them in his steady gaze. "Do you know how I can be so certain?"

They regarded him with wide, hopeful gazes. "How?"

"Because that is what Miss Sarah told me. Does that sound like a woman who fears to sleep at night?"

Willie slowly smiled. "No, sir."

Jimmy took a half beat longer, but at last he gave a shake of his head. "No, sir."

Knowing that only time and Sarah's unwavering love could heal their wounds completely, Raoul wrapped an arm around each of the boy's shoulders and steered them toward the nearby door.

"Now that is settled, perhaps we should continue our practice for the Christmas charades."

Chapter 15

Placing the large plate of sandwiches on the tray next to the warm scones and pitcher of milk, Sarah was pleased to discover her hands had stopped shaking.

A small victory, she wryly acknowledged, considering that her entire body still tingled with awareness of Raoul Charlebois.

He had been in the parlor with the boys for the past two hours, and while she had yet to catch sight of his impossibly beautiful face, the small cottage had been filled with the sound of his smooth, dark voice and occasional laughter. Gads, there were moments when Sarah thought she could actually catch the scent his warm, spicy skin.

A part of her wanted to be angered by his casual arrival. After all, it was only polite to await an invitation before simply appearing on the doorstep. And besides, she had made it quite clear in Chester that she would not allow herself to be lured into a scandal that would hurt the boys.

This man was a danger.

To her all too susceptible body.

To her reputation.

To her future.

To her heart.

But a larger part of her could not squash the thrill of excitement that made her heart race and her breath quicken.

Bustling from the small pantry, Maggie paused as Jimmy's laughter filled the air.

"Them boys are getting mighty attached to Mr. Charlebois," she murmured.

Sarah heaved a sigh. Yet another concern. "Yes, I do hope they will not be disappointed when he returns to London."

The maid sent her a speaking glance. "You are so certain he intends to leave?"

Sarah's breath threatened to tangle in her throat at the disturbing memory of Raoul holding her tightly in his arms, his expression one of determined nobility. She had known in that moment she had only to allow Raoul to be consumed by his guilt, and he would demand that she become his wife.

And for one brief moment of insanity, Sarah had been shockingly tempted.

Not because he was the renowned Raoul Charlebois. Or because her life could be one of elegant ease. Or even because she was certain he would do his best to ensure the future for both Willie and Jimmy.

No.

The temptation had been the simple desire of a woman who was utterly bewitched by a man.

Thank goodness her wits had returned in time to avoid such a disaster. Raoul had never been allowed to know the affection of his mother and father, and while he had managed to find success, Sarah sensed that beneath his arrogance was still a young boy in need of love.

When he wed it should be to a woman who would fill his heart with joy, not one he felt obliged to marry.

Meeting Maggie's curious gaze, Sarah forced herself to give a decisive nod, ignoring the pang of regret.

"Quite certain."

"Ah well, 'tis the season for miracles," Maggie said, refusing to concede defeat. "Who can say what the future might hold?"

Sarah squared her shoulders. Enough. She had never been one to mope over things that could not be changed, and she was not about to begin now.

"I do know the future will hold two hungry boys," she said, briskly lifting the tray. "I had better get this to them before they start gnawing on the furniture."

"I will finish the dishes. You join the boys with their tea tray."

Her heart banged against her chest. "There is no need. They are being well entertained."

"Perhaps, but they are still troubled by what the nasty Kohl woman said." Maggie crossed to the stack of dishes. "They need to have you near for a few days."

The pleasurable excitement was abruptly dampened by the memory of Jimmy's heartbreaking sobs that had woken her in the middle of the night. It had taken some prompting, but at last the boy had confessed what he had overheard Mrs. Kohl say to the Vicar.

Later Sarah intended to confront the horrid woman, but at the moment she was far more concerned with reassuring Jimmy.

He would not be allowed to believe, even for a second, that he was anything but a welcome member of her small family.

"You are right." She headed for the door, pausing to

glance over her shoulder. "Once the dishes are done, I want you to leave. It is too cold to be walking home in the dark."

"No fears," Maggie assured her. "Martin has promised to fetch me before nightfall."

Sarah smiled, wondering when the maid was going to put the young man out of his misery and agree to become his wife.

"Now that is a gentleman who knows how to win a woman's heart."

Maggie offered a pointed gaze. "He is not the only gentleman."

With a snort, Sarah stepped through the door and walked the short distance to the parlor.

She steeled her nerves before stepping into the cozy room, but that did not halt her stomach from clenching and her pulse from racing as her gaze landed on Raoul.

Seated on the sofa nearest the fire, he had one boy on each side of him, their faces turned upward as they regarded Raoul with a rapt adoration.

Sarah heaved a rueful sigh, knowing she would happily have joined the boys in their obvious enchantment if she were not sensible enough to accept what could not be changed.

As it was, she had to be prepared to comfort the boys when Raoul at last discovered the secret his father was hoarding, and returned to his life in London.

Conjuring a smile, she set the tray on a table near the sofa.

"And here I thought you were busy practicing your charades," she said, straightening to discover three gazes trained on her.

The boys, of course, were filled with a ready affection that always warmed her heart.

Raoul's, however . . .

She shivered as it swept over her with a heat that seared its way through her blue woolen gown.

If she thought that he had lost his peculiar fascination for her after their night of passion, then his grimly determined expression was enough to bring it to an end.

Struggling to recall how to breathe, Sarah was thankfully distracted as Jimmy bounced on the threadbare cushion.

"Mr. Charlebois was telling us about meeting the king. He shook his hand. Can you believe it?"

Of course she believed it. Why would the king be any more immune to this man's charm than everyone else?

"Astonishing."

Raoul held up a hand. "Before you presume me to be utterly vain, I also told them of the night I was driven from the stage by a barrage of rotten tomatoes."

Willie giggled. "He was hit right in the eye."

"Hmmmm." Sarah's smile became genuine. "Was he?"

"An experience I would prefer not to repeat," Raoul quickly added.

"I shall kccp that in mind."

"Mr. Charlebois says we need some stuff for our charades," Jimmy broke in, unaware of the intimate awareness that stirred in the air. Thank goodness. "Stage stuff . . ."

"Stage settings," Raoul supplied.

"I have begun with the costumes," Sarah said, readily allowing herself to be distracted. "But I confess I know nothing of stage settings."

Raoul lifted a shoulder. "As I recall, you have a number

of old pieces in your workroom. I can choose a few and have them hauled to the orphanage."

"You are welcome to whatever you need, but I warn you, they are bound to be covered in dust and cobwebs." Sarah wrinkled her nose. "It has been years since they have been properly cared for."

With a frown, Raoul caught and held her gaze. "I am not a gentleman of leisure who frets over the perfection of the knot in my cravat, Miss Jefferson. During my years in the theater, I have swept the grime from any number of stages."

Sarah hesitated, sensing he was attempting to reassure her. As if she would ever believe he was no more than a common actor.

"I think your cravat is bang-up," Jimmy proclaimed, his loyalty unfettered by the confusion of emotions that plagued Sarah.

"Thank you, Master Jimmy." Raoul ruffled the boy's hair, his gaze sliding to Sarah. "I can only wish that everyone shared your impeccable taste."

Sarah refused to rise to the bait. "If you boys wish to have your tea, then you must first wash your hands."

Jimmy bounced from the sofa. "Can Mr. Charlebois stay for tea?"

"Mr. Charlebois no doubt has other plans . . ."

"No plans, Miss Jefferson," he smoothly interrupted, rising to his feet. "I would be delighted to share your tea. So long as I do not intrude?"

Her lips thinned, well aware he had effectively maneuvered her into a corner.

"Hurry along, boys."

Vibrantly aware of the man standing at her side, Sarah watched in silence as the two boys tumbled from the room, their laughter echoing through the still air. She was so tense, she nearly leaped from her skin when he stroked a finger down her cheek.

"You do not seem as eager as the boys to have my company." He studied her with a searching gaze. "Are you not pleased to have me here?"

"It is not that."

"Then what is it?"

"This is all new to me," she confessed, her voice unsteady. "I am not certain how I should behave when you are near."

His grim expression eased. "How do you behave with your friends?"

"Friends?"

"I should like to believe that we are friends," he said softly. "Am I wrong?"

She paused before giving a shake of her head. "No."

"Not that I have abandoned my determination to have you as my wife."

"Mr. Charlebois . . ."

He pressed a finger to her lips. "But I am willing to give you time to become accustomed to your future."

She took a hasty step backward, feeling as if his simple touch had branded her skin.

"What of your father? Is that not why you came to Cheshire?"

His expression was brooding as he allowed her to put a bit of much needed distance between them. Not that it did a damnable bit of good. The entire room pulsed with his powerful presence.

"It was, although, I find it increasingly difficult to recall my original purpose."

"Surely you should be concentrating on discovering the truth he has hidden?"

"I am doing what I can." He grimaced. "My father has wrapped his past in so many layers of mystery, I am not certain I can ever unravel the truth."

Sarah frowned, suddenly sensing she was not the only one with conflicted emotions.

"Have you considered the possibility it might be best to leave the past alone?"

"More times than I can count, *ma belle*." A slow smile curved his lips, and without warning he had closed the small space between them to wrap his arms around her waist. "Unfortunately, once I set upon a path, I find it impossible not to see it to the end."

Sarah shivered, pleasure exploding through her body. "The boys . . ."

He buried his face in the curve of her neck, easily discovering that sensitive hollow just below her ear.

"I want to be with you."

She squeezed her eyes shut, resisting the powerful urge to melt against his hard body.

"You know that is impossible."

"The boys revealed they will go to the Vicar's tomorrow. We could spend the entire day together." He trailed a path of kisses down her throat. "Say yes."

Sarah could not deny the temptation that flared through heart. Her logic might whisper that she had taken enough foolish risks, but her body was already stirring with a need increasingly difficult to deny.

"I . . ."

The sound of approaching footsteps brought her back to reality with the force of a bucket of cold water. Giving a low moan, she wrenched herself out of Raoul's arms and took a hasty step backward as the boys rushed into the room.

Blithely unaware of Sarah's tension and Raoul's muttered curse, Willie and Jimmy headed straight for the tray of food.

"Martin promised he will come in the morning to take us to the Vicar's in his cart, and he says I can take the reins if I behave myself," Willie announced, filling his plate with sandwiches.

"Me too, me too," Jimmy piped in.

On the point of moving forward, Sarah came to a breathless halt as she felt Raoul run his fingers down the curve of her spine.

"Tomorrow, Sarah," he whispered.

December 20
Great House

Lord Merriot grimaced as he watched his wife pace the expensive carpet of her bedchamber, a petulant expression marring her once beautiful features.

He had purposely delayed this encounter until he had his belongings packed and the carriage called for. Over the past days, it had been increasingly difficult to meet his wife's bitter gaze, even with his mind fogged by brandy.

Reasonably sober, it was damned near impossible.

Spinning on her heel, she glared at his stoic countenance, her too thin body enveloped in a satin dressing gown that was the precise shade of lavender as the walls. The effect might have been charming if not for the gray pallor of her skin and the hectic glitter in her eyes.

"This is foolishness, Jonah," she accused, her voice shrill. "You cannot leave me here alone."

"Hardly alone. There are two dozen servants in the house."

Her expensive jewels shimmered as she waved her hand in dismissal. "And what do servants matter?"

"You were the one to insist that I do something."

"I never thought that you would abandon me for London."

His temper flared. This ghastly nightmare was as much her fault as his. Perhaps more.

"Listen to me, Mirabelle," he said, more harshly than he intended. "There is only person in this entire world who remembers the truth of Raoul. Once she is . . ." He smoothed a shaking hand down his exquisitely tailored black coat. "Dealt with, there will be no means by which the past can be known."

The faded brown eyes widened. "What do you intend to do, Jonah?"

He turned to hide his expression, unwilling to admit even to himself just what he was willing to do to keep the past hidden.

"I will send her to France," he muttered.

"And what if she refuses to leave?"

"Then I will have her transported, as I did that bloody gardener."

She moaned. "Do not speak of that."

With a growl he turned to glare at his wife. "She will go, and that will be the end of the matter."

"You keep saying that, but it never ends," Mirabella whined, wringing her hands in growing agitation. "Never, never, never."

He stepped forward to grasp her shoulders and give

her a small shake. "Gather your composure, Mirabelle. Or do you want the servants gossiping in the village? Raoul is suspicious enough."

She reached up to shove him away, any love she might have once felt for him now lost in the bitter recriminations.

Yet another price for his sins.

As if the death of Peter was not enough.

"He is more than suspicious, he is dangerous," she hissed. "You said yourself he managed to slip in the manor unhindered. How do you know he will not use your absence to sneak in and cut my throat?"

"If he wanted to harm us, he would have done so already." His jaw tightened with fury. Damn Raoul and his meddling. "Besides, he is too anxious to discover his past to risk putting us in our graves."

"Fine for you to say. You will not be here to . . ."

"Enough," Jonah sharply interrupted. "I have made my decision."

"You do not believe I have suffered enough from your decisions?" she demanded, her arms wrapping around her waist.

Jonah gave a weary shake of his head as he turned for the door. "Say what you will, Mirabelle, we are both in this together."

Leaving his wife sobbing in the middle of the room, Jonah made his way down the long flight of stairs, unable to enjoy the elegant marble that glowed in the morning light, or the exquisite chandelier that he had shipped from Venice near twenty years ago.

How the devil could he enjoy anything? Since Raoul's arrival in Cheshire, he had been plagued with a sense of doom that not even the finest brandy could dull.

Reaching the foyer, he smoothed his expression and regarded the footman with a cold composure.

"Is the carriage waiting?"

"Yes, my lord." The uniformed man opened one of the heavy oak doors.

Jonah shivered at the blast of frigid air. Damn, he hated traveling in the winter.

"I want the staff to remain on guard in my absence," he commanded as he moved forward. "And ensure that the windows and doors are kept locked at all times."

An unmistakable surprise crossed the footman's face before he was giving a hasty dip of his head.

"As you command, my lord."

Jonah grit his teeth, knowing he had no doubt stirred precisely the sort of curiosity he hoped to avoid.

"Lady Merriot is anxious at the thought of being here without me. I promised that the servants would see to her protection."

"Of course."

Dismissing the servant from his mind, Jonah swept through the door and walked down the steps. He had nearly reached the bottom when a man stepped from behind a large stone urn.

"So the great Lord Merriot at last crawls from his lair," the man snarled.

"What the devil . . ." Coming to an abrupt halt, Jonah ran a condemning gaze over the man's ragged clothing. A nasty beggar was his first thought. It was not until his gaze lifted to the filthy countenance that his heart gave a sharp jerk of alarm. Drabble. Standing on his property as bold as brass. Had the entire world gone mad? "Get off my land you nasty bit of rubbish."

"I may be rubbish, but I ain't got blood on me hands."

Drabble cackled, pointing a gnarled finger directly at Jonah's face. "You will pay."

Panic held Jonah paralyzed for a brief moment. Did the man have proof? Could he have spoken with Raoul?

No. Jonah gave a shake of his head. It was impossible. He had covered his tracks too well. This was nothing more than an effort to rattle his nerves.

Squaring his shoulders, he glared down at the pathetic toad. "Do you dare threaten me?"

"I warned you," the man hissed. "I said your evil would come back to haunt you."

"Leave before I have you hauled before the magistrate for poaching."

Drabble ignored the threat, his eyes glittering with a festering hate.

"Do you think I can't see how yer hands shake, or the fear in your eyes?" the man taunted. "Deal with the devil and he will demand his price."

"Shut your mouth. You know nothing."

"I know you as good as killed my brother."

"Your brother was a thief."

The man rasped in a sharp breath, his face flushing at the lie that tumbled so easily from Jonah's lips.

"Never you say that, you bastard. He was a decent and honorable man, and you will rot in the pits of hell for what you did to him."

Jonah felt another surge of alarm, wondering if the man had finally tumbled into insanity. God knew he had never been particularly stable.

"Sawyer," he called, relief scouring through him as the burly footman rushed from the carriage where he was securing the last of the luggage.

"Aye?"

"Get rid of this man."

"At once, sir."

Sawyer attempted to grasp Drabble, only to have the wily man dance out of reach.

"You can toss me from yer land, but you can't be rid of those you hurt. They will never leave you in peace."

His last warning delivered, Drabble turned and darted across the snow, swiftly disappearing into the hedges.

Sawyer muttered a curse. "Do you want me to call for the magistrate, sir?"

"No. I have no time for this nonsense."

Jonah strode angrily toward the carriage, more rattled by the encounter than he wanted to admit. Loose ends. Too many damned loose ends.

He felt as if his entire life were unraveling.

"Very well." The groom rushed to pull open the door of the carriage and let down the steps.

Settling on the soft leather seat and tugging the fur rug over his legs, he regarded his groom with a grim expression.

"Sawyer."

"Yes, my lord?"

"If Drabble returns, I want him shot." Ignoring the servant's shocked expression, he reached to slam shut the door. Then, digging beneath his coat, he pulled out the silver flask that held his brandy, and rapped on the ceiling of the carriage. "Drive on."

Chapter 16

December 21
Cheshire

Sarah was in the kitchen when she heard the front door open and then close.

Removing the apron, she smoothed her hands down the skirt of her pale amber gown and headed for the parlor. She knew precisely who would be waiting for her.

Of course, that did not ease the pounding of her heart as she stepped through the doorway to discover Raoul tossing his hat and caped greatcoat onto a chair.

At her entrance, he slowly turned, his lean muscles rippling beneath his tailored sapphire jacket and black waistcoat embroidered with silver thread.

Heavens, would she ever become accustomed to his golden beauty? Or the shocking power of his smile?

Obviously not, she wryly accepted, feeling her mouth go dry and her knees weaken as he moved forward and pressed her hand to his lips.

"Good morning, *ma belle*," he husked, his brilliant

blue eyes dark with a primal emotion that sent a thrill of excitement down her spine.

"Mr. Charlebois." She reluctantly pulled her hand from his grasp. "This is rather early to call."

"Early?" His lips twisted. "I spent the past three hours awaiting a decent hour. The boys have gone to the Vicar's, have they not?"

There was another tingle at the reminder that they were completely alone in the cottage.

Oh lord, this was dangerous.

"They have, but I have a number of chores . . ."

"Your chores can wait," he interrupted, stepping close enough to wrap her in his male scent.

"Easy enough for you to say."

"Come, Sarah, is there any task so pressing it cannot be delayed a few hours?" he demanded, his fingers toying with a curl that had come loose from her braid to lie against her cheek.

She stepped to the side, moving toward the window in an effort to catch her elusive breath.

"Where is your horse?"

"I left him in the woods." He prowled to stand at her side. "You seem reluctant to allow anyone to know of my frequent visits."

"The area is isolated, but there is always the chance that someone will stumble across Hercules and decide they have need of such a fine animal."

His chuckle brushed over her cheek. "I pity anyone foolish enough to try and steal Hercules. The last man who did so ended up with broken ribs and a number of teeth missing."

"You trained him to attack?"

"I had no need to train him. Hercules is merely fastidious in who he allows to handle him." He deliberately paused. "Much like his master."

She rolled her eyes. "I believe it of Hercules."

He grasped her shoulders to turn her to meet his fierce gaze. "You can be certain of it with me as well, *ma belle*. No hands but yours shall ever touch me again."

An aching need clutched at her heart. For all her determination to be sensible, there was a secret part of her that could not deny a wistful yearning that this man could feel more than guilt.

"Do not be absurd," she breathed.

"What is absurd about a man desiring to be faithful to the woman he has chosen as his wife?"

Once again she pulled away, turning to walk toward the fireplace, desperately needing to hide her expression.

"Please, do not."

"Why?" He moved until he could face her, his brows drawn together in a frown. "Do you not believe me sincere?"

She sighed, knowing he would not be satisfied until he had wrung the truth from her. For all his charm, he could be as stubborn as a mule.

"I believe you too honorable for your own good," she grudgingly muttered.

"Now that is an accusation I have never had thrown at my head before." His voice was tight, as if angered by her words. "Perhaps you should explain."

"You believe it your duty to wed me after . . ."

"After we shared a night of wondrous passion together?" he supplied as her words faltered.

"Yes."

He leaned an elbow on the mantel, his expression unreadable. "As you have repeatedly pointed out, you are not the first woman I have taken to my bed. I felt no compulsion to offer them marriage."

"No doubt they were far more sophisticated than myself."

"Perhaps, but I fail to comprehend what that has to do with my decision not to offer marriage."

She clenched her hands, annoyed by his refusal to simply admit the truth, acutely embarrassed by the entire conversation.

"They are experienced in the ways of men," she muttered. "They would have no expectations."

A golden brow arched. "But you did?"

"No, of course not."

"Then what is your point?"

"You are deliberately attempting to misunderstand me." She glared at his impassive countenance. "You feel compelled to wed me because I was a virgin."

Far from ruffled by her blunt accusation, Raoul merely shrugged. "And do you think I was not aware of your innocence before following you to Chester?"

"I have not the least notion."

"I knew, Sarah." His voice gentled, his gaze holding hers with an unnerving intensity. "And I would never have pursued you if I had not already made the decision that I desired you as my wife."

"You . . ." Flustered, Sarah gave a shake of her head. "You barely even know me."

"I know that you are intelligent and capable and always willing to put others before yourself. I also know that you will be a loving, devoted mother." Moving slowly enough that Sarah could easily avoid the arms that wrapped about her, Raoul pulled her against the welcome heat of his body. "What more could any man want?"

"Mr. Charlebois." She pressed her hands to his chest. "What are you doing?"

He moaned as he lowered his head to brush his lips down her cheek, halting at the edge of her mouth.

"Did I forget to mention that you also make me ache with my need for you?"

A violent shudder shook her body. His lightest touch was enough to scramble her brains and set her on fire.

There was something he said . . . something important . . . but each time she attempted to grasp onto the thought, it was like trying to catch a wisp of fog.

His tongue lightly traced her lips, his hands skimming up and down her back with a growing insistency.

Her breath tangled in her throat, a hum of pleasure vibrating through her.

"Sir, it is broad daylight."

His fingers tugged at the buttons that held her gown together, tugging down the bodice to reveal her corset.

"The better to admire your numerous charms," he growled.

"But anyone could . . ." Her words were cut short as her dress slithered down her body to pool at her feet.

"The door is locked, so unless you have someone hidden beneath the sofa, there is no one to know you are even home," he muttered, his voice unsteady as he yanked at the ties of her corset.

Sarah clung to the lapels of his jacket as her knees threatened to give way. A part of her felt decadent, perhaps even wicked to be indulging in this pastime at such an hour. Another part shivered with an acute longing.

She had spent the past two nights twisting and turning with a restless need that refused to leave her in peace.

And as much as she hated to acknowledge the truth,

it was not just desire that had kept her awake. If it were no more than passion, she might very well be capable of resisting temptation. She had learned after her mother's death how to find happiness in accepting what was possible, not longing for the impossible.

But the night with Raoul had revealed the sweet contentment to be discovered in having a pair of strong arms hold her close as she slept. And the delight of awakening with the knowledge she was not alone.

Those things . . .

They made her arch against the hardness of his body when she should be pushing him away, and to moan softly as he swiftly removed the remainder of her clothing and carried her toward the sofa.

"This is madness," she muttered, tangling her hands in his golden curls.

He kissed her with a stark longing, his ragged breath echoing through the silence of the cottage.

"Then we shall go mad together," he murmured against her lips, wrestling to remove his clothing. At last he managed to bare his chest, reaching to press her hands against his chest. "Touch me, *ma belle. Sacrebleu,* just touch me."

With a gasping moan, Raoul rolled to the side and tucked Sarah against his chest. The sofa was far too small, and the worn fabric scraped against his skin, but he would happily have remained in this precise position for the rest of the day.

Perhaps for the rest of eternity.

He had thought nothing could be so earth-shattering as his first night with Sarah. To at last have her in his bed, her nails digging into his back as he had slid into her welcoming heat had been nothing less than paradise.

But he had to admit that the pleasure that had just exploded through his body left him feeling stunned, and a bit humbled.

This beautiful, magnificent woman had given her body, and just as importantly, her trust to him.

He intended to ensure that she never regretted that decision.

Even if she were too stubborn to acknowledge that fate had bound them together.

Stirring in his arms, Sarah sucked in a shaky breath, clearly as rattled as himself by the shocking force of the passion.

"Good heavens."

"Not good," Raoul corrected softly, his lips stroking the tender skin of her temple. "Extraordinary. *You* are extraordinary."

Unexpectedly, she wriggled from his grasp, sliding off the sofa and hastily pulling on her clothes.

"Hardly extraordinary."

With a sigh at the realization that the intimate interlude was at an end, Raoul rose from the couch, hiding a smile at Sarah's covert glance over his naked body.

He enjoyed her bashfulness, so long as he was never left in doubt of her desire for him.

Gathering his own attire, Raoul pulled on his stockings and breeches as he sent his soon-to-be wife a stern frown.

"You can argue with me on any other matter but this, *ma belle,*" he warned. "You brighten the lives of everyone fortunate enough to cross your path."

With her corset tightened, Sarah pulled on her stockings before yanking the gown over her head.

"Nonsense," she muttered.

Stubborn. With a sigh, Raoul firmly turned Sarah around to button her gown, still attired in nothing more than his breeches.

"Listen to me, Sarah Jefferson, there is no one in this neighborhood who has not been touched by your generosity, whether it is with your healing herbs or a basket of food for those who are in need." Finished with his task, Raoul bent his head to brush a kiss over the silky skin of her nape. "And who else would have taken in two young boys abandoned by their mother?"

"*You* would have," she husked.

With a grimace, he turned her to face him. As much as he desired Sarah's good opinion, he would not pretend to possess her generous heart.

"I wish I could claim to be so selfless," he ruefully admitted.

"You admit you assist with orphanages, and you have plans to open a school," she insisted. "Do you know how many children depend upon such charity?"

"It is one thing to offer money, and quite another to open your heart and your home."

She shrugged. "I told you, they give me joy."

He hesitated, momentarily uncertain. It had all seemed so perfectly reasonable when he had been in Chester. Now he had to wonder if he had made the right decision.

At last he moved to pick up the expensive jacket he had tossed on the floor. Reaching into the inner pocket, he pulled out the folded sheets of parchment before returning to Sarah's side and pressing them into her hand.

"Then I hope you will be pleased with my Christmas present."

She frowned in confusion, glancing down at the papers. "Mr. Charlebois, I cannot accept a gift."

"My name is Raoul, and this is not precisely a gift." He cleared his throat. "Indeed, some would claim it a mixed blessing."

Slowly, almost warily, she unfolded the papers to regard the flourishing script.

"What is this?"

"Legal papers that give you guardianship of Willie and Jimmy."

There was a sharp, disbelieving silence as she shuffled through the papers, her brow furrowed.

"But . . ." Her eyes were dazed as she lifted her head. "It is signed by Polly."

"Yes."

"I do not understand. Where did you get this?"

"I had the papers written by a solicitor in Chester, and then traveled to Wallingford to meet with Mrs. Andrews."

"How did you find her?"

Raoul considered his words. Sarah was shocked enough without allowing her to know that the boy's mother was yet another victim of the gin bottle who was forced to sell her body to make ends meet.

"She was working in the local pub," he carefully skirted the truth.

Perhaps not quite so naïve as Raoul assumed her to be, Sarah snorted in disbelief.

"And she simply agreed to give me guardianship of her children?"

"She has little money and a new babe to care for. She

was grateful to know that the boys had discovered a home where they are loved."

She narrowed her eyes. "I am not a fool. Polly has given no more thought to those boys than she would to a couple of stray dogs. And she would never have willingly signed any papers unless she was offered a considerable reason to do so."

He smoothed a stray curl from her cheek. "You did claim my charm was irresistible."

Proving just how resistible his supposed charm truly was, Sarah waved the papers beneath his nose.

"If Polly thought a man of your means was taking an interest in the boys, she would demand more than charm. For all her silliness, she can be ruthless if she believes there is a quid to be had."

He sighed. Did she have to be so damnably clever?

"Does it truly matter, *ma belle?*"

"I need to know."

He would not deliberately lie. Never to this woman.

"Very well. Mrs. Andrews considered her signature worthy of a few pounds and I did not intend to quibble with her," he conceded.

"How many pounds?"

He framed her face in his hands, his uncertainty fading beneath a surge of determination.

He had done what was right. Not just for Sarah, but for those two boys. Whatever pity he might feel for Polly Andrews could not overcome the absolute knowledge she was no longer capable or even interested in being a mother to Willie and Jimmy.

There was no one on this earth who would love those boys more than Sarah. And certainly no one would give them better care.

"This is what you desire, is it not?" he prompted.

"Yes, but . . ."

"But what?"

She bit her bottom lip. "I do not like the thought that I have purchased the boys as if they are meaningless pieces of property."

He frowned at her ridiculous words. "You have done nothing but rescue two desperate children from the orphanage, or worse. You have given them a home and a future they could never have dreamed possible," he said sternly. "Any negotiations were conducted between myself and Mrs. Andrews."

Her lips thinned. "And that should absolve me of any guilt?"

"Why should there be any guilt?" he asked. "Polly Andrews has no desire to be a mother to those children."

"Still . . ."

"Sarah." He pressed a thumb to her lips, halting her argument. "Willie and Jimmy need you. This is the only means to ensure they cannot be taken from the only security they have ever known."

She was silent a long moment, her gaze searching his face as if seeking an answer to a perplexing puzzle.

"Why would you do this?"

"What do you mean?"

"I know you have become fond of the boys, but why would you go to such an effort to put them in my care?"

He smiled, his fingers lightly tracing the lush line of her lips.

"You are right, I am very fond of Willie and Jimmy, but while I would do everything in my power to keep them safe, my first thought was of you. I saw the fear in your eyes when you spoke of the boys' future. This paper will give you the comfort of knowing they are under your protection."

She trembled, her eyes darkening with an indefinable emotion. "You did this for me."

"I thought it would bring you happiness," he said, simply. "If I was wrong, then you need only say so, and I . . ."

"No, it brings me happiness," she interrupted.

"Then why do you look so troubled?"

She wrinkled her nose. "I am accustomed to being in charge of my life. Now I feel as if I have been caught in a whirlwind, never knowing what is to come next."

"You are not alone in that whirlwind." Unable to resist temptation, he bent his head to brush his mouth over her lips. "I never expected to discover such a woman when I came to Cheshire. You, *ma belle,* are a complication that consumes my every thought. And I do not doubt you will be consuming my thoughts for many years to come."

"A complication?" she charged, her shaky breath revealing a satisfying reaction to his caress.

"A most delightful complication," he murmured, scooping her off her feet to carry her back toward the sofa. The day was early and his need for this woman seemed to have no end. "Shall I prove just how delightful?"

It was a grudging Raoul who was finally shooed from the cottage to climb beside his groom in the waiting carriage.

Sacrebleu, he was too old to be conducting a secret affair, he wryly acknowledged. There might have been a time when a brief rendezvous was thrilling. It offered a few hours of pleasure he could walk away from without guilt.

Now, he wanted nothing more than to stay with Sarah. To curl up in front of the fire with her, and wait for the children to return.

Unfortunately, Sarah remained as wary as an untrained colt, and until he could convince her that his desire to wed her was genuine, he had little choice but to keep the reins light.

His aggravation, however, was swiftly forgotten as he climbed next to Pickens, and the groom revealed the latest village gossip as they barreled down the frozen lane.

"You are certain Lord Merriot left for London?" Raoul growled, his thoughts churning.

Pickens kept his gaze on the road, his big hands remarkably deft with the ribbons.

"That's what he told the servants."

Raoul frowned. What the devil was his father up to?

"Does he suspect that my nurse has been discovered, or is this simply coincidence?"

"Impossible to say, sir."

"Either way, Nico must be warned," Raoul muttered, his gaze skimming restlessly over the snowy countryside. Just because Merriot had claimed to be on his way to London did not mean he was not hidden nearby with a desire to lodge a bullet in his bastard's back. And even if he were gone, that did not mean he had not left behind someone to deal with such a gruesome task. What better opportunity to have Raoul killed than when he was far away? "We cannot risk having my father spiriting Francine away before we can get the information we need."

"Aye, I thought you would want Nico to know," Pickens agreed, his voice as slow and methodical as his movements. "I hired the blacksmith's son to carry a message to London as soon as I heard the rumors. With luck, he should reach Nico before Merriot's carriage ever reaches town. I hope I did right."

"You did exactly right." Raoul gave a sharp shake of his head. While he had been chasing after Sarah like a hound on the scent, his father had slipped away beneath his very nose. "Thank God I have servants who have not taken leave of their senses. I only wish I could the same for their employer."

Chapter 17

December 24
The Cottage

Sarah finished hemming the second of her father's old shirts and laid the voluminous linen garments on the floor to regard them with a critical frown.

The boys would be performing their charades for the orphanage on the morrow. The three short plays were based on famous Christmas stories, and it would be the task of the children in the orphanage to guess which tale the boys were performing.

It was a favorite occasion for all involved that also included sweet treats provided by the women in the village, as well as small Christmas presents.

Well, perhaps not so small this year, she wryly acknowledged. The Vicar had revealed yesterday that a generous donation from Mr. Charlebois ensured that they would be able to purchase new coats and boots for each of the needy children.

As always, the mere thought of Raoul was enough to make her shiver with delight.

Over the past few days, he had been a constant fixture in the cottage. Oh, he had been careful to arrive only when Maggie and the boys were in attendance, to assure that there could be no reason for gossip. And his occasional touches had been so casual that she would have no reason to complain.

It was growingly obvious he was attempting to court her in a proper manner, and while Sarah could not deny that every day he was stealing another piece of her heart, her body was increasingly frustrated.

She wanted—no *needed*—his kisses, the feel of his wicked hands stroking over her skin . . .

Even worse, she could no longer deny the deep yearning to accept his offer of marriage.

What other man would treat her as if she were some precious treasure? Or be willing to go to such effort to put Willie and Jimmy under her protection?

He was everything she could ever desire in a man.

But while her heart urged her to grasp the happiness she never thought possible, her sanity warned caution.

She knew that Raoul desired her. His searing glances and frustrated expression were proof enough. And she was certain that he held affection for her. Why else would he go to such lengths to please her?

Affection and desire, however, were not the same as love.

And of all the men in the world, Raoul Charlebois deserved a marriage that he could enter into with his entire heart. Only then would the wounds of the past truly be healed.

SEDUCE ME BY CHRISTMAS   249

At the sound of rushing footsteps, Sarah swallowed her wistful sigh and smoothed her expression.

Thus far, the boys had taken Raoul's frequent visits with the innocent acceptance that only children could possess. But she was constantly aware that any hint she was troubled, or unhappy, would unsettle the boys. Their sense of peace was still a fragile thing, and she would do nothing to jeopardize that.

Entering the parlor with their faces recently scrubbed of breakfast by Maggie, and their hair combed, they regarded the various piles of clothing scattered about the room.

That warm glow of contentment that had nestled in her heart since Raoul had brought her the papers making her the guardian of the boys flared through her body.

Whatever happened in the future, she could never repay the gift that Raoul had given her.

"These should do for your Magi costumes," she said, pointing to the shirts. Her father had been a large man, and the material would drape the boys from neck to toe in some semblance of robes.

"What about crowns?" Willie at last demanded.

"Hmmm." Sarah considered for a long moment. "I suppose we could make them out of evergreen branches."

Willie wrinkled his nose. "If we were really kings, they would be made of gold."

"With rubies," Jimmy added.

"Aye." Willie nodded. "And diamonds."

"It always seemed to be a silly tradition to me," Sarah said.

"Every king needs a crown," Willie protested.

"A good king tends to his people, not his vanity. Do

you know how many hungry citizens could be fed with those rubies and diamonds? Better an evergreen crown and people with full bellies."

"You should listen to Miss Sarah," a whiskey-smooth voice murmured from behind. "If our leaders possessed even a portion of her good sense, the world would be a finer place for us all."

With squeals of pleasure, the boys raced to Raoul, who casually leaned against the doorframe to the parlor, drawn to his compelling presence like moths to a flame.

She could sympathize, she ruefully acknowledged. It was only years of self-discipline that kept her from streaking across the floor and tossing herself into his arms.

As if sensing her inner conflict, Raoul glanced across the small space, his eyes dark with a raw awareness that sent a blast of heat over her skin.

Reminding herself to breathe, Sarah ran a shaky hand down her pretty cherry and black gown, vainly pleased she had chosen to attire herself in her Sunday best. Not that she could ever hope to compare to his golden beauty, she ruefully acknowledged.

In his black tailored jacket and gold waistcoat, he appeared more fitted for the elegant drawing rooms of London than a simple country cottage.

Reaching his side, Willie jumped up and down until Raoul glanced down at him with an indulgent smile.

"I don't want to be a king," he informed his current hero. "I want to raise horses."

"A fine career," Raoul swiftly approved.

"I should like to be a king," Jimmy said, his expression pensive. "I would do lots of stuff different."

Rather than laughing at the boy's impossible dream, Raoul squatted down until he was eye to eye with Jimmy.

"A wise man can wield power regardless of whether or not he is born into royalty."

"How?"

"First, he must be willing to study and learn as much as possible. Next, he must be determined to work harder than any other." Raoul smiled. "When I first began my acting career, I was willing to take on any role, no matter how small, for an opportunity to be on stage. And I let nothing dissuade me, not even rotten tomatoes, from following my path."

Jimmy tilted his chin. "I can be determined."

"Then I do not doubt you will succeed."

Possessing little interest in ruling the world, Willie grasped his younger brother's arm and dragged him through the doorway.

"Come on, Jimmy, we need to get the evergreen for our crowns."

There was the sound of the boys pulling on their winter garb before the front door was yanked open and then slammed shut.

Sarah winced. She had yet to convince the boys that the door could be shut as easily with a slight tug as with a vigorous bang.

Strolling forward, Raoul cast an amused glance over the various piles of clothing.

"Costumes?"

Her heart fluttered as he neared, her body tingling with a painful awareness. Dear lord, she felt *starved* for his touch.

"They cannot compare to what you are accustomed to, but they should do well enough," she husked.

"I have worn worse, I assure you."

Halting directly before her, Raoul cupped her face

in his hands and took her lips in a sweetly savage kiss. Sarah moaned, her hands reaching up to grasp his shoulders as her body went weak with need.

Oh . . . yes.

This was what she needed. What she craved.

All too soon, Raoul was pulling back, his rasping breath and the color staining his cheekbones the only evidence of his arousal.

Well, perhaps not the *only* evidence.

Delicious flames curled through the pit of her stomach as she felt the unmistakable thrust of his hard erection.

"You have been baking again," he whispered.

"I am making seedcakes for tea."

"Seedcakes." His gaze lingered on her lips, his eyes smoldering with a hunger that had nothing to do with food. "You shall have me as fat as Prinny if I do not have a care. I cannot imagine you would desire your husband to be trussed in a corset and creaking with every step."

"Behave yourself," she muttered, trying to ignore the stark longing that clenched her heart. "Maggie is in the kitchen."

"I have been behaving myself for days," he muttered, his fingers running a restless path down her throat and then boldly over her breasts, cupping them so his thumbs could tease the hardened nipples. "I very much want to misbehave, *ma belle*."

"Oh." She trembled, the need to tug off his clothing and press herself to his male heat nearly overwhelming. Unfortunately, one of them had to be sane. "No, you must halt."

"Must?"

"Yes." Wriggling out of his arms, Sarah shivered as a

cold chill replaced Raoul's welcomed warmth. "Did you have a purpose in calling?"

With a heavy sigh, Raoul scrubbed his hands over his face before regarding her with a rueful expression.

"The simple truth is that I cannot stay away," he admitted, his lips twisting at the blush that touched her cheeks. "But it does so happen that I did have a purpose."

"And that would be?"

"We shall have a need of a few pieces of furniture for tomorrow's performance. Two small chairs, and something large enough for the boys to hide behind to change their costumes."

Sarah frowned. "I had nearly forgotten. We can look now if you desire."

"You know what I desire."

She sucked in a sharp breath, heading toward the foyer. Another moment alone with Raoul Charlebois and she would not be capable of keeping her hands off him.

Good heavens . . . what had happened to her?

By nature, she had always been a happy, contented sort of person. But this giddy, almost dizzying joy whenever Raoul was near was utterly unfamiliar, and more than a little disconcerting.

"Come along." Pausing near the doorway, Sarah gathered her woolen cape and settled it around her shoulders as she led her companion down the short hallway to the kitchen. "I haven't had a fire lit, so it is bound to be chilly."

"The colder the better," he muttered, so low she barely caught the words.

"I beg your pardon?"

"Never mind."

Sensing it was best not to press for an answer, Sarah

crossed through the kitchen, ignoring Maggie's amused gaze as she tugged open the heavy wooden door that led to her long workroom.

"I have most of the furniture here."

Together they bypassed the small space she had claimed for her painting supplies and easel, moving to the very end of the workroom.

Halting in front of the numerous Holland covers that shrouded the various piles of furniture, cast-off ornaments, and tightly rolled carpets, Raoul's expression tightened with that familiar bitterness.

"You said these came from the Great House?"

"Yes, my father brought them here rather than allow the lot to be burned." As he stood rigid, Sarah reached out to tug a few of the covers off the furniture. "Do you have memory of them?"

"A few pieces," he grudgingly admitted, pointing toward a set of satinwood chairs with scrolled legs. "Those were in the foyer."

Sarah bit her lip, hating the shadows that darkened his eyes. "Perhaps it would be better if we ask the Vicar to bring . . ."

He gave a sharp shake of his head, his jaw tight. "No. These will do very well." He glanced toward the opposite corner. "What is hidden over there?"

"Mostly portraits, if I recall properly."

Pacing the short distance, Raoul yanked the sheet aside, revealing over a dozen framed portraits. They both coughed at the cloud of dust that filled the air.

"Odd that my father would wish to burn these. Usually dead ancestors are condemned to the attics, not to the bonfire."

Sarah tugged a handkerchief from her sleeve and

scrubbed at her nose. "Lord Merriot is obviously not a man devoted to the memory of his family."

"Lord Merriot is a man devoted to himself and his own pleasures."

"If that is true, then you are nothing like him."

He stiffened, then slowly turning his head, he met her steady gaze with a wrenching vulnerability.

"I might have been if not for Dunnington," he softly confessed. "He was a gentleman who inspired others to believe that they could accomplish great things, but also to understand that with success comes a duty to others."

She reached out to lay a hand on his arm. "I wish I could have known him."

"He would have adored you. In many ways you are alike."

"Oh." She blinked back a ridiculous urge to cry. "I believe that is the nicest compliment anyone has ever paid me."

With a rueful chuckle, he tucked a stray curl behind her ear. "You are a baffling woman, Miss Sarah Jefferson."

"No more baffling than you, Mr. Charlebois."

"Then we would seem to be a perfect match."

It felt perfect. Splendid and terrifying and utterly perfect.

"Perhaps," she whispered.

As if able to sense a weakening in her resolve, Raoul narrowed his gaze.

"Sarah . . ."

"You should have the portraits removed to your town house," she nervously interrupted, not yet prepared for the question hovering on his lips. "From what I recall, most of them were of indifferent quality, but there were one or two that appeared to be worthy of keeping."

Frustration glittered in his eyes, but with obvious effort, he returned his attention to the paintings.

"I have no more interest in the past Merriots than my father. Still, a few of the larger ones might be used as wings."

She frowned in puzzlement as he began shifting aside the small canvases to reach those hidden in the back.

"Wings?"

"To mark the sides of the stage," he explained, seemingly indifferent to the dust marring his beautiful jacket. "We can prop them against a chair, and the boys could change behind them."

"Ah." She stepped forward to assist him in shifting aside some of the smaller paintings. "There are a few at the back that should be tall enough to serve your purpose."

Raoul paused to study one of the portraits, grimacing at the forbidding gentleman who glared from the canvas.

"*Mon Dieu,* they were a motley crew."

"They do seem to be particularly miserable," Sarah agreed. "I remember playing here as a child and wondering why they were forever scowling at me. Although . . ."

He glanced at her with raised brows. "What?"

"Nothing." She gave a perturbed shake of her head. "I just have the strangest feeling there is something I should remember. Unfortunately, each time I try to call it to mind, it slips away."

His lips twitched. "No doubt a symptom of your advancing years."

"Advancing years?"

He ignored the dangerous edge in her voice. "Well,

ma belle, it does happen to all of us. Which is why you really should consider wedding without delay."

"I see." She fought back her smile. "And do you have anyone particular in mind I should consider wedding?"

"Obviously you have need of a gentleman who appreciates your young boys, and has a love for gingerbread."

"Truly? And I always assumed I desired a kind, modest sort of man. Perhaps a local farmer or merchant."

He snorted in disgust. "You would be bored to tears within a month. You are a woman who needs a challenge. Why else would you have taken in two high-spirited lads?"

She could not fault his logic. Although her life had been quite busy with her artwork and tending to her neighbors, she had still felt an emptiness. She had needed a purpose.

That did not mean, however, she was willing to leap blindly into danger.

"There are some challenges more risky than others," she muttered, grimly returning her attention to setting aside the small portraits to reach those in back.

"And some are worth the risk," he said, his hand cupping her cheek. "Sarah . . ." His words faltered as she abruptly stiffened in shock. "What is it?"

"That." She pointed at the portrait she had just uncovered, her mouth dry and her heart refusing to beat. "Oh, my God."

Grudgingly turning his head, Raoul cast an indifferent glance over the exposed canvas, clearly unimpressed by the painting of the pretty honey-haired woman holding a baby in her arms and the elegant gentleman standing at her side, gazing at the child with obvious devotion.

At least he was unimpressed until he caught sight of the gentleman's familiar countenance.

"*Mon Dieu,*" he breathed.

Instinctively, Sarah reached to touch his arm, not surprised to discover his muscles as hard as granite beneath her fingers.

Who wouldn't be shocked?

Raoul might have posed for the picture himself, if not for the clothing that revealed it had been done some years ago. And of course, the large French chateau that was prominently displayed in the background.

"I knew you reminded me of someone, but I could not recall why," she at last managed to say.

"You have known me since you were a child," Raoul rasped. "Of course you remembered me."

"I was very young when you left for London, and I rarely caught sight of you on the few occasions that you did return." She shivered as an inexplicable chill trickled down her spine. "This is why you are so familiar. It is astonishing." She turned her head, her stomach twisting with fear at Raoul's alarming pallor. "Mr. Charlebois?"

There was a long, brittle silence. Then, with a shake of his head, Raoul appeared to come out of his trance.

"Who are they?" he demanded, his voice thick with emotion.

"Wait." Leaning down, Sarah brushed the dirt off the small plaque at the bottom of the frame. "The Comte and Comtesse de Suriant," she read aloud. "They must be relatives of your father. Do you know of them?"

"No, and I am certain they are not related to the Merriots."

She frowned, glancing from Raoul's beautiful countenance to the man in the portrait.

"They must be. The resemblance is uncanny."

"My father rarely spoke of his family except to condemn them as prolific wastrels, a charge that possesses a great deal of merit according to most," he said. "But as a youth, I spent many rainy afternoons hiding in the library where the family Bible was left to gather dust. My recollections might be vague, but I assure you I would have recalled mention of French nobility."

Sarah felt a pang of sadness, easily able to imagine a young Raoul sitting alone in a vast library, unloved and unwanted.

"Perhaps there was some sort of falling out, and this Comte was disowned," she suggested softly.

Raoul snorted. "It would not matter if he cavorted with the devil, my father is too great a preening peacock to ever deny a relationship with members of the aristocracy." His voice was low, but there was no mistaking the edge of bitterness. "Besides, unlike many English families, the Merriots have no claim to any foreign nobility."

Sarah chewed her bottom lip, trying to sort through the various possibilities. A task that would be a great deal easier if her brain was not refusing to cooperate.

"Then they must be related to your mother."

"Yes."

"Your family."

His expression tightened. "A family who sent me to England and promptly forgot I existed."

"You do not know that for certain," Sarah protested, wanting more than anything to ease this man's pain. "Just consider the turmoil in France thirty years ago. They might have sent you away to keep you safe."

"They have had a great deal of time since the bloody

revolution to contact me," he gritted, his jaw clenched. "I am not, after all, entirely unknown in France."

She bit back the obvious explanation that they had not survived the revolt. Surely fate could not be so cruel as to offer him the hope of a family, only to steal it away?

"You at least have a name to assist in your investigation."

"True. There has to be someone who can tell me what happened to them."

"Yes, there does." She squared her shoulders, ignoring the crippling pain that wrenched her heart. "But so long as your father refuses to speak, you must find your answers elsewhere."

"Sarah . . ." Abruptly turning, he grasped her face in his hands. "I do not want to leave you. Come with me."

She wanted to. Dear heavens, she wanted to be with Raoul more than she had ever wanted anything in her life.

"You know I cannot," she husked.

Even in the shadows, his eyes shimmered with the rare beauty of sapphires.

"We could take the boys," he urged. "They would love London, or even Paris if I am forced to seek information there."

"Mr. Charlebois, even you must comprehend the scandal such a journey would cause."

"Not if you were my wife."

Chapter 18

Sarah closed her eyes, battling against the wave of longing that threatened to overcome her common sense.

It would be so easy to say yes.

She loved him. Perhaps even more important, she *liked* him.

He was intelligent, thoughtful, amusing, and capable of great kindness to others. And of course, she desired him with a desperation that was downright embarrassing.

Unfortunately, the past few moments had only hardened her determination.

Until Raoul had healed his wounds, he would be incapable of offering his heart.

To anyone.

"You are not thinking clearly . . ."

"I have never been more clear in my life," he interrupted, his fingers tracing lightly over her face. "Sarah, whatever truth I might discover in my past is meaningless if I do not have a future." He lowered his head to brush her lips in an achingly gentle kiss. "*You* are that future."

She trembled, savoring his touch. "If I am your future,

then there is no need for a hasty marriage. We have all the time in the world."

His lips thinned before he was heaving a rueful sigh. "I suppose this is only justice."

"What is?"

He slid his arms around her, leaning his cheek on the top of her head.

"I was the one to lecture Ian on patience when Mercy refused to elope with him. Now I know precisely how he felt."

Unable to resist, Sarah snuggled closer, breathing deeply of his enticing scent.

"And did they eventually wed?"

"Yes, but it did not make the wait any easier."

She smiled, amused in spite of herself at his peeved tone. He was not a gentleman who was often denied what he desired.

"This is not a decision to be made lightly." Her smile faded as she considered a future that suddenly seemed far too uncertain. "By either of us."

"My decision has already been made, *ma belle.*" His arms tightened until she had to struggle to breathe. "You will be my wife."

"Then go wherever it is you have to go to discover your past, and then return," she urged, proud that her voice was nearly steady. "The boys and I will be here."

Pulling back, Raoul regarded her with a searching gaze. "You promise?"

"Promise what?"

"That you will be here."

A wistful smile touched her lips, her hand lifting to touch his beautiful face.

"We are not going anywhere, Mr. Charlebois," she whispered.

With a tormented groan, he swooped down to capture her lips in a desperate kiss she felt all the way to her toes.

"I swear I will come back to you," he muttered against her lips.

"I will be waiting."

With a last, passionate kiss, Raoul was pulling away and gathering the large portrait, awkwardly hauling it to the side door that led directly to the back garden.

Blinking back the threatening tears, Sarah turned to make her way back into the cottage. She would not watch him climb into the waiting carriage and drive away. Not when she might toss sanity to the wind, and chase after him like a madwoman.

She crossed through the kitchen, ignoring Maggie's curious gaze as she paused in the hallway to hang up her cloak and give herself a moment to gather her composure.

Only when she was certain that she had battled back her tears and smoothed her expression did she enter the parlor where the boys were sitting beside a pile of evergreen branches.

"Where is Mr. Charlebois?" Willie demanded, looking beyond her shoulder as if expecting Raoul to magically appear. "I want him to help us make the crowns."

Conjuring a smile, Sarah moved to kneel next to Jimmy. The sensitive boys were bound to be disappointed by Raoul's abrupt departure, but she was determined it would not ruin their Christmas.

"I am afraid he had to leave."

Jimmy wrinkled his brow. "But he just got here."

"Yes, he was called away unexpectedly."

Always keenly perceptive, Willie studied her with an unwavering gaze.

"Called away by who? There isn't anyone here but us."

"His business is his own, Willie," she reminded him gently. "And we should respect his privacy."

"He'll be back won't he?" Jimmy demanded. "He promised to help with the charades."

She reached to ruffle his hair. "And he has helped. Indeed, he has ensured your performances will be far better than they would have been otherwise. Now he has other duties that demand his attention."

Jimmy's bottom lip trembled. "But I wanted him to be there."

"He would be, my dear, if it were at all possible. He has become very fond of the both of you."

Willie heaved a disappointed sigh. "It won't be the same without him."

"Of course it will," she promised, her tone bracing. "We must remember we are performing for the children at the orphanage, and they are all very excited. Do you think Mr. Charlebois would ever disappoint his audience?"

"No," Willie grudgingly agreed.

"Jimmy?" she prompted.

There was a pause before he bravely tilted his chin. "No."

"Good." She offered an encouraging smile. "Then we will do our very best and when you are done, we will go to the Vicar's house for dinner and then we shall all go caroling. It will be a lovely evening."

"Aye," Willie agreed, although he could not entirely hide his disappointment.

Searching her mind for a means of reassuring the boys, Sarah was distracted as Maggie entered the room.

"What are these gloomy faces?" the maid demanded, her hands on her ample hips.

"Mr. Charlebois had to leave," Jimmy said in a small voice.

"Did he now?" A hint of a smile touched Maggie's mouth. "Well, perhaps he would not mind if I told you his secret."

As one, the two boys were on their feet.

"What secret?" Willie demanded.

"When he first arrived this morning, he popped into the kitchen for a chat, and while he was there he hinted there might be Christmas presents hidden in the back garden."

"Presents?" Jimmy breathed.

"For us?" Willie demanded.

Maggie nodded. "I believe so."

Willie turned his excited gaze to Sarah. "Can we go look for them, Miss Sarah?"

Jimmy bounced up and down, barely capable of containing his anticipation.

"Yes, please."

"Only if you put on your coat and boots. And do not forget your mittens," she warned, knowing the boys were quite capable of charging outside without any thought to the cold.

Presents of any sort were a rare treat.

With a noisy whoop, they raced from the room, tugging on the outer attire they had so recently shed. Then arm in arm, they dashed down the hallway.

Following at a much slower pace, Sarah frowned, attempting to sort through her feelings.

There was the expected bittersweet pain at the thought

of Raoul. And a warm pleasure at his thoughtful gesture. But there was also . . . uncertainty.

Why would he have brought the presents the day before Christmas?

Entering the kitchen, Sarah moved directly to the window that overlooked the back garden, her brow still furrowed as she watched the boys dash through the snow.

"I hope you do not disapprove?" Maggie asked, moving to stand beside her. "It seemed as if the boys could use a treat."

"They could, indeed," Sarah murmured. "I am just surprised."

"That Mr. Charlebois would have bought Christmas presents for the boys?"

"No, he is a very generous gentleman, especially towards children. But . . ."

"Aye?"

She kept her gaze trained on the boys, hoping to keep her expression hidden from the overly curious maid.

"His decision to leave Cheshire was quite abrupt, or so I thought," she said, her voice a shade too casual. "Why would he bring the gifts today?"

Maggie chuckled. "He said something of young boys being overly eager on Christmas morn, and that while he was quite fond of them, he refused to rise at some ungodly hour to play Father Christmas. He did ask that I tell you that he had hidden them. I also have a gift that he helped the boys to purchase for you, but I am under strict orders not to reveal it to you before the boys have the opportunity to hide it in your stocking."

She released the breath she did not even realize she was holding. Good lord, she was a fool.

Or perhaps she was merely like any other young

woman who had suddenly tumbled into love, she wryly conceded.

Giddy. Confused. And terrified that it was all a dream that could not possibly be real.

"I see."

Maggie cleared her throat. "He left rather abruptly, did he not?"

"He recalled business he needed to attend to."

"Did his business include a portrait from the Great House?"

Turning, Sarah met Maggie's gaze with a somber expression. Lord Merriot had already proven he was a danger. Sarah would do nothing to alert him to Raoul's discovery.

"For now it is best no one know those portraits were ever in the workroom, Maggie."

Maggie gave a wise nod of her head. "Like that, is it?"

Sarah snorted, unable to imagine what the woman was implying. "I am not entirely certain what it is."

"Is he coming back?"

She gave a slow shake of her head, returning her attention to the boys as they discovered the two wooden sleds that had been hidden among the hedge. A sad smile curved her mouth as their shouts of joy echoed through the frozen air.

"I do not know," she whispered. "I truly do not know."

December 25
London

Raoul was cold and weary as he pulled his carriage to a halt in front of the London town house.

He had purchased the mansion on Hertford Street a dozen years ago, and devoted a near fortune to having it enlarged and remodeled. There was little to be done with the exterior that was styled with a plain stonework and Doric porch, but within the house, the once cramped and dark rooms had been combined to form state rooms lined with lavish gold-veined marble and gilt, as well as long galleries with Grecian columns and arched windows that overlooked the formal gardens.

Raoul had never given a tinker's damn about the elegant French furnishings or the works of art his secretary had chosen. For him, no amount of renovations could make the house seem any less empty.

Tonight, however, as he climbed the shallow steps and watched the front door being pulled open, he was suddenly fiercely pleased that he had such a fine home to offer Sarah. Her dark, exotic beauty would be perfectly framed by the stark, classical style.

Stepping into the vaulted foyer with a domed ceiling and shallow alcoves that held Grecian statues, he turned his attention to the short, nearly bald butler with a gaunt face and the dignified expression expected of a London servant.

He was also fiercely loyal, and embarrassingly protective of his master.

"Welcome home, sir, and a Happy Christmas to you," the servant murmured with a stiff bow. "I fear we were not expecting you for another day or so. Still I am certain that Cook can . . ."

"You were expecting me?" Raoul demanded in surprise. For all of Burke's skill, he had never before displayed a talent for clairvoyance.

The older man sniffed. "That valet of yours said he

sent a message demanding your return to London. Gets above himself, that one. What right does he have to order about his master?"

Raoul ignored the outburst. Burke had always been bitterly jealous of Nico's close relationship with Raoul. Instead, he concentrated on the realization that Nico must have discovered something. He would never have sent word without reason.

"Where is he?"

"Do you think he would bother to tell me?" Burke said tartly. "He left a message for you in the library."

Raoul swallowed a weary sigh, sensing that his hope for a warm brandy before the fire was about to be delayed.

"Come with me," he commanded, bypassing the stairs to head toward the back of the house.

He entered the library and crossed the Oriental carpet to the massive oak desk that was set beside a long bank of windows overlooking the back garden.

Unlike the majority of the house, this room had been personally overseen by Raoul, who had commanded the walls be lined with sturdy shelves to hold his ever growing collection of books. He had also hired an unknown artist, one who had begun his career creating scenery for the theater, to paint the ceiling with toga-clad actors on a Roman stage.

It was the one room where he felt utterly comfortable.

Easily finding the folded scrap of parchment, Raoul snatched it from the desk and smoothed it to read the brief message:

Meet me at Shakespeare's Boudoir. I have your Christmas present waiting.

Raoul's lips twitched. Clearly Nico feared the message would fall into the wrong hands, and had written it in a code that only Raoul could decipher.

Well, at least partially decipher.

He knew that Shakespeare's Boudoir was a small hotel just off Drury Lane that was actually called the Swan's Nest, although it was used so often by actresses entertaining their noble patrons, it had gained a less respectable nickname among the theater community.

As for his Christmas present . . .

Well, he could only hope that it had something to do with the mystery that was his past.

Accepting that his brandy was indeed going to have to be postponed, Raoul turned toward the hovering butler.

"There is a painting in my carriage that I wish to have taken to my private chambers."

"Of course, sir."

"I also wish two armed footmen to keep a constant guard on Lord Merriot's town house. Tell them to be discreet, but I want to know his every movement, and if he has any visitors."

Burke lifted his brows in surprise, but was wise enough to keep his questions to himself. "Did you wish them to begin their duties tonight?"

"Is that a problem?"

"Well, it is Christmas," the servant explained in apologetic tones. "Most of the staff have been given the day to spend with their family. There is only myself, Cook, and a groom here."

Raoul experienced a flare of frustration, swiftly followed by a stab of regret.

Dammit, he wanted to be in Sarah's small cottage, watching the boys play with the sleds he had been so eager to give them. He wanted to be sipping warm cider, and roasting chestnuts, and making plans for a swift wedding.

"Of course." With an effort, Raoul turned his thoughts to his more immediate problem. Sarah had promised to wait for him. He could do nothing but trust her word. "Send word to Pickens's family," he at last commanded. He had left his servant in Cheshire to keep watch on Sarah and her brood, but the majority of his groom's family resided in the seamier part of London. "He has a half dozen brothers who are always desperate for extra coin. Tell them I'm willing to pay each a pound for their efforts."

Burke pinched his lips, as jealous of Pickens as he was of Nico.

"Rather generous."

Raoul shrugged. "I am willing to pay for loyalty, as you know Burke."

"Indeed, sir."

"Have a horse brought from the stables."

"At once."

Returning to the foyer, Raoul was forced to wait only a few moments for the one under-groom on duty to bring around a spirited stallion.

He vaulted into the saddle and offered the lad a coin before urging his horse to a brisk pace.

The day had been chilly, but with the setting sun, the air had become downright frigid. Of course, the inhospitable weather, combined with the promise of Christmas dinner, ensured the streets were all but empty, allowing Raoul to swiftly cross town with no fear of being recognized.

Reaching the small, whitewashed hotel, Raoul rode directly to the back stables, leaving his horse in the capable hands of the groom before entering the establishment through the back door.

With remarkable speed, a gentleman with distinguished gray hair in a modest black coat and gray breeches appeared from a side office, his eyes widening with shock as he offered a deep bow.

"Mr. Charlebois, this is an honor. A great honor," he murmured.

"I believe Mr. Dravali is expecting me."

"Yes, of course." The man motioned toward the front lobby. "I will take you to him."

Raoul gave a shake of his head. "I would prefer my presence not attract notice."

"Ah, of course. This way." Leading Raoul to the servants' staircase, he glanced over his shoulder. "Without modesty, I may say that I am well-known for my discretion, sir. You can depend upon me."

Raoul did. It was not just the proximity of the hotel to the theater district that made it a favorite among the nobles and politicians.

Reaching the third-floor landing, the man moved down a short hallway. "This way." He halted at a door, turning to regard Raoul with a hopeful smile. "Shall I have tea sent up? Or perhaps you prefer brandy?"

"No." Raoul's tone made it obvious he did not want to be interrupted. "That will be all, thank you."

"A pleasure, sir."

With another bow, the man turned to leave Raoul alone in the hallway, and lifting his hand he rapped on the door.

"Nico?" he called softly.

There was the muffled sound of footsteps. "Charlebois?"

"Yes, open the door."

He heard the scrape of the bolt being drawn, then the door was tugged open to reveal a decidedly tousled Nico.

"How the devil did you return so swiftly?" his servant demanded.

Stepping into the room, Raoul shut the door behind him and studied his companion. Nico always appeared disreputable, but with his linen shirt loose and wrinkled, and his jaw unshaven, he looked as if he had spent the past few days in the gutter.

"Well I did not sprout wings and fly," Raoul assured him.

Nico snorted. "So much for the legend that Raoul Charlebois is an angel come to earth."

"More likely I was spit from hell."

Nico ran his fingers through his tangled hair. "You still have not told me how you came to be in London."

"I will explain later." Raoul turned his attention to the small parlor of the suite. It was a refreshingly plain room with sturdy English furnishings and applewood paneling. Clearly the Swan's Nest understood that most gentlemen detested the cheap opulence attempted by so many dens of iniquity. "You said in the message you left at the town house that you had a Christmas present for me?"

"Aye, and I intend to see that you pay dearly for the suffering I have endured over the past two days." Nico narrowed his eyes. "Can you imagine being trapped in this suite with an outraged French woman?"

Raoul sucked in a sharp breath. "You have Francine here?"

"I had no choice," his servant growled. "When I arrived in London, I discovered she was making plans to leave England. It seemed best to convince her to remain."

"By kidnapping the poor woman?"

"Poor woman? I still have the bruises from where she beat me with a parasol."

Raoul's lips quirked. It was little wonder his valet was looking so harassed. Nico preferred to deal with his problems with a knife, not charm.

"Did she say why she was leaving?"

Moving toward a low walnut table set between two wing chairs, Nico grasped a silver flask and returned to Raoul. Taking a sip, he handed it off to Raoul.

"She was suspicious of Fredrick's questions," he said. "She harbors a belief that her life is in danger."

Raoul took a thankful drink of the brandy, hoping it would ease the chill that had seeped to his bones.

"My father?"

"It must be." Nico met his gaze steadily. "I had to lug her here kicking and screaming, but when I received word from you that Lord Merriot was on his way to London, she abruptly decided she was quite satisfied to remain hidden in these rooms."

Raoul nodded, gratified that Nico had the sense to hide Francine before his father could get his revolting hands on her.

"Does she know that you work for me?"

Nico's expression hardened. "I tried to assure her, but she claimed she would not believe me until she laid eyes on you."

Raoul chuckled. "You should not look like a cut-throat."

"I *am* a cutthroat."

"True enough. Can I assume she refused to admit she was my nurse?"

"The nasty old bat has done nothing but hurl French insults at me."

"Does she know you speak French?"

An evil glint entered Nico's dark eyes. "Not yet."

"Do not be too hard on her, *mon ami*," Raoul urged. "She must be frightened out of her wits."

Before Nico could respond, the sound of a door opening had both men turning to watch as a short, decidedly round woman with a puff of silver-streaked brown hair and hazel eyes stepped from the attached bedchamber and into the parlor.

Raoul discovered he was holding his breath as he studied the round face that was faintly wrinkled, and the eyes that held a gleam of wary intelligence.

It would be a lie to say that he recognized her, but there was a stir of familiarity that was more a feeling than logical conclusion.

Taking a timid step forward, the woman smoothed her hands down the satin of her elegant green gown.

"Raoul," she said softly, the thick French accent abruptly bringing Raoul back to the soft lullabies sung in his ear as he fell asleep. "Is it truly you?"

Chapter 19

Struggling to find his breath, Raoul moved forward, careful to do nothing that might frighten the woman.

"Francine? You were my nurse?"

"*Oui.*" She pressed her hands to her ample bosom. "My beautiful boy. How I've longed to speak with you."

Raoul gave a shake of his head, his numbing shock being replaced by the stark realization that this woman had been in London for all these years without once approaching him.

Mon Dieu. She must have known he would want to visit with her, if only to learn more of his mysterious mother.

"Your longing could not have been too overwhelming, considering that I have been living in London for years," he said, unable to disguise the hint of bitterness in his voice. "You had only to walk a few blocks to speak with me."

A hint of genuine sorrow darkened her eyes. "You cannot conceive how difficult it has been for me. I used to go to your every performance, and even stood before your home on more occasions than I wish to recall." Her voice broke as she battled back her tears. "But I was too frightened to approach."

His anger faded as swiftly as it had risen, replaced by a pained sense of confusion.

"Frightened of me?"

"Never you," she breathed. "You will always be my sweet Raoul."

"Then why?"

Francine paused, her eyes darting toward the door as if fearful that someone was about to barge in.

Nico had been right. The poor woman was terrified.

"Lord Merriot," she at last whispered. "I could not risk him discovering that I revealed myself to you."

"Why would my father be concerned whether or not my nurse speaks with me?"

Some indefinable expression rippled over her face before she nodded her head toward the sofa.

"Perhaps we should sit down."

Raoul wrestled with his surge of impatience. Francine was obviously wary enough. The last thing he desired was pressing her to the point that she refused to reveal what she knew of his past.

"If you wish."

Taking her arm, he gently led her toward the sofa, ensuring she was comfortably settled before taking a seat beside her.

The forgotten Nico moved across the room to tug open the door leading to the hotel corridor.

"I will leave the two of you to speak alone."

Raoul nodded, sympathetic to his valet's need for fresh air. Nico, a man of the streets, was never happy when he was confined for any length of time.

Waiting until Nico had exited the room and closed

the door, Raoul returned his attention to the woman at his side, rather unnerved to find her regarding him with evident adoration.

"Do you remember me at all?" she demanded softly.

"Only your voice a little," he confessed. "I am sorry."

She waved her hands in a Gallic gesture. "*C'est bien,* it was a long time ago."

"You came with me from France?"

"*Oui.* You were just a baby and already so beautiful. It broke your mother's heart to put you in my arms."

Raoul's heart squeezed with pain. No young boy should ever be without his mother.

"So . . . you knew her?"

"Since she was very young." A wistful expression touched her countenance. "My mother was a chambermaid for the family, and never have I encountered such a lovely, more sweet-tempered woman. You have her smile."

"Her name." Raoul licked his dry lips. "What was her name?"

"Miranda, the Comtesse de Suriant."

It took a moment for him to realize why the name was so familiar.

"Comtesse?" He gave a shake of his head. "That makes no sense. I have seen her portrait."

Francine widened her eyes with surprise. "Ah, then it was not destroyed?"

"No, but I look nothing like the woman in the painting."

"As I said, you have her smile, but it is true you greatly resemble your father."

He held up a hand, his thoughts in turmoil. "Lord Merriot . . ."

"Lord Merriot. That pig." The woman made a sound of disgust. "That he claimed to be your father makes me ill."

Raoul sucked in a sharp breath. "Claimed?"

"*Mon enfant,* you are the son of the Comte and Comtesse de Suriant."

Surging to his feet, Raoul gazed down at the woman with a bewildered sense of disbelief.

"No," he rasped.

"*Oui,* Raoul. You are their only child and heir." She tilted her chin. "Which now makes you the Comte de Suriant."

He shook his head even as the memory of the portrait flared with agonizing clarity through his mind.

The mother and father gazing with such love at the small child in the woman's arms. Those parents would not have tossed aside their baby as if it were no more than a bit of rubbish.

Not for any reason.

"That is not possible," he gritted. "You have made a mistake."

She shook her head, her expression one of absolute certainty. "I assure you, *mon enfant,* there is no mistake. Even if I had not been present when you were born, I would know you were Hugo's son. As you have seen from the portrait, you are so much like him, it makes my heart ache to look at you."

Raoul shoved his fingers through his hair, pacing toward the fireplace.

"This is insanity."

"I know this must be difficult to accept."

"Not difficult, bloody impossible," he corrected, his voice harsh as he was forced to consider the realization that his entire life was a lie. "French aristocrats do not abandon their only heir to an Englishman so he can claim him as his bastard. It is absurd."

He heard her soft gasp. "They never abandoned you."

Spinning around, he met her reproachful gaze. "They deliberately condemned me to hell."

"No, Raoul, they adored you. Which is why they would do anything to protect you."

His harsh laugh echoed eerily through the room. "And they have done such a fine job of it, have they not?"

"Please listen to me."

"Why should I?" he demanded. "You are speaking nothing but gibberish."

Without warning, her mouth thinned and she stabbed a finger in his direction.

"You are being childish, Raoul," she snapped. "Sit down and I will explain."

Caught off guard by the sharp command, Raoul discovered himself moving to perch on the edge of the sofa, his expression wry.

"You at least have the manner of a nurse."

She reached to lightly pat his cheek. "I have loved and cared for you since you entered this world, but I will not allow you to insult your parents. They gave their lives to keep you safe."

Raoul flinched, feeling as if he had taken a blow.

The earth was shifting beneath his feet.

The man who he had always thought to be his father was suddenly not. His mother had not willingly discarded him. And far from being a bastard, he was a supposed heir to a French title.

Abruptly, however, nothing mattered except the icy fear that it was all too late.

"Their lives?" He was forced to halt and clear his throat. "Then they are dead?"

A vast sadness darkened the hazel eyes. "They were taken by the guillotine."

"*Sacrebleu.*" He reached to take one of her hands, as much to seek comfort as to offer it. "Tell me what happened."

She gave a tiny shake of her head. "It is difficult, *mon enfant.* Only those who lived through the revolution could understand the constant terror and uncertainty we endured." Her eyes grew distant, a shiver shaking her body. "You woke in the morning never knowing if this was the day the mob would arrive at the door and carry you to the Tribunal. Neighbors turned against neighbor, willing to offer any lie, with the hopes of keeping their heads. Even family members were willing to betray one another." She clutched his hand as if it were the only thing that kept her anchored to the present. "Such dark times."

Raoul grimaced, suddenly feeling ashamed by the bitterness that had plagued his life. He had grown up alone and unloved until he had been placed in Dunnington's care, but it could not compare to the tragedy of his parents.

"I am sorry for making you recall such a painful time," he said, squeezing her fingers.

"You do not make me recall," the woman denied, her hazel eyes haunted. "I never forget. Not ever. We all suffered, your parents most of all."

His parents. It still was difficult to accept.

"Why?"

"They were well-known to be fully committed to the king. It was even hinted that they were involved in plotting to assist the Royal Family from France."

"That could not have been popular among the *Montagnards*."

"It was only the devotion of the local villagers, and of course your parents' tenants and servants, that held the wolves at bay. Even then, the Comté and Comtesse realized it was only a matter of time."

"Why did they not leave France?"

"By the time the full danger was known, it was too late." Francine heaved a deep sigh. "The estate was constantly being watched, and any effort to slip away would have given Robespierre the excuse he desired to have them executed."

Aching regret pierced his heart.

Not regret for having been denied his life as a legitimate aristocrat, or even for the grand inheritance that no doubt might have been his.

No, it was the regret of a young boy who had never been allowed to know his family.

"They were trapped," he rasped.

"*Oui,* but they never lost hope that they could save you."

He fought back the childish urge to cry. "How did they accomplish it? It could not have been easy."

"Actually, it was remarkably simple in the end," the nurse corrected. "Your parents let it be known they were traveling to Paris to visit your mother's family who were already imprisoned, and after the usual fuss, a dozen carriages that included your parents and most of the servants left the estate. They took with them the *armées révolutionnaires* who were keeping watch on the house."

It took a long moment before Raoul realized what must have occurred.

"They left me behind."

Francine nodded. "*Oui.* Your mother carried the child of a tenant in her arms so no one would suspect, and left you in my care. They also left behind as much money as they could gather, along with the family jewels and a few of the most precious works of art."

Raoul's eyes widened, a sharp fury flooding through his body.

The money, the jewels, the works of art . . .

Lord Merriot's mysterious inheritance.

"*Mon Dieu,* that bastard," he gritted, his eyes narrowing as he imagined the pleasure of choking the life from the man. Obviously it was not enough to make Raoul's existence a misery, he had stolen his inheritance as well. Belatedly recalling the woman at his side, Raoul gave a rueful shake of his head. "Forgive me, Francine. Please, continue with your story."

"There is not much more to tell." She shrugged. "A handful of servants and I waited a few days to make certain we were not being spied upon, and then we loaded a cart with what we could, and covered it with hay before heading for the coast. Your father had already arranged to have an English boat waiting for us south of Calais."

Raoul was not fooled for a moment by her dismissive tone. Although he had never endured the terrors of a revolution, he could easily imagine the fear of a young woman who was not only forced to brave certain death if she was caught, but also obliged to leave her family and all she knew behind so she could flee to England to save a child that was not her own.

He quite literally owed her his life.

"You were extraordinarily brave," he said, his voice thick with emotion.

A flustered blush touched her round cheeks. "Not brave. I assure you that I was terrified the entire journey."

"And yet you continued on," he pointed out gently. "That is the true measure of courage."

She shook her head, her expression profoundly sad. "No, in the end, I failed. My courage was not enough when Lord Merriot demanded I leave you."

"I understand your flight to England, but why did you take me to Merriots?" Raoul demanded, careful to keep any hint of recrimination from his voice.

"Your parents feared that even if I managed to escape with you, there would still be those who would hunt you down and attempt to kill you. They could not send you to family or those friends that might be known by the revolutionaries."

"Understandable, I suppose, but that does not explain why they chose Lord Merriot."

Francine grimaced. "They had met him briefly while he was in Paris, and he had written to your father more than once implying that he would be delighted to help in their fight against Robespierre."

"You must be jesting." Raoul snorted in disgust. "Lord Merriot is a spineless coward. Why would he risk his neck for a cause that he had no stake in?"

"Because he understood that there was no danger to him so long as he was in England, and he hoped that his offers of friendship would allow your father to look more favorable on his constant requests for money."

"Ah. Now it makes perfect sense." Raoul had no difficulty imagining Lord Merriot dunning a near stranger for blunt, but he had to admit he was disappointed by the thought that the Comte de Suriant was foolish enough to be taken in. "But surely my father must have realized that by sending a cartload of wealth to a man known to be in desperate need of funds was like asking the fox to guard the chickens?"

Francine clicked her tongue. "Your parents never intended Lord Merriot to know of your inheritance. Before we left France, the Comte sent Lord Merriot a bank draft to pay for his assistance and to reveal that we would soon be in England. It was intended that the money and personal property would travel on to London and be kept hidden by your parents' most loyal servants until we could return to France, or you came of age."

Raoul was ridiculously relieved by the knowledge his parents had done their very best to keep him and his inheritance safe.

It surely proved just how much they loved him.

Unnerved by the realization of how desperately he needed to believe in his parents' devotion, Raoul sternly focused his mind on the questions that still clamored to be answered.

"What happened?"

Francine's eyes filled with tears. "Lord Merriot came in person to meet the boat, which we had not expected. He commanded that the cart be brought to Cheshire and that the other servants return to France. I was so desperate to see you safe that I did not argue. Forgive me."

"It was not your fault, Francine," he soothed, patting her hand. "You risked everything for me and I shall never forget your sacrifices."

"I never dreamed that his lordship could harbor such evil," Francine declared. "And in the beginning, he was quite kind. He took you in and allowed others to believe you were his bastard son. He gave you the name Charlebois, which prevented any speculation that you might have ties to French nobility. He even treated me as a welcomed guest."

"When did it change?"

"After we received word that your parents had been taken to the guillotine."

Raoul's heart clenched with a combination of regret at his parents' untimely death, and weary resignation at Merriot's treachery.

"But of course," he scoffed, easily capable of imagining Lord Merriot's delight at the news. "Until then, there was always the possibility my parents might arrive on the doorstep and demand their son, as well as their wealth."

"*Oui.* Once, however, he realized that there was no one to halt him from stealing your inheritance . . ."

"No one but you," Raoul pointed out.

"And what am I?" Francine gave a wave of her hands. "A meaningless servant from France who willingly repeated the lie that you are Lord Merriot's bastard son. Who would believe anything I said? Too late did I realize the danger of our masquerade. So foolish."

"Never that," Raoul denied.

"But I was." The round face hardened with self-disgust. "The moment I realized that the pig intended to steal your inheritance, I should have taken you from Cheshire."

"Why did you not?" he gently demanded.

"I had no money and nowhere to go. I thought it was best to ensure you at least had a home and food to eat."

Sensing the woman's lingering guilt, Raoul caught and held her gaze. "I do not blame you for Lord Merriot's sins, Francine. Indeed I am extremely grateful for all you did for me."

"It was not enough," she whispered. "I will never forgive myself for having left you alone in that ghastly house."

"You had your future to think of, Francine. I understand."

Her eyes widened, as if she were shocked by his words. "*Non, mon enfant.* You cannot believe I ever left willingly."

"You did say Lord Merriot had no fear of you convincing others I was nothing more than his bastard," Raoul reminded her.

"He did not believe that any English court would accept the word of a French servant against that of a nobleman, but as time passed, the revolution came to an end." A bittersweet smile touched her lips. "The government remained unsettled, but I became determined to return you to France so you could claim your place as the Comte de Suriant."

Raoul lifted his brows in surprise. Francine was obviously a woman of uncommon resources and courage.

Much like another woman he knew.

The mere thought of Sarah was enough to ease the chill that was lodged in the pit of his stomach.

Mon Dieu, he wished she were here with him.

"Did you reveal your plan to Lord Merriot?"

"Of course not," Francine denied, her tone indignant. "I knew he would do anything to keep secret his theft of your inheritance. Even if he were not judged guilty by English law, his name would certainly be tarnished."

"Then how did he discover your plans?"

An unexpected blush touched her cheeks. "I was still young and foolish enough to be susceptible to the charms of a handsome young gentleman."

"The gardener," Raoul breathed.

"How did you know?"

"I spoke with his brother. He claimed that Lord Merriot had Drabble transported."

"*Oui.* We fell in love, and I confessed all to him. I also told him of my plans to return to France, and he was determined to assist me." Her lips trembled with a reminiscent pain. "Ah, such a good man. I will always miss him."

Raoul gave her a moment to gather her composure, only distantly aware of the crackle of the logs in the fireplace and the muted sound of laughter from the street below.

"I still do not understand how Lord Merriot discovered your plans," he at last prompted.

She drew in a shaky breath, her hands clenched in her lap. "Frank and I made a habit of meeting in the nursery after Lord and Lady Merriot went to bed to discuss our journey to France. I do not know if Lord Merriot became suspicious, or if he came to the nursery for some other purpose, but he overheard us speaking and . . ."

Her words trailed away, and Raoul reached out to once again take her hand.

"Francine, you need not say any more."

"*Non,* I wish you to know." She determinedly squared her shoulders, her expression grim. "We were in the nursery when Lord Merriot entered with a gun. He forced Frank and I to follow him downstairs, and then he called for the servants, telling them he had caught Frank stealing." She was forced to halt and clear her throat. "Of course, they did not believe his absurd accusations, but what could they do? They sent for the magistrate, and

Frank was taken into his custody. I was never allowed to see him again."

Raoul bit back a curse. Of course Lord Merriot would think nothing of ruining the life of an innocent man. Selfish ass.

"He was transported," Raoul muttered.

"And it was all my fault."

"No," he rasped, refusing to allow this woman to hold herself to blame. "The fault lies with Lord Merriot, not with you."

She studied him with a wistful smile. "You are so much like your mother. So kind and prepared to forgive others."

Raoul shook his head. "I fear I am not nearly so kind as you believe, and I assure you there is nothing to forgive."

She abruptly ducked her head, hiding her expression. "But you have not yet heard the whole."

"You can tell me, Francine."

There was a long pause, as if she were inwardly gathering her courage. Then she raised her head to regard him with open regret.

"After Frank was taken away, Lord Merriot locked me in the nursery."

Raoul widened his eyes, astonished to discover that just when he assumed his opinion of Lord Merriot could not sink any lower, there was yet another trough to be discovered.

"He held you captive?"

Francine nodded. "He told me that he would allow me to leave the Great House, and even promised to provide me a yearly allowance, so long as I would swear not to ever approach you or reveal the truth of your past."

"And if you would not swear?"

She licked her lips, the hazel eyes darkening with fear. "He said he would kill me."

"A promise I intend to keep," a harsh, shockingly unexpected voice assured them.

Chapter 20

Raoul was on his feet and placing himself between the intruder and the shrieking Francine in one smooth movement. He was swift but not swift enough, he acknowledged in disgust, glaring at Lord Merriot, who stood in the doorway with a dueling pistol pointed straight at Raoul's heart.

Damn.

He was an utter idiot. He knew Merriot was in London. And that he was desperate to locate Francine. That alone should have kept him prepared for disaster.

Instead, he had readily allowed Nico to leave rather than keeping him on guard, his pistol was tucked in his coat pocket rather than having it in hand where it might have done some bloody good, and worse of all, he had allowed himself to be so distracted by Francine's confessions that he had never even heard the door being opened.

Furious with himself, Merriot, and the world at large, Raoul allowed his contemptuous gaze to flick over Lord Merriot's expensive caped coat, and the glossy Hessians that had no doubt been purchased with Raoul's stolen inheritance.

"Do not be a fool, Merriot," he growled. "It is over."

"No." The beefy face that was still red from the cold twisted with a violent hatred. "I have come too far to have what is rightfully mine stolen by a tawdry actor."

"Rightfully yours?" Raoul scoffed. He was not indifferent to the gun pointed at his heart, or the realization that Merriot was a superior marksman. Indeed, he was acutely aware of the danger. At the moment, however, his only hope was to distract the frantic nobleman long enough to retrieve his own gun, or hope for Nico's timely return. "And pray tell me what possible claim could you have to my inheritance?"

"If not for me, you would have gone to the guillotine."

Raoul snorted. "You might have offered me refuge, but you had already been well compensated, had you not?"

"I risked my life . . ."

"You did nothing more than take a small child and nurse beneath your roof," Raoul cut in, his tone revealing his revulsion. "If there had been the slightest danger, you would have tossed us out with no more thought than if we were a bit of rubbish. You will always consider your own neck, you spineless maggot."

The nobleman's eyes glittered with something very close to madness, and Raoul shifted to ensure that he was between Merriot and the softly sobbing Francine, who remained cowering on the sofa.

The man was clearly unstable.

"I did everything asked of me, and I deserved my reward."

"You are a common thief and a liar, and the only thing you deserve is the gallows."

"Never," Merriot hissed. "I have suffered more than you will ever comprehend. Now I only want this business to be at an end."

Raoul's sharp laughter echoed through the room. "And what have you suffered?"

"My son is dead. Taken from me when he was just a child."

"And that is my fault?"

The hand holding the pistol trembled. The bastard had truly convinced himself that all his troubles were Raoul's fault.

"You have brought nothing but ill fortune since you arrived in England."

"I also brought considerable wealth, that you have squandered with obvious pleasure," Raoul taunted.

"And what could I do?" Merriot demanded. "My father left me on the brink of ruin."

"Again, I fail to see how the fault can possibly lie with me."

"It was too much temptation to resist," Merriot blustered, his eyes protruding as he sought to justify his evil. "No man in my position would have chosen differently."

"Unless he happened to possess a few pesky morals," Raoul mocked, unable to feel anything but disgust for the weak-willed fool. Lord Merriot had stolen more than his inheritance. He had stolen his life. "Tell me, Merriot, did you have the least sense of remorse when you bartered off my father's artwork and my mother's jewels?"

"It had to be done." He licked his fat lips, beads of sweat marring his brow. "I . . . I had no choice."

"There is always a choice." Raoul paused, wrestling against the rage that flowed like lava through his veins. He still had questions that only this man could answer. "I am curious."

"Curious?"

"Dunnington was obviously blackmailing you." Raoul kept his voice indifferent. "What did he know?"

"That fool."

"Hardly a fool," Raoul corrected. "He managed to lighten your stolen bounty by twenty thousand pounds."

Fury twisted Merriot's expression, but thankfully he appeared unaware of the significance of his answer to Raoul.

"Only because Mirabelle refused to comprehend the delicacy of our situation," he muttered. "She was determined to keep the finer pieces of jewelry and, even after I warned her not to flaunt them, she refused to heed my warnings."

"I presume she draped herself in my mother's gems and waltzed through London?"

"Not London. A house party we had been invited to near Winchester."

"Winchester," Raoul breathed. It had been Fredrick who had discovered their old tutor had spent several years in the town. Obviously he had uncovered more than just the fact that Fredrick was the eldest son and heir of Lord Colstone. "Dunnington taught at the local college."

Merriot curled his lips. "Had I known that Sir Easterby was so lacking in refinement as to invite a commoner to his gatherings, I should never have agreed to attend."

"You have no need to prove your repulsive arrogance, Merriot," Raoul snapped, refusing to have Dunnington insulted. Not by this worthless cad. "Perhaps if you had more sense and less pride, you could have avoided your inevitable decline into disgrace."

Merriot stiffened. "You will notice that I have the sense to be the one holding the gun."

"So you are," Raoul drawled. "I am still baffled. I have no doubt that Lady Merriot was stupid enough to prance around in stolen goods, but how could Dunnington possibly have known they were filched?"

"The interfering jackass had spent several years in Paris when he was young."

"As a student?"

"As if I care. I only know he was employed to run errands for the owner of a *salon* where the Comtesse de Suriant often visited."

Raoul's lips twisted. He could easily imagine Dunnington traveling to Paris to surround himself with those who possessed a passion for learning. Obviously his mother had made a lasting impression on the tutor.

"So he was in a position to personally recognize her jewelry. How unfortunate for you."

"Encroaching muckworm."

Raoul kept his expression unreadable, despite the pounding of his heart. The next question meant more than he wanted to admit.

"Did he know I was the Comtesse's son?"

"Of course not," Merriot denied, unwittingly easing the one lingering dread that haunted Raoul. "He had never met your father."

"So he only knew you somehow possessed my mother's jewelry?"

"The idiot was convinced that I had stolen them while I was in France. As if I were a common thief."

Raoul shuddered with relief. Dunnington hadn't known that he was the legitimate son of Comte de Suriant. Thank God. He was not certain he could bear the thought that the man he held in such esteem could have hidden the truth from him.

Still, he was careful to disguise his reaction behind a sneer. "But that is precisely what you are."

Merriot gritted his teeth, taking a threatening step forward. "It no longer matters. Dunnington is dead, and soon enough you and your meddlesome nurse will join him in the grave."

From behind, Raoul heard the sound of Francine's groan, but he never shifted his gaze from Merriot.

The encounter was spiraling toward a bloody conclusion unless he could convince the lunatic that killing them was a poor notion.

"So you will add murder to your sins?" he demanded.

"I have no choice."

"As I said, there is always a choice."

"No." Merriot shook his head, his eyes wild in the flickering firelight, sweat dripping from his face. "Once you are gone, it will be over."

Raoul held up his hands in a calming motion. "You believe you can shoot two people in a hotel, and walk away without being seen?"

"I . . ." He swallowed heavily. "I shall say that you traveled to Cheshire in an attempt to demand money from me, and when I refused, you lured me to London to have your revenge. Only I was wise enough to shoot you first."

"Very clever." He shrugged. "And Francine?"

"She was obviously a partner in your nefarious plot."

"Ah."

"There will be no one left who can speak of the past."

Raoul summoned a condescending smile, calling upon his years upon the stage. He had never needed his acting skills more than he would over the next few minutes.

"Now that is where you are out, Merriot."

The older man frowned. "What do you mean?"

"Your crimes have already been exposed."

"Impossible."

"You were not nearly so careful as you believed," Raoul drawled, casually crossing his arms over his chest. "Or perhaps you merely underestimated Jefferson's frugal nature."

"What the devil did my gamekeeper have to do with this?" Merriot snapped. "He knew nothing."

"No, it is true he did not suspect your treachery, but he could not bear to witness perfectly decent furnishings condemned to the bonfire. He instead donated them to the local villagers," he informed the wary nobleman. "Except for a handful that he took to the cottage . . . along with several portraits."

There was a shocked silence as Merriot considered the implications, then his ruddy face paled to a sickly ash as he realized the dangers of Jefferson's interference.

"A lie."

Raoul shook his head. "I have seen them with my own eyes, including the portrait of Comte and Comtesse de Suriant with their child."

"That proves nothing."

"It proves everything," Raoul countered. "No one who views the portrait could possibly overlook my resemblance to Comte de Suriant."

"And who will view it?" Merriot rasped, clearly shaken. "As soon as I finish here, I will return to Cheshire and burn it myself. I should have done so in the first place."

Raoul's smile widened. "You can return to Cheshire if you desire, but you will not discover the portrait."

"Where is it?"

"It should be in the hands of Lord Liverpool by now. And I must warn you that he has always been particularly fond of me."

Merriot's chest heaved up and down as he battled against his rising panic. Raoul's attention, however, remained firmly fixed on the trembling hand that held the pistol.

The last thing he desired was for the man to accidentally squeeze the trigger.

"Impossible."

"Why impossible?"

"I was watching your house when you arrived in town. You came straight here."

Raoul felt a stab of self-disgust. In his haste to find Nico, he had led Merriot straight to the hotel.

"So we may add spying to your unsavory habits," he growled.

"I knew when I could not find Francine, you must be somehow involved."

"And so you followed me here."

"Exactly." Merriot made a visible effort to gather his faltering composure. "So now I need only to travel to your town house to retrieve the damnable thing."

"I fear you are too late." Raoul dropped his hands to his side, ensuring his hand was close to the pocket holding his pistol. The more he pressed Merriot, the more dangerous the situation, but it also offered the only opportunity to distract him long enough to get his hand on his weapon. "I never claimed that I personally delivered the portrait to Liverpool."

Merriot shook his head. "This is nothing more than a ruse to distract me."

"Not at all," Raoul smoothly lied. "Once I arrived at the hotel, I commanded my valet to return to the town house to collect the portrait before calling upon Liverpool, and revealing the entire story."

Merriot's horrified expression revealed that he had spotted Nico leaving the hotel. Now Raoul could only hope he would soon return.

"Lord Liverpool will never believe such a Banbury tale," he said, more determined to convince himself than Raoul.

"Perhaps not on the word of my servant, but he will be intrigued enough by my likeness to the Comte de Suriant to investigate the claim. There must be at least a few of my family's servants still living to assure him that the Comte did indeed send his only heir, and a considerable amount of his wealth, to Lord Merriot in England."

"No." Merriot took a stumbling step backward, unaware the door was silently swinging open behind him. Nico . . . at last. "I will not believe you."

Raoul covertly slid his hand into his pocket, his fingers closing around the hilt of his gun.

"You said you wanted this business over and done with. I fear it is only beginning."

"You bastard . . ."

"I may be many things, but a bastard I am not," Raoul interrupted, his voice as cold as the frigid night air.

Merriot waved his pistol, his entire body shaking with fear. "Do you think I will let you get away with this?"

The words had barely left his lips when Nico stepped through the door. With one swift motion, he hit Merriot on the back of his head with the butt of his gun, and the nobleman crumbled onto the floor in an unconscious heap.

"I wondered when you would choose to make your appearance," Raoul chided, turning to help a still shaking Francine to her feet.

"I hated to interrupt such a touching family reunion."

"Very thoughtful."

Nico chuckled, kicking the oblivious Lord Merriot with the toe of his boot.

"What do you wish to do with him?"

Raoul hesitated, torn between the vengeful need to wrap his hands around the foul man's neck to choke the life from him, and a desire to put the painful past behind him so he could concentrate on his future.

It was the image of a raven-haired beauty with exotic eyes and lips that tasted of gingerbread that helped make his decision.

"Leave him."

Nico cursed, his brows drawn together in outrage. "Have you taken leave of your senses? He intended to murder you."

"What would you have me do? Slit his throat?"

In less than the beat of a heart, Nico had a dagger pulled from his sleeve.

"If you are squeamish . . ."

"No, Nico," Raoul hastily commanded, knowing that his valet would not hesitate to put an end to Lord Merriot.

"I intend to take my case to Liverpool, and then to the French Embassy. Once the story is known, Merriot will not dare to harm me."

Nico snorted. "You cannot imagine that the authorities will hang this imbecile? Noblemen are above the law."

"He might not be arrested, but he faces utter ruin when the truth is spread throughout society. There will not be a door left open to him."

"And you consider that ample punishment?"

Taking Francine's arm, Raoul carefully negotiated her around the unconscious form toward the door. The poor woman had endured enough for one night.

"For a gentleman such as Lord Merriot, it will be a fate worse than death," he pointed out, not above taking pleasure in Lord Merriot's coming downfall from grace. He might not face the gallows, but being the laughing stock among society would be infinitely worse. "Nothing means more to him than his pride."

Nico slid the dagger back into his hidden sheath, not at all satisfied. "Bah."

"Are you quite certain, Raoul?" Francine timidly demanded, her face still wet from her tears. "He did seem determined to do you harm."

Urging his old nurse through the door, he led her down the empty corridor.

"I will not deny it is tempting to toss him in the Thames, but I will not lower myself to Merriot's standards," he said, a slow smile curving his lips. "Besides, Sarah would never approve."

Nico fell into pace beside him, his gun still out as he remained on guard.

"I knew that woman had made you soft in the head."

Ignoring his servant, Raoul smiled down at Francine. "I know you must be weary, but I do hope you will join me in offering Lord Liverpool a Christmas he will not soon forget?"

"Of course." She tilted her head to the side. "Is he truly fond of you?"

"So he has said." Raoul smiled as he thought of what Liverpool's reaction would be to his shocking story. "We are about to discover just how fond."

Chapter 21

Twelfth Night
Cheshire

The snow that had threatened to come most of the morning began to fall just after lunch.

Standing in the kitchen surrounded by the scent of apple spice cake, Sarah gazed out the window, thankful the boys had left earlier to make their way to the Vicar's. They would never have forgiven her if she had refused to allow them to walk through a near blizzard to assist with decorating the vicarage for the Twelfth Night Ball.

And in truth, she was in dire need of a few hours of peace.

The effort to appear properly cheerful for the boys had taken its toll. More than once, she had been forced to leave the room to blink back the tears that would form without warning.

Not that she had any reason to cry, she reminded herself sternly.

When the Vicar had called yesterday to reveal the

shocking elevation of Raoul from bastard to the Comte de Suriant, she had been too stunned to feel anything. Even with the knowledge that Raoul was searching for a secret from his past hadn't prepared her for such a shocking revelation.

But then, who could possibly have dreamed that Lord Merriot could be so vile?

It was unthinkable that anyone could not only steal a young child's inheritance, but that he would steal his very identity.

As her shock had faded, however, a stark reality had set in.

Raoul was no longer the handsome scoundrel that had acted his way to success on the stage and in the drawing rooms of London society. Or even the vulnerable young boy who had hidden his wounds behind an irresistible charm.

He was now a French aristocrat, with all the benefits and responsibilities that came with the title.

Responsibilities that did not include the mere daughter of a gamekeeper and two stray boys.

And as much as she might be pleased for Raoul's wondrous discovery, a part of her was selfish enough to mourn the loss of what might have been.

Unaware of the passing time, Sarah was wrenched from her dark thoughts by the sound of the front door being opened and closed.

Frowning in confusion, Sarah made her way into the parlor to discover Maggie removing her snow-dusted cloak and knit scarf.

Sarah's confusion only deepened as she studied her maid. Surely she had specifically told Maggie that she was at liberty to enjoy the numerous festivities that were planned for Twelfth Night?

"Maggie, what are you doing here?" she demanded, wiping her hands on the apron that covered her shabby gray gown. "I told you to spend the day with your family."

Unlike Sarah, the maid was attired in her finest wool gown, with her curls tucked becomingly beneath her bonnet. No doubt she had just come from the Squire's house, where Christmas tea was traditionally held for the villagers.

"I came straight over as soon as I heard the news," the maid breathed, her cheeks flushed from more than just the crisp air. "I could barely believe my ears. Can you imagine? Why it's just like one of those novels you love to read."

It was precisely the knowledge that Raoul would be the inevitable source of gossip at the tea that had kept Sarah from attending.

Ridiculous, of course.

She should have known that she could not avoid the painful subject for long.

Still, she could not resist attempting to divert the inevitable conversation.

"Oh, then you know that Mr. Arment has announced his engagement to Miss Gregory?" she said, her expression innocent. "Yes, it was all very romantic."

"Lord, that was hardly news. He has been making calf eyes at her for the past year," Maggie swiftly dismissed the announcement, not about to be diverted. "Surely you must know I am speaking of Mr. Charlebois . . . oh, I suppose I should call him the Comte de Suriant?"

Sarah swallowed a sigh. Obviously there was no halting the woman.

"There was no need for you to come, Maggie. The Vicar came by yesterday to tell me of Mr. Charlebois's elevation to the French aristocracy."

Unaware she was painfully scraping against Sarah's raw nerves, Maggie smiled with satisfaction.

"Not that I am entirely surprised, you know. Such a handsome, elegant gentleman. It was obvious he was born to be among the finest of society."

"Yes, quite obvious."

"I heard tell that he has claim to some fancy chateau, and a half dozen smaller estates spread all about France. Vineyards and everything."

Sarah's heart sank even as she told herself she was delighted that Raoul was blessed with such a windfall. He would be an extraordinary landlord to his people. Generous, caring, and capable of appreciating those who labored to provide his comfort.

"A handsome inheritance to be sure," she murmured. "He must be very pleased."

"So, I should say. And it could not have happened to a more worthy gentleman." Maggie regarded Sarah with a coy expression. "I shall never forget his particular kindness to you and the boys."

Sarah clenched her teeth, refusing to reveal the bitter regret that was settled in the pit of her stomach.

"Yes, well, I am certain he has more important matters to attend to now that he has become a comte."

"Perhaps for now," Maggie agreed, although she clearly was laboring beneath the absurd assumption that Raoul would return to Cheshire as if nothing had changed. "Whatever do you think will happen to Lord Merriot? Not that I am particularly surprised that he would prove to be the villain of the piece. He was never liked in the neighborhood, with all those false airs of his, and always lording it over others. Still, it is one thing to be disrespectful to the common folk, and quite another to steal a young boy's inheritance." She shook her head in disgust. "Shameful."

"It is more than shameful, it is pure wickedness," Sarah snapped, unable to halt the revealing words. "When I consider his cruelty to Mr. Charlebois . . . the Comte de Suriant, I mean, when he was just a child, it makes me wish he could be properly punished."

Maggie nodded in sympathy. "And of course, he had poor Frank Drabble transported to hide his shocking behavior."

With an effort, Sarah gathered her composure. Lord Merriot might be the worst sort of villain, but his punishment was out of her hands.

A pity.

"It can only be hoped that someday Lord Merriot will be judged for his sins," she muttered.

"According to the squire's wife, we won't have to wait quite so long," Maggie revealed in satisfied tones. "She says that society has already turned their backs on Lord and Lady Merriot, and that they dare not show their faces in London. Or anywhere else for that matter."

Sarah grimaced. "I suppose one should feel sorry for them, but I confess I cannot claim the least amount of sympathy."

"I should say not." Maggie appeared startled at the mere notion of pity. Like many in the neighborhood, she had always held Lord Merriot in contempt. "They deserve every misery they might suffer."

Sarah shrugged, more concerned with Raoul than with the appalling Merriots.

Pretending an indifference she was far from feeling, she straightened the frayed cuff of her gown.

"Have you heard if the Comte de Suriant has traveled to France?"

"Not that I can determine, but I suppose he shall have to eventually travel to his home," Maggie said, almost as if it were a thought that had never crossed her mind. Strange when Sarah had been dwelling on it for hours. "I wonder if any of his relations survived the revolution?"

"I hope for his sake that they did," Sarah said without hesitation. She might be selfish enough to regret the loss of Raoul, but she would never wish him anything but utter happiness. "I think he has always longed for a family."

"Poor man." Maggie clicked her tongue. "'Tis bad enough to have his fortune stolen, but to be told he was a bastard and treated with such contempt . . . well, it breaks my heart."

Lifting her chin, Sarah pasted a brave smile on her lips as she met Maggie's gaze.

"Fortunately, he can now be reunited with his true family."

"Aye, that is true enough," Maggie slowly agreed, a frown wrinkling her brow. "But surely . . ."

"What?"

"Do you think he intends to live in France?"

"Why would he not?" Sarah demanded. "As you said, he has a number of homes to choose from, and perhaps relatives who will be anxious to have him near."

For the first time realizing the full implications of Raoul's transformation from actor to aristocrat, Maggie's expression fell.

"Oh."

"Besides, there is nothing to keep him in England,"

"There is you and the boys."

"Hardly a temptation when compared to a grand chateau and a place among the highest of societies," Sarah said grimly, preferring that the maid realize there was no reason to hold on to foolish hope. It was far better to accept the truth and make the best of their situation. "If that is all, Maggie, I should finish decorating the cake for the children's ball before the boys return."

Maggie sighed, but with visible effort resisted the urge to continue her arguments.

"I do hope you remembered to put in the bean."

Sarah brushed back a curl that had strayed from her braid. "Of course," she assured her companion. Tradition held that the Twelfth Night cake would be baked with a hidden bean. Whoever was fortunate enough to receive the slice of cake with the bean would be named king or queen of the ball. "What would the ball be without the proper royalty?"

There was another sigh as Maggie turned to pull on her cloak and scarf.

"Then I will see you at the vicarage."

"Yes, I shall be there."

Moving to the window, Sarah watched until Maggie was safely seated on Martin's cart, then with a shake of her head, she turned to make her way back to the kitchen.

She hadn't simply been attempting to rid herself of Maggie's presence. She did have to finish the cake before she could have her bath and prepare herself and the boys for the ball.

There were also the dishes to wash, and the firewood to be brought in for the night, and the dogs to feed . . .

An hour later she had finished the cake and the dishes,

and was busily sweeping the floor when a male arm reached around her to pluck the broom from her hands.

"I see you still have not learned to lock your doors," a low, intoxicatingly familiar voice whispered close to her ear.

With a small screech, Sarah whirled around, her heart halting with shocked disbelief.

Raoul.

There was no mistaking the golden curls that were tousled to fall against his brow, the brilliant blue eyes that were so lushly framed by black lashes, the perfect nose, and sensuous lips. Her gaze lowered, skimming over the elegant gold jacket and silver waistcoat that were matched with black breeches and glossy Hessians.

She slowly shook her head, torn between elated disbelief and horror at being caught wearing her oldest gown, covered in flour.

"Mr. Charl . . ." She caught her impulsive words, a flush staining her cheeks. "I mean Comte de Suriant."

He tossed aside the broom, wrapping his arms around her waist as he regarded her with a compelling gaze.

"Do you suppose there will ever come a day when you can bring yourself to call me Raoul?" he demanded, his voice low and smoky. "I very much desire to hear my name on your lips."

She trembled, acutely aware of the heat and scent of him surrounding her.

"What are you doing here?"

His lips touched her brow. "I told you I would return. Did you not trust me to keep my word?"

"But . . ." She shook her head, her mouth dry, her heart hammering in her throat. "Everything has changed since you left."

"Ah, that is where you are wrong. There are some things that will never change." He shifted to brush his mouth over her lips in a teasing motion. "You still taste of spice. And you still feel perfect in my arms." He groaned, his arms tightening around her. "*Sacrebleu,* I have missed you."

Instinctively, Sarah pressed her hands to his chest, her head swimming as she sought to comprehend what was occurring.

Only moments ago she had been resigned to the notion that she was destined never to see Raoul again. She had even convinced herself that she could be content with her small cottage and the boys to love.

She could not bear to have her hopes raised, only to be dashed again.

"Wait," she breathed.

He rested his forehead against hers, his breath rasping through the air.

"I have done nothing but wait, *ma belle.*"

"Surely you should be in France?"

As if realizing that she would not be content until he had convinced her that this was no illusion, Raoul pulled away and studied her with a brooding gaze.

"I intend to travel there eventually," he conceded, his tone revealing a remarkable lack of interest in his vast inheritance. "For now, however, my claim to the title is still being investigated by the proper authorities. Until a ruling is made, my presence is decidedly unwanted."

Sarah tugged off her apron, trying to ignore her disheveled appearance as she concentrated on his confession.

"Is there a chance it will be denied?" she demanded.

He shrugged. "I am assured this is only a formality,

but to be honest, I have more important matters to claim my attention."

"Yes, I suppose you do," she said, abruptly realizing that he might have more than one reason for traveling to Cheshire. "Is Lord Merriot to be charged with a crime?"

A hard smile touched his lips. "The Foreign Minister is considering what should be done, and Prinny is rumored to be furious. He would rather have his tongue removed than to offer a formal apology to the French government on behalf of one of his noblemen. No doubt he would send Merriot to the gallows if he could."

"Is that what you desire?" she asked softly.

"I no longer have the least interest in Lord Merriot, or his fate. All I desire is to put the past behind me."

She studied his expression, caught off guard by his complete lack of fury.

Lord Merriot had done everything in his power to destroy Raoul's life. For God's sake, he had tried to kill him.

Surely any gentleman would be eager for blood?

"But after the misery he . . ."

His hand reached to cup her cheek. "Sarah, I now understand that I had parents who loved me enough to give their lives to save me. That is all that matters."

Sarah understood, she truly did. For a man who had lived his entire life believing he was unwanted and unloved, the knowledge that he had two parents who were willing to sacrifice their lives for him must be a powerful force.

Perhaps powerful enough to heal his deepest wounds.

And yet, her own festering anger toward Lord Merriot, and his cold cruelty toward Raoul, was not at all satisfied.

"It is still grossly unfair he should go unpunished," she muttered.

His smile became one of genuine amusement. "So Nico assures me with tedious regularity."

"It is a wonder he did not take matters into his own hands," she said, recalling the sense of lethal danger that clung to the servant.

"He wished to, but I refused to offer him leave to slice the bastard's throat."

"Why?"

His thumb teased the corner of her mouth, his gaze darkening with a heat that sent a dangerous thrill of excitement sizzling through her.

"Because I did not think you would approve," he husked.

She blinked. He had denied his opportunity for a well deserved revenge and stayed Nico's hand because he was concerned what she would think?

"I . . ."

He chuckled as the words stuck in her throat. "Yes?"

She swallowed the lump forming in her throat, not prepared to admit just how touched she was by his words.

"Well, I would not wish for Nico to hang for having murdered Lord Merriot, but I would not mind the horrible man spending at least a few years in Newgate prison," she muttered.

Raoul grimaced. "I suspect he is already living in a prison of his own making."

Sarah slowly nodded, unable to deny the truth of his words. Lord Merriot might never face the gallows, but his years of guilt had taken their toll. He was a broken man who could not so much as leave his house.

"You are very forgiving."

"No," he denied, his fingers trailing down the length of her jaw. "I simply refuse to waste any more of my life fretting over a man who is not worthy of my attention."

She hastily stepped away from his distracting touch. The urge to toss sanity aside and give in to his seduction was a potent temptation.

One of them had to cling to a bit of reason.

Ignoring his growing scowl, Sarah smoothed her hands down her skirt, wondering why the kitchen suddenly seemed far smaller than usual.

"Have you discovered if you have any relatives in France?"

With a resigned sigh, Raoul leaned against the edge of the wooden counter, his expression that of a predator willing to give his prey a brief reprieve before pouncing for the kill.

"A few distant cousins who have written to ingratiate themselves with the new Comte de Suriant, and my mother's sister, who seemed genuinely pleased to know I survived," he said, his thoughts clearly distracted.

"Of course she is pleased." A genuine happiness stirred in her heart. Raoul would at least have some connection to the parents he had never known. "You must seem like a Christmas miracle to her. And you must be happy as well. You discovered the truth of your past, and now have a family of your own."

His gaze swept down her tense body before returning to regard her with an unnerving intensity.

"I hope they are not to be my only family," he said, his voice low and compelling. "If you will recall, I asked you to be my wife before I was forced to return to London."

Her breath caught, a helpless yearning tugging at her heart. "Yes, but you must realize that it is utterly impossible now."

His jaw tightened. "I realize no such thing."

She frowned. He was being deliberately obtuse. But why? Surely he had to comprehend that the situation between them could never be the same?

"You are the Comte de Suriant."

"I am Raoul," he stubbornly countered. "The same man who played Snapdragon with the boys, and stole plum cakes from your kitchen, and held you in my arms as you . . ."

"That was before you knew you held a title," she interrupted, her voice harsh as a raw pain jolted through her. "A French aristocrat will be expected to wed a woman of his own world. You must see that."

He straightened, stepping forward to grasp her shoulders in a firm grip.

"All I see is that *you* are the woman I intend to make my Comtesse, no one else. Sarah, you are everything I desire in my wife." He peered deep into her eyes, as if willing her to believe his sincerity. "Never before have I known a woman with such a kind heart and giving spirit and, of course, I have not failed to notice that you also happen to be exquisitely beautiful. But just as importantly, you are the only woman in the world with whom I can truly be myself. No barriers, no masquerade. Just me."

Her heart melted. Dear God, she did understand him. To her he was more than a brilliant actor, or charming rake, or a wealthy and powerful Comte.

He was a man who had endured a lonely, barren childhood, and yet with courage and a refusal to give into bitterness, had created a life that was not only the envy of London, but was filled with a generosity of spirit that allowed him never to forget those less fortunate than himself.

That was the man she loved and respected and desperately desired.

Still, she could not forget the gaping chasm that now stood between them.

"You are not thinking clearly," she muttered, her voice unsteady.

His hands shifted to cup her face. "I love you, Sarah Jefferson, and more than that, I *need* you."

Trembling, Sarah regarded him with a longing that she could not disguise. He loved her?

She had known that he was fond of her, and that he desired her. She had even suspected that a part of him was comforted by her presence.

But love?

It was . . . unbelievable.

"Just think of the scandal," she forced herself to point out. "I am the daughter of a simple gamekeeper. Do you think society will ever accept me?"

"Scandal?" Without warning, he tilted back his head to laugh with a rich amusement. "*Mon Dieu.* I spent my life as the bastard son of Lord Merriot who made my living upon the stage. Do you truly believe I shall be able to take the title of Comte de Suriant without scandal?"

"Which is all the more reason that you should choose a proper wife. She will give you the respect you need."

He shook his head, his hands tightening on her face. "I do not want a proper wife. I want a raven-haired gypsy who can give something far more important than respect."

"And what is that?"

"Happiness," he said, the simple sincerity touching her in a manner that no amount of flowery speeches could match. "It is something that has eluded me for too long. Only you can give me that, *ma belle.*"

Her arms instinctively lifted to wrap around his neck, all the hope she had held at bay beginning to swell and fill her heart with a near painful intensity.

Raoul *did* deserve happiness. Perhaps more than any man she had ever known.

And if he truly believed that she was the one to offer him such an elusive treasure, then who was she to argue?

Arching closer to the welcome strength of his body, she allowed all the doubts and worries to fade away.

She had tried to be self-sacrificing and offer Raoul the opportunity to reconsider his proposal. Had she not refused to agree to a swift marriage before he had discovered the truth of his past? And even now, she had pointed out all the reasons he should seek a wife among society.

Clearly he was not to be dissuaded.

Thank God.

There was only one issue left to be discussed.

"What of the boys?"

His expression softened at the mere mention of Willie and Jimmy.

"You must know they will always be welcome in my home, although I hope we can discover a proper school so they can grow into young men capable of following their dreams." An affectionate smile curved his lips. "You are not the only one who cares about them."

"Or perhaps we shall have to establish a proper school,

so we can be certain they are being given the very best education possible."

She felt him stiffen, his jaw clenched as if fearing he might receive an unwelcome blow.

"Is that a yes, *ma belle?*" he rasped.

She smiled, her fingers tangling in the satin-smooth curls at the nape of his neck.

"I suppose it is."

"Sarah?"

"Yes, Raoul," she breathed. "Yes."

He groaned, his head swooping down so he could steal a heart-stopping kiss.

"I knew I would eventually hear my name on your lips," he muttered, his voice rough with emotion.

"You were so very certain of me?" she teased.

"You know very well I have never been so uncertain of anything in my life." He kissed her again, then nipped her bottom lip in gentle punishment. "You have led me in a merry chase."

She pulled back to meet his gaze with a somber expression. "All I have ever desired is your happiness, even if that meant allowing you to walk away."

He shuddered, his arms wrapping around her as if to assure himself she was going nowhere.

"Without you, my life would be nothing more than an empty shell." He buried his face in the curve of her neck. "I love you."

She brushed her lips over his smooth cheek, her entire body filled with a shimmering happiness that she could barely contain.

"We are going to make a very odd Comte and Comtesse de Suriant."

He nuzzled a tender spot at the base of her throat.

"No more odd than any number of aristocrats I have known. I assure you, society will willingly accept a raving madman into their parlors, so long as he carries a title."

She grimaced, daunted by the mere thought of facing the London *ton,* let alone the French aristocracy.

"I suppose that is true enough," she attempted to re-assure herself. "They did, after all, welcome Lord Merriot to their homes."

His lips became more insistent as they skimmed up the line of her throat, his hands exploring the curve of her spine.

"I believe our best choice is to mix as little as possible among the fashionable hypocrites," he husked.

Heat swirled through the pit of her stomach, making her toes curl in anticipation. No longer plagued with those pesky doubts, she made no effort to deny her reaction to his touch.

"Whatever would we do?" she asked, her lips brushing his ear.

He sucked in an unsteady breath, his erection abruptly pressing against her stomach.

"I have a few suggestions."

She kissed a path to the edge of his mouth, a thrill of pleasure racing through her as she felt him tremble beneath her soft caress.

She might never comprehend why this beautiful, fascinating, intelligent man had chosen her to love, but she intended to appreciate each and every day she had with him.

"Do you?" she whispered.

He muttered beneath his breath, his fingers digging into her hips.

"Where are the boys?"

"At the vicarage preparing for the Twelfth Night ball."

"Then we are alone?"

"For an hour or so."

"Time enough," he declared, scooping her off her feet in one smooth motion to cross toward the kitchen door.

Sarah chuckled, happily snuggling against his chest. "Time enough for what?"

His stride never slowed as he gazed down at her flushed face, a wicked smile curving his lips.

"To unwrap the finest Christmas present I have ever received, *ma belle*."

Epilogue

September 26
London

The town house tucked in Lombard Street was a perfectly respectable brick structure, with a perfectly respectable garden, in a perfectly respectable neighborhood.

Just as Dunnington had left it.

Well, not precisely as Dunnington had left it, Raoul acknowledged with a wistful pang.

Over the past months, he had paid a fortune for a large crew of workmen to renovate the house, as well as add several rooms onto the back.

Not that he regretted one single quid.

A sense of satisfaction eased the bittersweet regret that Dunnington was not here to see the revival of his school. Slowly he allowed his gaze to roam over the small front garden that was overflowing with children, teachers, and several of the most important politicians in London.

Although the school had been opened nearly three

weeks ago, Sarah had insisted that they host a gathering to celebrate the event. She had also been the one to insist that they include those gentlemen who were in a position to assist children in need.

Raoul had attempted to warn her that those who might accept his invitation were more likely there to gawk at the elusive Comte and Comtesse de Suriant than to share any true interest in the plight of orphaned boys, but she had refused to budge. She could not believe that anyone, no matter how frivolous, could fail to be moved by the near dozen urchins who now called Dunnington's School for Boys home.

A flare of contentment warmed his heart at the mere thought of his wife.

They had been wed quietly in Cheshire with only the boys, Nico, and Maggie in attendance. A part of him had regretted denying Sarah the lavish wedding that many women desired, but she had assured him she was far more pleased to hold the ceremony in the small country church, with the local vicar presiding over the vows. And, in truth, he had been too impatient to at last have her as his wife to have to wait for a more formal London affair.

Besides, Sarah would have hated having a hundred near strangers gaping and whispering during such an intimate moment.

On the point of going in search of Sarah, who had disappeared along with Mercy and Portia (Ian and Fredrick's wives), Raoul was halted as Ian suddenly appeared at his side to thrust a glass of champagne in his hands.

Slender and dark with whiskey-gold eyes, Ian Breckford had once been a hardened gamester, and an even more hardened rake. Now he was a devoted husband who spent his days making an embarrassing fortune with his numerous business affairs.

More importantly, he was one of Raoul's largest contributors to the school.

"Dunnington would be proud," Ian murmured, his expression revealing his lingering pain at the loss of their old tutor.

Raoul nodded. "Yes, I think he would."

They both turned their attention to the crowd overflowing from the house.

"However did you ever lure Kingston from Cambridge?" Ian demanded, referring to the red-haired teacher who was currently surrounded by a strange combination of avid young boys and several elderly statesmen, many of whom had long been attempting to convince the brilliant young scholar to choose a career in the government.

"Actually he approached me," Raoul confessed. "He was acquainted with Dunnington, and when he heard I was opening the school, he asked to be included."

"Astonishing."

"I have every expectation he will be an extraordinary teacher."

Ian chuckled as Willie and Jimmy streaked past them to join the throng around Kingston. It had only been a week since a tearful Sarah had left the boys in the care of the meticulously chosen staff at Dunnington's, but already they were delighted with their new home.

"Your boys seem happy enough with him."

Raoul smiled with rueful amusement. "I fear I have been replaced as the most bang-up chap in the world."

"Kingston does seem to possess Dunnington's magic touch when it comes to wayward brats."

"He is not the only one." Raoul heaved a dramatic sigh. "I am fairly certain that I have also been cast in the shade by the assistant teacher, Mr. Stewart, who has just returned from China with an endless number of adventures to share with the students."

"It was bound to happen, you know," Ian drawled. "You are not nearly so interesting as the Comte de Suriant as you were as the infamous Raoul Charlebois."

"Thank you."

"I am always delighted to be of service."

Raoul snorted, although he was inwardly pleased by his friend's teasing. He knew that he could always count on Ian and Fredrick to treat him as the same Raoul Charlebois they had always known.

It was a considerable improvement on those in society who were eager to ingratiate themselves with the Comte and Comtesse de Suriant.

Sipping his champagne, Ian frowned as yet another carriage halted to allow several elegant noblemen to alight.

"Where the devil is Fredrick?" he muttered.

"The last I saw, he was surrounded by eager boys in the basement as he demonstrated his latest invention."

Ian shuddered, recalling clearly the last occasion they had visited Fredrick's warehouse and had nearly been decapitated when the steam engine he was perfecting had exploded.

"Let us hope the house is not destroyed."

"I had the walls throughout the basement reinforced, as well as a water pump installed, in the case of an unexpected fire," Raoul assured his companion. "Besides, Fredrick assures me that he has not caused an explosion for several weeks."

"Have you warned the staff that Fredrick will be creating havoc on a regular schedule?"

"They are aware that Fredrick is to be a welcome guest whenever he chooses." Raoul deliberately paused. "As are you."

Ian jerked in surprise. "Me?"

Raoul clapped his friend on the shoulder, his smile sly. "Who better to teach the boys the importance of mathematics?"

"What makes you think I will not fleece them of the few coins they possess?" the one-time gambler groused.

"Because you are no more immune to the charm of those boys than Fredrick."

Ian's lips twisted as he realized Raoul would not be fooled. "Or you."

"Or me," Raoul readily agreed.

Lifting his glass, Ian sipped the expensive champagne. "It would seem your work here is done."

Raoul sighed, pretending a resignation he was far from feeling.

"That was my thought as well. Unfortunately, Sarah has decided that such a fine school should not be solely for the benefit of boys. She is busy planning a similar school for young girls."

Ian snorted. "Yes, Mercy has already demanded that I donate an inordinate sum of money to the cause."

Raoul chuckled, easily able to imagine the sweet, soft-spoken Mercy receiving whatever she desired. All of London knew she had Ian wrapped around her little finger.

"Wives can be quite persuasive," he murmured.

"In the best possible way."

"Oh, yes." Raoul shivered as he recalled his morning

spent in the arms of Sarah. Marriage, he was discovering, suited him to perfection. "Who would have suspected when Dunnington left his legacy, it would end with the three of us wed?"

"I shouldn't be at all surprised if the wily old fox had planned it from the beginning."

"Not even Dunnington could have suspected that our journeys into the past would influence our futures."

Ian shrugged. "Who can say?"

"Who indeed," Raoul agreed, raising his glass in a toast to the man who had been willing to devote his life to offering young boys a future that would never have been possible without him. "To Dunnington."

Ian readily raised his own glass in tribute. "Dunnington."

"Speaking of the future, should you not be making plans to travel to France?" a familiar voice demanded.

Both men turned to discover Fredrick standing beside them, his handsome countenance marred by a streak of soot on his cheek, his pearl-gray coat covered in dust.

"Sarah has insisted that we leave at the end of the month," Raoul admitted, offering his companion a fond smile. "Are you in a hurry to be rid of me?"

Fredrick's silver eyes danced with amusement. "I am more interested in enjoying watching someone besides myself being plagued with the endless duties of overseeing an estate."

Raoul grimaced. His elevation to the Comte de Suriant had been officially approved last month, but he had done his best to ignore the inevitable journey.

It was not that he dreaded the responsibilities of his new position, or his introduction to French society, although he did regret the knowledge it would interfere with the time he could devote to Sarah and the boys.

No, it was more a need to prepare himself for meeting the family he had never known existed.

Hardly surprising. Having been raised with the belief that Lord Merriot was his father, his opinion of families was not particularly pleasant.

It was taking a great deal of effort to gather the courage necessary to accept complete strangers into his life, and his heart. If not for Sarah's steady presence, he might never have conceded to his aunt's growingly insistent invitations.

Not that he was alone in his confused emotions toward his family, he ruefully acknowledged, studying Fredrick's resigned expression.

"Can I presume that your father has been pestering you to return to Wessex?"

Fredrick sighed. "He is convinced that I might kill myself in my workshop before I have an opportunity to inherit."

"Shocking," Ian drawled. "Wherever did he come by such an absurd notion?"

Accustomed to Ian's teasing, Fredrick quirked a honey-gold brow. "The odds of me putting an end to my existence with one of my inventions are considerably less than you having your throat slit during one of your visits to the docks."

Ian shrugged. Unlike many gentlemen, Ian made a habit of personally inspecting every detail of his investments, whether it was the crew hired for his fleet of ships or the workers in a brick factory. Nothing was too small to escape his attention.

"I happen to prefer ruffians to aristocrats, not including present company," Ian retorted, his gaze shifting to Raoul. "And speaking of ruffians, I warn you that I intend to use all my powers of persuasion to lure Nico from your employ."

Raoul frowned. He did not doubt for a moment that Nico would be of tremendous service to Ian. Not only did he have contacts among the criminal underworld, but there was not a rumor in London that did not reach his ears.

Unfortunately for Ian, Raoul had no intention of losing such useful skills. Not when he did not yet know who was friend or foe in France.

"You possess your own cutthroat for a valet, and I doubt that Reaver would be pleased to be replaced."

"Nico's talents are wasted as a mere valet," Ian argued. "He could make me a fortune . . ."

"Do not even think about it, *mon ami,*" Raoul smoothly interrupted. "Nico stays with me."

Ian assumed a wounded expression. "Rather selfish of you, Raoul. There are some of us who do not possess the benefits of a title and vast estates to keep their coffers full. We must rely on our wits to survive." His eyes narrowed as both Raoul and Fredrick tilted back their heads to laugh at his ludicrous words. "What is so amusing?"

Fredrick was the first to regain his composure. "Your investments have earned you more wealth in the past year than my father's estate has earned in the past decade," he retorted. "It is nothing less than indecent that one man should hoarde such a fortune."

"Hoarde?" Ian gave a regretful shake of his head. "My wife donates to every charity in London. I shall be lucky to keep a quid."

As one, the friends turned to regard the three women

who were busy charming those noblemen who were foolish enough to stray across their paths. Raoul did not doubt that they would manage to extort a fortune for the school by the end of the day.

"Yes." Fredrick chuckled. "I begin to wonder if we made a mistake by allowing those three to become such close friends."

Ian heaved a sigh of mock resignation. "As if we had a choice in the matter."

Raoul's gaze lingered on Sarah, his heart bursting with happiness as he watched her move confidently among the most elite of London society, her dark, sultry beauty attracting the noblemen like bees to honey.

Whatever her misgivings had been of becoming the Comtesse de Suriant, she had proven to be a favorite among society. The blue bloods were no more immune to her charm than Raoul.

"No," he murmured softly, "there was never a choice."

"Thank God," Ian added, his attention centered on Mercy as she bent to speak with one of the young lads.

"And Dunnington," Fredrick added. "Without his legacy, none of this would have been possible."

Raoul's gaze shifted to the house that once again was filled with the sounds of laughter. Without warning, a shaft of spring sunlight glinted off the upstairs window, almost as if the old tutor was assuring Raoul he was pleased with what he had accomplished.

A smile curved his lips.

The past had at last been laid to rest, offering all three men the opportunity to concentrate on the future.

A future that offered something none of them had ever thought possible.

A family . . .

And for a taste of something different,
please turn the page for an exciting sneak peek of
DARKNESS UNLEASHED,
the latest novel in Alexandra Ivy's
Guardian of Eternity series,
coming December 2009!

Prologue

Jagr knew he was creating panic in Viper's exclusive nightclub. The elegant establishment with its crystal chandeliers and red velvet upholstery catered to the more civilized members of the demon world. Jagr was anything but civilized.

He was a six-foot-three vampire who had once been a Visigoth Chief. But it wasn't his pale gold hair that had been braided to fall nearly to his waist, or the ice-blue eyes that missed nothing that sent creatures with any claim to intelligence scurrying from his path. It wasn't even the leather duster that flared about his hard body.

No, it was the cold perfection of his stark features, and the hint of feral fury that smoldered about him.

Three hundred years of relentless torture had stripped away any hint of civility.

Ignoring the assorted demons that tumbled over chairs and tables in an effort to avoid his long strides, Jagr concentrated on the two Ravens guarding the door to the back office. The hushed air of sophistication was giving him a rash.

He was a vampire who preferred the solitude of his lair hidden beneath the streets of Chicago, surrounded by his vast library, secure in the knowledge that not a human, beast, or demon possessed the ability to enter.

Not that he was the total recluse that his vampire brothers assumed.

No matter how powerful or skilled or intelligent he might be, he knew that his survival depended on understanding the ever-changing technology of the modern world. And beyond that was the necessity of being able to blend in with society.

Even a recluse had to feed.

Tucked in the very back of his lair was a plasma TV with every channel known to humankind, and the sort of nondescript clothing that allowed him to cruise through the seedier neighborhoods without causing a riot.

The most lethal hunters knew how to camouflage when on the prowl.

But this place . . .

He'd rather be staked than mince and prance around like a jackass.

Damn Styx. The ancient vampire had known that only a royal command could force him to enter a crowded nightclub. Jagr made no secret of his disdain for the companionship of others.

Which begged the question of why the Anasso would choose such a setting to meet.

In a mood foul enough to fill the vast club with an icy chill, Jagr ignored the two Ravens who stood on sentry duty near the back office, and lifting his hand, allowed his power to blow the heavy oak door off its hinges.

The looming Ravens growled in warning, dropping

their heavy capes, which hid the numerous swords, daggers, and guns attached to various parts of their bodies.

Jagr's step never faltered. Styx wouldn't let his pet vampires hurt an invited guest. At least not until he had what he needed from Jagr.

And even if Styx didn't call off the guards . . . well hell, he'd been waiting centuries to be taken out in battle. It was a warrior's destiny.

There was a low murmur from inside the room, and the two Ravens grudgingly allowed him to pass with nothing more painful than a heated glare.

Stepping over the shattered door, Jagr paused to cast a wary glance about the pale blue and ivory room. As expected, Styx (a towering Aztec who was the current king of vampires), was consuming more than his fair share of space behind a heavy walnut desk, his bronzed features unreadable. Viper (clan chief of Chicago, who, with his silver hair and dark eyes, looked more like an angel than a lethal warrior), was standing at his shoulder.

"Jagr." Styx leaned back in the leather chair, his fingers steepled beneath his chin. "Thank you for coming so promptly."

Jagr narrowed his frigid gaze. "Did I have a choice?"

"Careful, Jagr," Viper warned. "This is your Anasso."

Jagr curled his lips, but he was wise enough to keep his angry words to himself. Even presuming he could match Styx's renowned power, he would be dead before ever leaving the club if he challenged the Anasso.

"What do you want?" he growled.

"I have a task for you."

Jagr clenched his teeth. For the past century, he'd managed to keep away from the clan who called him brother, never bothering others and expecting the same in return. Since he'd been foolish enough to allow Cezar to enter his lair, it seemed he couldn't get rid of the damn vampires.

"What sort of task?" he demanded, his tone making clear that he didn't appreciate playing the role of toady.

Styx smiled as he waved a slender hand toward a nearby sofa. It was a smile that sent a chill of alarm down Jagr's spine.

"Have a seat, my friend," the Anasso drawled. "This might take a while."

For an insane moment, Jagr considered refusing the order. Before being turned into a vampire, he had been a leader of thousands. While he had no memory of those days, he had retained all his arrogance. Not to mention his issue with authority.

Thankfully, he had also kept the larger portion of his intelligence.

"Very well, Anasso, I have rushed to obey your royal command." He lowered his hard bulk onto a delicate brocade sofa, inwardly swearing to kill the designer if it broke. "What do you demand of your dutiful subject?"

Viper growled deep in his throat, the air tingling with his power. Jagr never blinked, although his muscles coiled in preparation.

"Perhaps you should see to your guests, Viper," Styx smoothly commanded. "Jagr's . . . dramatic entrance has disrupted your charming entertainment, and attracted more attention than I desire."

"I will not be far." Viper flashed Jagr a warning glare before disappearing through the busted door.

"Is he auditioning for a place among your Ravens?" Jagr mocked.

Pinpricks of pain bit into his skin as Styx released a small thread of his power.

"So long as you remain in Chicago, Viper is your clan chief. Do not make the mistake of forgetting his position."

Jagr shrugged. He wasn't indifferent to the debt and loyalty owed to Viper. The truth was he was in a pissy mood, and being stuck in the *chichi* nightclub where there wasn't a damned thing to kill beyond a bunch of dew fairies wasn't helping.

"I can hardly forget when I am forever being commanded to involve myself in affairs that do not concern me, and more importantly, do not interest me."

"What *does* interest you, Jagr?" He held Styx's searching gaze with a flat stare. At last the king grimaced. "Like it or not, you offered your sword when Viper accepted you into his clan."

He didn't like it, but he couldn't argue. Being taken into a clan was the only means of survival amongst the vampires.

"What would you have of me?"

Styx rose to his feet to round the desk, perching on a corner. The wood groaned beneath his considerable weight, but didn't crack. Jagr could only assume Viper had all the furniture reinforced.

Smart vampire.

"What do you know of my mate?" Styx abruptly demanded.

Jagr stilled. "Is this a trap?"

A wry smile touched the Anasso's mouth. "I'm not a subtle vampire, Jagr. Unlike the previous Anasso, I have no talent for manipulating and deceiving others. If there comes a day when I feel the need to challenge you, it will be done face-to-face."

"Then why are you asking me about your mate?"

"When I first met Darcy, she knew nothing of her heritage. She had been fostered by humans from the time she was a babe, and it wasn't until Salvatore Giuliani, the current king of the Weres, arrived in Chicago that we discovered she was a pureblood who had been genetically altered."

Jagr flicked a brow upward. That was a little tidbit that the king had kept secret.

"Genetically altered?"

"The Weres are increasingly desperate to produce healthy offspring. The pureblood females have lost their ability to control their shifts during the full moon, which makes it all but impossible to carry a litter to full term. The Weres altered Darcy and her sisters so they would be incapable of shifting."

Jagr folded his arms over his chest. He didn't give a damn about the worthless dogs.

"I presume you will tell me why you have summoned me, before the sun rises?"

Styx narrowed his golden eyes. "That entirely depends on your cooperation, my brother. I can make this meeting last as long as I desire."

Jagr's lips twitched. The one thing he respected was power. "Please continue."

"Darcy's mother gave birth to a litter of four daughters, all genetically altered, and all stolen from the Weres shortly after their births."

"Why were they stolen?"

"That remains a mystery Salvatore has never fully explained." There was an edge in the Anasso's voice that warned he wasn't pleased by the lack of information. "What we do know is that one of Darcy's sisters was discovered in St. Louis, being held captive by an imp named Culligan."

"He's fortunate that she's incapable of shifting. A pureblood could rip out the throat of an imp."

"From what Salvatore could discover, the imp managed to get his hands on Regan when she was just a child, and kept her locked in a cage coated with silver. That is, when he wasn't torturing her for a quick buck."

Torture.

The Dutch masterpieces hanging on the walls crashed to the floor at Jagr's flare of fury.

"Do you wish the Were rescued?"

Styx grimaced. "Salvatore already freed her from Culligan, although the damned imp managed to slip away before Salvatore could eat him for dinner."

Jagr's brief flare of hope that the night wasn't a total waste was brought to a sharp end. Slaughtering bastards who tormented the weak was one of his few pleasures.

"If the woman was rescued, then why do you need me?"

Styx straightened, his bulk consuming a considerable amount of the office space.

"Salvatore's only interest in Regan was installing her as his queen and primary breeder. He is determined to secure his power base by providing a mate who is capable of restoring the purebloods' dwindling population. Unfortunately, once he freed Regan, he discovered she was infertile."

"So she was of no use."

"Precisely." The towering Aztec was careful to keep his composure, but even an idiot could sense he wouldn't mind making a snack of the Were king. "That is why he contacted Darcy. He intended to send Regan to Chicago so she could be under my protection until he established her in the local Were pack."

"And?"

"And she managed to escape while he was conferring with the pack master."

Jagr grunted in disgust. "This Salvatore is pathetically inefficient. First he allows the imp to escape, and then the woman. It's little wonder the Weres are declining in number."

"Let us hope you are more efficient."

Jagr rose to his feet, his expression cold. "Me?"

"Darcy is concerned for her sister. I want her found and brought to Chicago."

"The woman has made it fairly obvious she doesn't want to come."

"Then it will be your job to convince her."

Jagr narrowed his gaze. He wasn't a damned Mary Poppins. Hell, he would eat Mary Poppins for breakfast.

"Why me?"

"I've already sent several of my best trackers to St. Louis, but you're my finest warrior. If Regan has managed to run into trouble, you will be needed to help rescue her."

There were no doubt worse things than chasing after a genetically altered Were who clearly didn't want to be found, but he couldn't think of one off the top of his head.

In the outer room, the sound of a string quartet resumed, along with the soft "ohhs" and "ahhs" of the audience as the dew fairies resumed their delicate dance. Jagr could suddenly think of one thing worse than chasing the Were.

Remaining trapped in this hellhole.

"Why should I do this?" he rasped.

"Because what makes Darcy happy makes me happy." Styx moved until they were nose to nose, his power digging into Jagr's flesh. "Clear enough?"

"Painfully clear."

"Good." Styx stepped back and released his power. Slipping his hand beneath his leather coat, he pulled out a cell phone and tossed it to Jagr. "Here. The phone has the numbers of the brothers who are searching for Regan, as well as contacts in St. Louis. It also has my private line. Contact me when you find Regan."

Jagr pocketed the phone and headed for the door. There was no point in arguing. Styx was struggling to force the vampires out of their barbaric past, but it wasn't a freaking democracy.

Not even close.

"I will leave within the hour."

"Jagr."

Halting at the door, Jagr turned with a searing fury. "What?"

Styx didn't so much as flinch. "Do not forget for one moment that Regan is precious cargo. If I discover you have left so much as a bruise on her pretty skin, you won't be pleased with the consequences."

"So I'm to track down a rabid Were who doesn't want to be found, and haul her to Chicago without leaving a mark?"

"Obviously the rumors of your extraordinary intelligence were not exaggerated, my brother."

With a hiss, Jagr turned and stormed through the shattered opening. "I'm not your brother."

* * *

Viper monitored Jagr's furious exit with a wary gaze.

Actually it hadn't gone as bad as he had feared. No death or mutilation. Not even a maiming.

Always a plus.

Still, he knew Jagr too well. Of all his clansmen, he had always known that the ancient Visigoth was the most feral. Understandable after what he'd endured, but no less dangerous. He was beginning to regret having brought the tortured vampire to Styx's attention.

Slipping past the seated demons who were once again enthralled with the dew fairies, Viper returned to the office, finding Styx staring out the window.

"I have a bad feeling about this," he muttered, his gaze taking in his priceless paintings, shattered on the floor.

Styx turned, his arms folded over his chest. "A premonition? Shall I contact the Commission and inform them they have a potential oracle?"

Viper arched a warning brow. "Only if you want me to lock you in a cell with Levet for the next century."

Styx gave a sharp bark of laughter. "A nice bluff, but Levet has decided that he is the only one capable of tracking Darcy's missing sister. He left for St. Louis as soon as Salvatore informed me that Regan had slipped from his grasp."

"Perfect, now we have two loose cannons charging about Missouri. I'm not sure the natives will survive."

"You believe Jagr is a loose cannon?"

Viper grimaced, recalling the night that Jagr had appeared at his lair requesting asylum. He had encountered any number of lethal demons, most of whom wanted nothing more than to kill him. He'd never, however, until that night, looked into the eyes of another and seen only death.

"I think beneath all that grim control, he's a step from slipping into madness."

"And yet you allowed him to become a clansman."

Viper shrugged. "When he petitioned, my first inclination was to refuse. I could sense he was not only dangerously close to the edge, but that he was powerful and aggressive enough to challenge me as clan chief. He's by nature a leader, not a follower."

"So why allow him into Chicago?"

"Because he swore an oath to disappear into his lair and not offer any trouble."

"And?" Styx prodded.

"And I knew he wouldn't survive if he were without the protection of a clan," Viper grudgingly admitted. "We both know that despite your attempts to civilize the vampires, some habits are too deeply ingrained to be easily changed. A rogue vampire with that much power would be seen as a threat to any chief. He would be destroyed."

"So you took mercy."

Viper frowned. He didn't like being thought of as anything but a ruthless bastard. He hadn't become clan chief because of any sensitivity bullshit. He was leader because the other vampires were scared he'd rip out their undead hearts.

"Not mercy—it was a calculated decision," he growled. "I knew if the need ever arose, he would prove an invaluable ally. Of course, I assumed that I would need him as a warrior, not as a babysitter for a young, vulnerable Were. I'm not entirely comfortable sending him on such a mission."

Styx grasped the medallion that always hung about his neck, revealing he was not nearly as confident in his decision as he would have Viper believe.

"I need Regan found, and Jagr has the intelligence and skills that are best suited to track her and keep her safe. And he possesses an even more important quality."

"It can't be his sparking personality."

"No, it's his intimate knowledge of the anguish Regan has suffered." Styx regarded him with a somber expression. "He, better than any of us, will understand what Regan needs, now that she has been freed from her tormentor."

Romantic Suspense from
Lisa Jackson

See How She Dies	0-8217-7605-3	$6.99US/$9.99CAN
Final Scream	0-8217-7712-2	$7.99US/$10.99CAN
Wishes	0-8217-6309-1	$5.99US/$7.99CAN
Whispers	0-8217-7603-7	$6.99US/$9.99CAN
Twice Kissed	0-8217-6038-6	$5.99US/$7.99CAN
Unspoken	0-8217-6402-0	$6.50US/$8.50CAN
If She Only Knew	0-8217-6708-9	$6.50US/$8.50CAN
Hot Blooded	0-8217-6841-7	$6.99US/$9.99CAN
Cold Blooded	0-8217-6934-0	$6.99US/$9.99CAN
The Night Before	0-8217-6936-7	$6.99US/$9.99CAN
The Morning After	0 8217-7295-3	$6.99US/$9.99CAN
Deep Freeze	0-8217-7296-1	$7.99US/$10.99CAN
Fatal Burn	0-8217-7577-4	$7.99US/$10.99CAN
Shiver	0-8217-7578-2	$7.99US/$10.99CAN
Most Likely to Die	0-8217-7576-6	$7.99US/$10.99CAN
Absolute Fear	0-8217-7936-2	$7.99US/$9.49CAN
Almost Dead	0-8217-7579-0	$7.99US/$10.99CAN
Lost Souls	0-8217-7938-9	$7.99US/$10.99CAN
Left to Die	1-4201-0276-1	$7.99US/$10.99CAN
Wicked Game	1-4201-0338-5	$7.99US/$9.99CAN
Malice	0-8217-7940-0	$7.99US/$9.49CAN

Available Wherever Books Are Sold!
Visit our website at **www.kensingtonbooks.com**

Thrilling Suspense from
Beverly Barton

__Every Move She Makes	0-8217-6838-7	$6.50US/$8.99CAN
__What She Doesn't Know	0-8217-7214-7	$6.50US/$8.99CAN
__After Dark	0-8217-7666-5	$6.50US/$8.99CAN
__The Fifth Victim	0-8217-7215-5	$6.50US/$8.99CAN
__The Last to Die	0-8217-7216-3	$6.50US/$8.99CAN
__As Good As Dead	0-8217-7219-8	$6.99US/$9.99CAN
__Killing Her Softly	0-8217-7687-8	$6.99US/$9.99CAN
__Close Enough to Kill	0-8217-7688-6	$6.99US/$9.99CAN
__The Dying Game	0-8217-7689-4	$6.99US/$9.99CAN

Available Wherever Books Are Sold!

Visit our website at **www.kensingtonbooks.com**